# *cold girls*

"A haunting, heart-wrenching story about finding the strength to live after unimaginable loss. Maxine Rae shows the lonely, internal journey one goes on when grappling with grief and fighting for joy. *Cold Girls* absolutely shook me."

—Jenna Miller, author of *Out of Character*

"Heartbreaking and healing, Maxine Rae has crafted an exceptional debut that isn't afraid to explore the heaviest parts of our humanity and, in turn, how deeply we can love."

—Sarah Ainslee, author of *That Wasn't in the Script*

"An honest and hard-hitting tale of friendship, family, and grief that is as beautiful as it is raw."

—Brenda Rufener, author of *Where I Live* and *Since We Last Spoke*

"Eloquently crafted, this story of grief, friendship, and self-awareness will crack you open like ice in spring, sweep you into turbulent waters, and deliver you, shaken but safe, to the shores of hope."

—Shana Youngdahl, author of *As Many Nows As I Can Get*

# cold girls

a novel by
Maxine Rae

# cold girls

Maxine Rae

flux

Mendota Heights, Minnesota

First Edition
First Printing, 2023

Book design by Cynthia Della-Rovere
Cover design by Cynthia Della-Rovere
Cover illustration by Alisha Monnin

Flux, an imprint of North Star Editions, Inc.

**Library of Congress Cataloging-in-Publication Data (pending)**
978-1-63583-089-7

Flux
North Star Editions, Inc.
2297 Waters Drive
Mendota Heights, MN 55120
www.fluxnow.com

Printed in Canada

s—for you.

we weren't liv and rory, but we
were magic.

thanks for keeping me on my toes,
chin up, angled toward the sun.

# author's note

*Cold Girls* is a work of fiction, and is separate from my own personal experiences with loss and identity. This novel explores teenage friendship, queerness, grief, mental health, and healing. These topics come up in the book and may be difficult for readers: the loss of a loved one, the memory of sexual harassment, and the experience of panic attacks. I know that reading about these topics can at times be cathartic and healing, but can at other times be triggering. Please take care of yourself first!

If you are struggling with mental health and/or the loss of a loved one, you are not alone. Here is a list of resources you can contact:

- Teen Line: www.teenline.org Call 1-800-852-8336, or text TEEN to 839863.

- The Compassionate Friends, an organization for grief: www.compassionatefriends.org. Call 1-877-969-0010.

- The Trevor Project, an organization for LGBTQ+ young people: www.thetrevorproject.org. Call 1-866-488-7386 or text START to 678-678.

- The National Suicide Prevention Lifeline: Call or text 988.

If you're a young person struggling with your sexuality and/or your gender: You are valid. You are beautiful. Keep breathing, and never apologize for who you are.

*I*'m staring at myself in the bathroom mirror when Mom bursts in, garbage bag in tow, and starts rummaging around.

"Oh," I say. "Cool. I guess knocking's out of fashion?"

Mom ignores me and, despite her fierce devotion to thriftiness—despite the fact that she yells at us if we buy anything fully priced, or really if we buy anything *at all*—starts throwing bathroom products in the trash at random. I watch in silence, too stunned to bid a silent farewell to my Aveeno lotion, which I *just* bought. My younger sisters Saige and Willow stand behind her, mesmerized by this grand ransack of our bathroom.

"Mom," I finally explode. "Hello? Hi. What are you doing?"

"Shrink said to." Mom's grinding her teeth.

"I haven't met the shrink yet, but I'd bet *all* my savings that she didn't tell you to pillage the bathroom."

"Rory," Mom says. "I'm done. If you can swallow it, it's going away. Period."

"Are you serious? Do you really think I would drink"—I gesture furiously at what she's holding —"Saige's fucking *anti-dandruff* shampoo?"

"Hey now," Saige objects from behind Mom. "We all use that."

Mom gives me the death glare to end all death glares. "Rory, I don't know anymore. You tell *me* what you're capable of doing. And give Willow a dollar for the swear jar."

I fish a single out of my jean shorts, drop it into Willow's hand. She grins at me before diligently leaving the bathroom. My youngest sister is eight, but sometimes, she's the most mature member of our family.

Saige, who's sixteen, takes the opportunity to interrogate me. "When my friends ask how college is going for you, what am I supposed to tell them? What will they *think*?"

"The truth." I shove my fists into my pockets and lean against the bathroom counter. I don't know why Saige cares about what her vapid lacrosse friends think. They're all the same. There's truly not a *single* unique thought among them. "You can tell them your weird older sister's stuck in this bullshit town, because Ridgewood College apparently decided to pull her scholarship for no fucking reason."

Mom straightens up with her garbage bag and wipes sweat from her cheek. "No reason? No bloody *reason*?" After living in the States for two decades, she's nearly lost her British accent, but it always shows up when she's pissed.

"No *real* reason," I say as Willow returns. Instead of using literally any of the empty space around us, my little sister sidles up right next to me, leaning against the counter like I am. Except that she's much shorter, obviously, so she's on tiptoe. She looks up at me with her big eyes and gives me a hopeful, anxious smile.

Mom pushes past me into the hallway. "You know, I'm not even going to discuss this with you. Not today."

"You're punishing me because I'm sad," I call after her.

"Oh, cut the shit," Mom responds.

Willow glances up at me again, seeming torn, before running after Mom for another dollar.

\* \* \*

The whole Xanax thing was an accident. I never thought taking three would knock me out like *that*. I mean, was I taking more than I usually took? Yes. Did I want to fall into a relatively deep sleep? Yes.

FOR A *BIT*.

But I wasn't trying to send myself to the hospital. Or . . . worse. Mom, Saige, Willow, and my grandparents, Nonni and Nonno—would be heartbroken. Not to mention extremely pissed at me. And as Mom likes to remind me, my family has already been through enough "Rory-related horseshit" this year even before the Xanax Incident. It's been eight months since the Worst Night, January 5th, when I *actually* almost died. I mean, in the car accident. Mom's like, "I didn't go through forty-eight *bloody* hours of labor to bring you into this world so you could snuff it early, Rory. Quit it already with the drama."

\* \* \*

"I'm going to pause you right here," says April, i.e., the shrink who instructed Mom to raid the bathroom.

For the first time since coming into the office, I look up at her. April is unfairly gorgeous and put together: a middle-aged Black woman with long braids and chic glasses, who dresses in colorful, printed clothes. Kind of elite-Zen-bohemian vibes. A lot of moms in Clarksdale who want you to think they're boho *try* to dress like this, but April actually has it nailed.

She takes a breath and says, "Your mom's reaction to the pills incident seems a little—"

"Wild? Like *she's* on drugs?"

"I was going to say angry, but . . . is she on drugs?" Her tone remains remarkably casual, like she's asking about the weather.

"No, she's just bitter about her life."

"Okay. I'm hearing some potentially harbored resentment, but first, I want to address—"

"They think I did this on purpose to hurt myself, but that's not what happened," I say, suddenly out of breath.

"Can you tell me what *did* happen?"

I can feel my heart pounding in my throat. *Calm down.*

"I already told you. I took a few more pills than I should have because I wanted to sleep."

"Why did you want to sleep?"

"That's generally what people do at night," I respond, irritated.

April moves on, looking down at her notes. "And it was your mom's Xanax. How long has she been on it?"

"Since my sister Willow was born."

April nods. "Had you ever taken her Xanax before?"

"Yeah. Sometimes she'd let me have one, if I couldn't sleep."

"But you've always asked your mom first."

"Well, yeah," I say, twirling my finger through my bangs. They're getting way too long, but it's been a hot minute since I cared about my appearance.

"Why didn't you ask her this time?"

I'm going cross-eyed, looking at my increasingly purple finger, yanking my hair tighter and tighter around. I don't answer April's question.

"I just want to know how I can best help you, Rory," she continues, after it must become obvious that I'm staying silent. "And to do that, I need to know how you got here."

"I biked," I say, hating myself.

"You know what I mean."

"It's a long story."

"We have thirty-eight more minutes."

April and I then have a staring contest that lasts about five eternities. I learn a few new things, such as: April's skin is flawless. Therapists don't blink. I am suffering.

Finally I say, "Aren't you supposed to, like, ask me questions?"

April smiles, uncrossing and recrossing her legs. "Ideally, we could have a conversation. But we can go with more questions, if you'd like."

I take a deep breath and prepare. I'm not as ignorant as I'm acting in this appointment: I know exactly why I'm sitting in April's office overlooking the woods near Evergreen Lane. Saige found me unconscious in my room three weeks ago, and now I'm seeing a therapist. Mom's on a mission to fix me. She wants to make me return to who I was Before—the quiet, chill daughter with no social life, who babysat for free and preferred to listen to Britpop with her while watering the plants on Friday nights.

I know therapy is a waste of time at this point, but I have sob stories prepared anyway: Body insecurities. General anxiety. Dad dying, even though it happened when I was three and I can't remember him much.

I think, *Ask me anything. I'll talk about anything,
as long as it's not—*

"Tell me about Liv," April says.

A chill spreads from my chest down my legs to my
feet. I try not to look down at my hands, which are
starting to go numb.

"That isn't a question," I say.

"You're shaking," she says, a thin crease forming between her eyebrows.

"How do you know her name?" I try not to sound
accusatory. Try to be calm, remember my breath. *I am
cold*, I tell myself steadily. *April can't touch me.*

Despite myself, I ask, "Did you . . . did you Google
me?"

"I didn't have to Google you, Rory. I heard about
the accident back in January. Your faces and names
have been all over Clarksdale, as you know. It's hard to
live here and *not* know about it."

*You're fine. You're fine.*

*Push it away.*

"I'm here because I accidentally swallowed too many
pills," I say. "Nothing about that has to do with Liv."

Even as I say it, the falseness of my statement hits
me so hard that I almost smile.

Everything about everything has to do with Liv.

April's smile is the very small and sad type that I've
become used to in the eight months since the Worst
Night. "I know it's difficult," she says. "But I want you
to at least try."

"I'm fine. It's not difficult."

April doesn't respond right away. Instead, she stares
at me, which makes me have a long, honest think about
what I must look like. My dirty blond hair is piled

uselessly at the top of my head, half-grown-out bangs shoved behind my ears. The sleeves of my worn-out sweater are rolled up, revealing the rash caused by my hospital bracelet from the Xanax Incident. My jeans are torn, and underneath, we can both see the eight-month-old gash across my knee, one of my souvenirs from the Worst Night. I haven't worn makeup in eight months. Again: Who cares at this point? But although there are no mirrors in April's office, I can almost *see* through her eyes the dark circles under my own.

I am a complete dysfunctional mess.

"It's not difficult," I repeat, amazing even myself with the lie.

"Okay."

More silence.

"This isn't about me doing my job, Rory," she says finally. "This is about you being able to have a good night's sleep."

I have to give her some credit for the drama, but I press my lips tighter together. We sit and sit and sit, and time stops and the sun sets and the world ends, and when I look at the clock, only three minutes have passed.

Thirty-five to go.

I don't want to think about Liv, so I grab on to the next thing that comes to mind. "I wonder who Ridgewood gave the scholarship to. You know. After they took it away from me."

"Rory," April says.

I feel my cheeks heating with anger. Also with shame, but I try to push that down. *You're fine.*

If you asked me last New Year's what I thought my life would be like by now, by early fall, I would have answered that I'd be a freshman at Ridgewood College in upstate New York, wearing bulky sweaters and going to English seminars, writing papers on feminist authors. There was no alternate universe in which this *wouldn't* happen.

Except that there was, and it was this current one, the shittiest universe in the world. In which, four days after New Year's, the Worst Night happened.

In which I spent the next three weeks in the hospital, and eight more in physical therapy.

In which I spent the summer numbly drifting, half-heartedly doing my physical therapy, just thinking, *September. September. September.*

*In September, I will still go to college at Ridgewood. In September, I will escape Clarksdale.*

*This* shitty universe, in which Mom told me last week that, because of my deteriorated grades from spring semester, my Presidential Merit Scholarship at Ridgewood had been taken away. So, no, I would *not* be attending college in September. I would be living at home for another year, still "recovering." Surrounded by everything, and everyone, that made me want to burrow under the covers and sleep.

"I hope you're not feeling guilty, Rory," April says. "The accident, your scholarship—none of that was your fault. Yes?"

I only stare at her.

"And it's not like Ridgewood's out to get you. Colleges can only give so much aid to each of their students. It sounds like removing your scholarship was just a procedural thing. Your mom told me that if you took community college classes this year and got back up to a steady GPA, Ridgewood would reconsider your scholarship for next year. And from what she told me about your grades in high school before the accident, that shouldn't be a problem." She smiles again. "Straight-A student?"

"No," I say, before I can stop myself. "I got a B+ in pre-calc. Liv was the one with straight As, not me."

"Well, it doesn't sound like getting your grades up will be difficult for you. And then, like your mom said, you'll be reconsidered for the Ridgewood scholarship next year."

I don't know what to do, so I nod slightly, but I'm still shaking. "My mom—she seemed so casual, telling me about the scholarship. It's like she's *glad* I can't go to school this year. And then she makes me go to this bullshit." I gesture vaguely to April's lines of diplomas on the wall. "Like she can just fix me."

April gracefully ignores that I've just called her line of work bullshit, sighs, and looks down. "Listen, I know it's not what you want to hear right now. But your mom loves you, and she didn't really have a choice but to send you here." She looks at me hard. "I think you know that."

I grind my teeth.

"Rory, your mom almost lost you twice this year. First, the accident in January. Then, a couple weeks ago, with the Xanax." Her eyes pierce me. "She's scared."

I think, although I don't want to, about this morning. The way Mom seized up when I walked into the kitchen, how she cut her finger slicing bananas for Willow's cereal, swore, brought her bleeding finger to her lips.

"Off already?" she asked roughly, looking down. "Without breakfast?"

"I'm not hungry."

We looked at each other then, because this would normally be the beginning of a fight: you just *don't* use that tone with Mom. But she pursed her lips and looked away, wrapping her finger tightly in a towel. Willow slurped her milk behind us, watching us. Willow is like a tiny version of me: wide-eyed and bony, quiet, observant. Always taking mental notes. In the past few weeks since the Xanax Incident, it's gotten even more extreme: she's with me every moment, observing everything I do. I've woken up to her staring at me more than once.

"Wear a helmet," Mom said. "And stay away from the street."

I couldn't remember the last time Mom said the words *stay away from the street*. Or the last time she even cared to look me in the eye and ask if I was being safe.

"Can you chill?" I seethed, although what I really wanted to say was, *Where were you for eighteen years?* "I'm not five."

Again: you can't sass Mom like that. I've been grounded for less. But this time, she just looked at me. And her blue eyes were gray. And the circles beneath them were black.

April is watching me relive it, this small, pointless memory. She crosses her arms, peering at me critically.

"I know you don't like this, Rory. But your mom signed you up to see me, once a week, for the foreseeable future," she says. "I'm not saying your mental health is a problem we can just *fix*, but if your mood improves at home, she might get off your back." She waits until I meet her eyes. She raises her eyebrows pointedly. "We can sit here in silence, or we can talk about Liv. Your choice."

I try to sit, remain cold. And when I finally can't stand it, I look at April and communicate through my eyes: *Just because I'm going to start talking doesn't mean you won.*

*one year before*

*L*iv Martinez was late to fifth period, and to my life.

I could have really used her before that frigid Monday in January when she walked into choir wearing a bathrobe and a scowl, but unfortunately, that was the first time I'd ever seen her.

There are lots of *unfortunately*s in my story with Liv. This one's just the first.

\* \* \*

Hours earlier, I stood outside waiting for the first bell to ring at Telsey College Prep, where my status as the New Kid but Also a Junior Whose Mom Is a Science Teacher Here had rendered me basically friendless. As I brooded in the cold, a girl in my homeroom ran full-speed into me on the way to greet a friend.

"Sorry, Lori!" she said.

*Crushing it, Rory,* I told myself.

I had begged Mom to let me keep going to my old school when she took the job at Telsey, but she bit back with the classic *Telsey-is-the-thirteenth-best-high-school-in-the-country-and-you'd-better-be-grateful-for-this-opportunity* bullshit. To this day, I cannot explain how little I fit in there: the place was overflowing with preppiness, trust fund babies, and an absurdly high level of school spirit. In fact, everyone in our whole town of Clarksdale seemed to be rich, tan, and beautiful, and come from a "golf family" with "Ivy League ties," and have "parents who've paid off their mortgage" and "moms who don't get wine-drunk and stress-cry periodically while blaming their dead husband's career choices." I mean, I didn't care *too* much about what other people thought, but it's hard for even the most self-assured kids to go to this school and *not* feel insecure when they're wearing beat-up sneakers from eighth grade.

I kept my eyes trained on my high-tops, shoving as much of my face into my jacket as humanly possible, concentrating on the song pulsing through my headphones: Bowie's "Modern Love." These vintage headphones had been with me from the beginning—and by that I mean sixth grade, when I bought them off our old neighbors at a garage sale with my babysitting money. Mom raged, asking what was wrong with the $9.99 knockoff earphones she'd bought me from Walgreens, but I've always insisted on having as much of my head covered as possible. I like to be *enveloped* by the music. It's much easier to disappear.

I had a few minutes of uninterrupted me-time, standing near the front door and listening to Bowie, before a long arm swooped around my neck and tightened.

Speaking of "basically friendless": I did have *one* friend. Sort of.

"You're so emo," Stoff said, loosening his grip on my neck a little so that I could breathe.

I rubbed my neck. "You're such a bully."

"Oh, you're fine," he said, resting his chin on top of my head. "Keep me warm, Rory. I'm fucking dying."

"You're not scared of my germs?" I responded, my voice muffled. It worked. Stoff twitched and extracted himself from me, shivering. The very first thing I ever learned about Stoff: major germophobe.

Stoff waited for the first bell with me, sharing some winter break tea he'd gathered from the various parties he'd attended. In the first week of school, when I knew absolutely no one, I'd partnered with Stoff for a French project. We spent one delirious night throwing together an awful poster, and the rest was history. It was hilarious that Stoff was the one friend I'd made since starting at Telsey, because he was also (separately from me) very popular. Everyone seemed to want an extroverted, designer-wearing, *Riverdale*-watching gay best friend, and that's precisely what Stoff was. He was tall and glamorous; he wore mostly Ralph Lauren or J. Crew with the small exception of Gap on his "ugly days." He even worked at J. Crew during the summers. He knew everything about everyone all the time, and no one ever got mad at him for it.

"WAIT!" he shouted straight into my ear, in the middle of a story. "You haven't told me what you decided for fifth period yet!"

I rolled my eyes. For the fall, I got to have fifth period as an "adjustment period" (read: study hall), but my advisor forced me to pick an elective for second semester instead. I cleared my throat and mumbled a response, hoping he wouldn't be able to distinguish my words.

"You joined fucking *choir*?" he screamed.

"You convinced me," I joked, but much quieter than him, and kind of not joking. Stoff is very, very much a theater kid, and I had decided to just stick with him.

But I didn't want to make it too obvious.

"Rory Quinn-Morelli *sings*?" he said.

"Oh my god. It's not that big of a deal."

"That means you *auditioned*. I'm all over this. Okay—did you sing a Simon & Garfunkel song or something?"

"I ran, like, one scale with Mr. Wong."

"I'm picturing you walking in with your gray sweat-shirt, like"—he hunched his shoulders and lowered his eyes—"'Hey, I'm Rory. I haven't smiled since I was ten. I like old bands and staying at home.'"

"Please get over yourself. At least I'm not wearing turquoise pastel pants."

"Don't hate me because I'm thriving right now. These are vintage Ralph Lauren."

I lightly hit him, and he elbowed me back. Because of our major discrepancy in size, this actually hurt.

"Dick," I said, rubbing my arm as the first bell rang.

"Please. You need to bulk up."

I rolled my eyes and followed the crowd into Prep Hell.

\* \* \*

Mom told me an easier A than choir would have been taking home ec, but I flat-out refused. I figured choir would be a blow-off, and I would have Stoff to keep me company. But when I entered the music hallway before fifth period, I started to wonder if learning how to fry an egg with thirty-five future Clarksdale housewives would've been better than this. Stoff was immediately engulfed in hugs from a group of overexcited kids who looked like they just finished filming an episode of *Glee*. Ducking underneath their arms, I leaned on the wall with my headphones, attempting to look chill.

I tried very hard not to listen to Bowie again, but it happened anyway.

After a few minutes, the door swung open and the teacher, Mr. Wong, beckoned us in with a beaming smile. I hoped he wouldn't notice me, but when I trudged through the door, he grabbed one of my shoulders and squeezed.

"Welcome, Rory!" he exclaimed, as the rest of the kids filed past.

I did my usual thing for when people showed me kind or pleasant gestures: my body turned into a weird pointy rock, and I looked away.

I thought it would end there, but he kept his hand on my shoulder and turned to the class. "We have a new student joining us this semester!" he called out, and my insides evaporated. "Friends, this is Rory Quinn-Morelli. And I'm super jazzed she's here, because"—he turned back to me theatrically—"you might not realize it, Rory, but you're single-handedly saving us. Well, you and one other girl, but she's usually late."

Everyone laughed.

"We have a slight shortage of men singers this year, am I right?" Mr. Wong said in a bubbly voice, which caused some more laughs from the other kids. "So—listen to this—you're going to join the *tenor* section."

I stared at him blankly. I neither knew nor cared what that meant; at that point I just wanted to sit down and sink through the floor.

Mr. Wong cleared his throat at my lack of response. "I mean, you'll be singing with the guys. Is that okay?"

I mumbled, "Sure."

"Great!" Mr. Wong shouted, and he pointed me to-

ward two empty chairs in the middle of the guys' section. "Everyone up! Let's get those voices warm!"

I mutely walked to one of the chairs he'd gestured to,
taking some time to hang my flannel over the back so
that my face could return to a normal color.

We were halfway through our second warm-up—a
weird rendition of "Do Re Mi" that had people holding
on to different notes and had me sweating profusely,
trying to keep up—when the door opened. As if the
bell hadn't rung two minutes ago, as if no one on earth
was expecting her anywhere, this girl kind of just meandered in.

My first thought was, *This chick is wearing a bathrobe.*

It looked like something Nonni wore around the
house: it draped over her shoulders and fell to her
knees, shivering with hand-sewn flowers and beads, bil-
lowing around her as she walked, partially obscuring a
black patterned jumper and tights. When I got over the
fact that she was wearing a robe, I looked up and saw
a scarlet printed scarf tied around a messy-but-also-
perfect bun at the crown of her head. Wrapped around
her neck were chunky beige headphones, almost as old
as mine. Long silver and gold earrings dangled from her
ears, which contained at least three piercings each, and
her wrists and fingers were lined with jewelry.

"Nice of you to join us, Liv," Mr. Wong said, barely
looking up as he pointed to the seat next to me. "You
finally have a fellow girl tenor."

Her eyes flicked up to me then, and from across
the room I could see layers of impeccable makeup on
her vaguely annoyed-looking face: Identical dark brows.
Maroon lipstick. Thick, catlike wings of eyeliner, curv-

ing upward into identical, cunning smiles.

I can't remember what I actually thought, in that first moment that we made eye contact, but it must have been vaguely along the lines of: *Cool.*

Then she started walking directly toward me, so I had to fix my gaze back on my feet.

She slid into the chair next to me and jumped into the middle of a scale as if she knew the warm-up by heart. At the very top note, she yawned, and then she turned and saw me gaping at her.

Color rose to my cheeks at the horrifying accidental eye contact, but she didn't seem embarrassed. "Is there something on my face?" she asked, her perfectly shaped eyebrows rising slightly.

*A lot of bold-ass makeup,* I thought.

"No," I said. "I just like your sweater . . . jacket. Thing."

"Oh, thanks," she said. "I thrifted it."

We faced forward and kept warming up.

When Mr. Wong sat us down and started passing out music, Liv turned to me again.

"You're the new tenor," she said. It wasn't a question.

I swallowed, trying not to stare at the wings lining her eyes. "Um, yeah."

"Cool." She faced front again without smiling. "Choir's a blow-off."

I didn't know how to respond, so I eventually said, "Word."

We sat in silence for a bit, and then she said, "Gum?"

She handed me a stick and folded another into her mouth. Within a minute, she'd blown a bubble bigger than her face. It popped very loudly.

"Spit it out, Liv," Mr. Wong said lightly, without looking up.

Liv took her time to walk to and from the garbage can. When she got back to her seat, I tried to face the front, but couldn't. I watched, intrigued, as she unwrapped another piece of gum and popped it into her mouth. Then she met my eyes. I flushed deeper—*God, you learned not to stare at strangers in, like, kindergarten. Get it together, Rory.* Excuses flew through my mind, things I could say to make it less weird, like, *Sorry, you have an eyelush on your cheek,* or, *Is there an outlet over there?* But before I could muster up the courage, she smiled—a mischievous-looking half smile, like she knew something I didn't—and then she was back to staring at her music.

*eight months after*

"I think we're done now," I say, looking at the clock. April sighs. "Just a few minutes left. Should we set goals?"

I say nothing because I know I don't really have a choice.

"What are two things you can do for yourself this week?"

I want to say *take a bath*, but I realize that my mom would have to be present, lest I attempt to drown myself. "Read," I say instead.

"What are you reading?"

"*The Girl with the Dragon Tattoo.*"

April cocks her head. "Isn't that a murder mystery?"

"Yes, but it's really unrealistic and . . . distracting," I say, picking adjectives that I hope she'll want to hear.

My real answer is: *It gives me nightmares, but it's also Liv's favorite series.*

My heart plunges into cold.

*Was.*

*Was* her favorite series.

April stares at me with her big eyes. I try to keep my entire body still. *If I move, the avalanche will come,* I think wildly to myself. *Don't move. Don't speak.*

"One more self-care goal," April says, as if everything is fine. As if the world hasn't already ended. "What about . . . seeing friends?"

I look at her coolly.

"Stoff?" she asks hopefully.

I take a breath, trying to move on. It doesn't work, so I take another.

"He's at Northwestern now," I say eventually. "He doesn't want to hang out with me."

April leans forward, resting her elbows on her knees, and fixes me with an intense stare. "Rory. You need to work on eliminating this type of self-talk. Why wouldn't he want to hang out with you?"

I don't give her an answer, but an uncomfortable feeling of guilt seeps through my chest.

She leans back in her chair. "You should check in with Stoff. And I know you have some other friends who go to school around Chicago. You mentioned them to me earlier. What about Natsuki?"

"She goes to Michigan."

"That couple—Devon and Grace? Aren't they going to Northwestern?"

"U of Illinois," I say. "Three hours away."

"Okay . . . Saige?"

"She's not my friend. She's my sister."

April grimaces, and I can see embarrassment etched across her face.

"It's okay," I say, before she has a chance to apologize. "You have a lot of names to remember."

"Thanks. My brain did a little mix-up."

"Me every day," I say, attempting to sound relatable.

April smiles, and it seems like a sad one.

"I'll text my friend Jem," I say, and I realize it's only

to try and make April feel good about doing her job.

"He goes to U Chicago."

"Great!" says April. "I'll check in on Monday. I want you to make some social progress before then, okay?"

"Fine." I stand up and sling my bag around my good shoulder.

"One last thing," April says.

"We did those questions at the beginning." At the start of our session—like, truly *right* after April introduced herself and we exchanged a highly awkward handshake—she interrogated me: *Have you had any self-injurious thoughts? Have you taken any self-injurious actions? Are you feeling self-injurious right now?* She says we have to do that every time, just in case.

"I know we did the questions," April says. "But we haven't done the mantra. I always do a mantra at the end of each session with my clients."

I have to physically restrain myself from rolling my eyes.

"Come on," April says. "Repeat after me: I survived, and I am here."

"I survived, and I am here," I say tonelessly.

"I am here for a reason."

I grind my teeth. "I am here for a reason."

"It's not my fault."

"It's not . . . it's . . ."

"It's not my fault," she repeats, fixing me with an intense stare, "for being the one who survived."

I try that last part. I really do. But the words do not come out.

chapter four

*one year before*

The night after I met Liv in choir, I ignored my three hours of homework ("It's the *first day back!*" screamed Stoff as we took the bus home) and decided to sit in the fetal position on my floor watching *Bob's Burgers* instead.

"RORY!" Mom shouted from downstairs. "DINNER!"

"NOT HUNGRY!" I shouted.

"DON'T CARE!"

I turned off the show, but then started scrolling through Instagram. Not that I gave it much thought, but most girls at Telsey had thousands of followers, and all they did was post pictures of themselves and then delete them an hour later. There was this one girl, Kennedy, who modeled for Urban Outfitters and literally just posted photos of her ass in different-colored leotards. In fact, it was the first thing I saw when I opened the app: the tanned curve of Kennedy Jones's butt cheek, with 864 likes. The caption: *senior's* 😊 🍑.

I didn't care that much about the butt cheek, or even the likes. The apostrophe, though, made me want to die.

"RORY! NOW!"

"I'M *COMING!*"

I grabbed my cracked phone and bounded down the

stairs. Saige, Willow, Mom, and Nonno sat at the table in the kitchen, while Nonni bustled around, shoveling pasta onto each plate. Everyone was talking at the same time, and no one was really listening to each other. I plopped onto my seat across from Mom and started scrolling through Instagram again.

My family's structure is—to put it lightly—weird. My dad's parents, Nonni and Nonno Morelli, moved here from Italy right before Dad was born. Dad was their only child, and they wanted him to become a doctor and marry another Italian, or at least a Catholic. But, as most plans in my family do, this backfired comically: Dad became an anthropology professor. He met Eve Quinn, a British, atheist biology teacher with tattoos up and down her arms. They got married. They had me, and then Saige. Mom grudgingly let Nonni take us to church on holidays and feed us lasagna on Sundays. For a while, things sort of worked out.

Then Dad had a premature heart attack and died.

I was three, so I remember almost nothing except for flowers: flowers everywhere, all the time. I don't remember my mom reacting. I don't remember *myself* reacting. I just know that, before Dad died, Mom liked to smile and squeeze us, swinging us around, burying her nose in our hair. And after Dad died, Mom became more, well, *Mom:* rough around the edges, sarcastic, stressed, and bone tired. All through elementary and middle school, I *lived* for the times when Mom cracked one of her twisted, one-sided smiles at an art project I brought home, or gave an out-of-character guffaw at a joke I told. I loved having fevers or the stomach flu, because she'd kiss my forehead and let me sleep with her.

But those moments were rare, because after Dad

died, Nonni and Nonno moved in, and they ended up staying permanently. And they got old. And when I was eleven, Mom had Willow with a doorknob boyfriend who promptly left, and then there was a baby to care for. Mom takes care of five people now, has sworn off men for life, and isn't necessarily keen on "showing affection."

So, there we all were: Nonni and Nonno, who— despite having moved to the States almost fifty years ago—still barely spoke English. Mom, as atheist and tattooed as ever. Saige and me, hybrids of Mom's and Dad's opposite worlds. And Willow, who we pretended was just immaculately conceived. Six people in a bungalow on the outskirts of town, sharing all meals and two bathrooms: the precise opposite of an average Clarksdale family.

"Rory, phone," Mom said, and I clicked it off, stuffing it into my pocket.

"Nonni, I don't want any more," Saige said, as Nonni allowed a small avalanche of meat sauce to fall onto her plate.

"Is okay," Nonni said, continuing to serve Saige.

"Rory, will you play *Minecraft* with me after dinner?" Willow asked me.

"Don't you have homework?"

"She doesn't, but you do," Mom said, motioning to me with her wine glass.

"*Nonni*," Saige said again. "No more."

When Nonni sat down and dinner officially began, conversations flew across the table, each person trying to be louder than the next. Nonno and I, as usual, stayed quiet on opposite ends.

I shoved a forkful of pasta into my mouth and took

my phone back out, holding it in my lap. Stoff had posted an edgy picture in the snow; I liked it.

From across the table, Saige sent me an unflattering selfie that gave me a view straight up her nose, and I almost choked. For the past six years, we'd been playing a single game of Chicken, seeing who can make the other laugh when we're in the same space and not supposed to be on our phones. I narrowed my eyes at her across the table, and she smiled mischievously.

*I win*, she mouthed.

*Barely*, I mouthed back, before returning to Instagram. I couldn't help but grin. Since we'd moved to Clarksdale, these moments between Saige and me had kind of diminished, because as soon as she started her freshman year at Telsey, my sister gained about six thousand friends. Between that and her new, unexplainable obsession with lacrosse, she was rarely even home for dinner most nights.

On the other hand, I had made precisely one friend and spent all my free time at home. My sister did lacrosse; I now, apparently, did choir.

I did choir next to a girl who wore a colorful robe to school, just because.

Without thinking much, I went to the search bar and typed *Liv*.

"—physics teachers changed their test day to Wednesday, which screws up my entire spring semester plan for the sophomores—" Mom was ranting.

"—if you just put less aioli on it, Nonni—"

"*Ti piace, bambina?*"

About thirty different Olivias popped up under my search, all looking the same. I scrolled disappointedly through them until, at the brink of giving up, I found the username *@bullshitwitch* and, underneath, the name *liv martinez*. Bio: *she/her \*\* filipinx \*\* irritated*.

It was her.

Her Instagram page was nothing and everything that I expected it to be, the most random and obscure pictures: Lipstick scrawled on a mirror. A frantic, sprinting cat. A goblin-like creature from the depths of Twitter. A huge wasp next to a manicured foot. Each picture had over a thousand likes, most with comments like *this is sending me* or *not the goblin liv i'm dead* or just a simple *whyyyy*.

"Even kids in *my* class have phones, Nonni," Willow was saying. "First grade!"

"Brats," Mom whispered under her breath. "Let me help you with that, Nonno."

I was now ten months deep into Liv's Instagram. My thumb hovered over a shot she must have taken in the mirror of a very dark room—her reflection turned away, the wing of one eye sparkling underneath her hair.

My thumb brushed the screen, and a white heart popped up. I'd accidentally liked it.

Panic flooded through my body. My eyes started to cloud over. I un-liked it, but it was too late. Liv would get the notification: *@rory.q-m liked your photo.*

"*Fuck* me," I said under my breath.

"Swear jar, Rory," Willow said brightly, bathing her spaghetti in parmesan.

Rapidly, my hands shaking, I went to *Settings. Change Username.*

*Anything*, said my brain. *Anything but this.*

I fumbled blindly, ending up with *@spaghetti123*.

*Great, Rory. Very cool.*

"Rory. *Phone*," Mom said again, this time reaching

across the table. Resigned, I gave her my phone and let her place it on the counter.

* * *

The next day during choir, I kept my eyes on my shoes for the entire forty minutes, just in case Liv wanted to say something about my weird, stalker-like social media move. I waited for her to say, "Hey, so this account called *@spaghetti123* liked one of my old pictures last night, and when I went to the page, it looked like you." Waited for her to notice what a complete loser I was.

Turns out, she didn't. The next day, she simply sent me a follow request, and I accepted. In choir, I stared at my shoes again until she offered me more gum.

We didn't talk for the rest of the week.

Meanwhile, Stoff was aggressively carving out my social schedule for the month. "You're blacking out with me on Friday," he said as we sat at our table at the edge of the cafeteria. I was holding my peanut butter sandwich with my right hand, while a spiral notebook sat open to my left. At first, I didn't process what he said, because I was trying desperately to come up with any awards or recognitions I'd received in my seventeen years that would look relatively impressive on a college essay. Even though it was the middle of junior year, Mom already had me working my ass off on applications. As she kept reminding me, it wasn't as much about the college as it was about the scholarship. If I wanted to leave Illinois, I had to pay for it.

"Would you say getting a sportsmanship trophy in fourth-grade softball would constitute an achievement award?" I asked Stoff, wiping some peanut butter off the corner of my mouth with my pinkie finger.

Stoff choked on his salad and sprayed me with a bit of iceberg lettuce.

"You did *not* play softball in fourth grade," he said.

"Hella more believable than you playing basketball in eighth," I said as the bell rang for choir.

"You won the *sportsmanship trophy?*" he continued. "So you were, like, *good* at sports. Rory!"

"Yeah, it's no big deal, but I was the best one on the team," I said casually as we picked up our books.

I was not. I was perhaps the worst one on the team. I won the sportsmanship trophy because I was unpopular, and therefore didn't participate in the illegal gum-trading ring in the batting cage, and therefore never got in trouble, and therefore displayed sportsmanship. It was too complicated trying to explain this to Stoff.

It wasn't until we walked through the slush to the bus stop later that he informed me, once again, of my weekend plans.

"We're getting *fucked up* on Friday," he said as we hunched under the bridge. We stood uncomfortably close to the Cancer Corner, where the Telsey stoners lurked in their tight black clothing staring stoically at nothing, nodding along to whatever pulsed out of their AirPods. They were the "problem kids" at Telsey, but even they had expensive shit.

"Fucked up?" I asked. "As in . . ."

"As in *drunk*, Rory," Stoff said. "It's the Duvall twins' party, and this is the first time I'm invited, and you're coming with me."

I laughed out loud. The Duvall twins were seniors whose parents owned the Clarksdale Lighthouse on Lake Michigan. Every year, apparently, they threw a

party that was *the* social event of our school. The way
Stoff had explained it, if you hadn't been seen at a
Duvall twins' party by the time you graduated, did you
even attend Telsey?

"Stoff," I said. "My *mom.*"

"The queen of wine, science, and British sass?"

"Yeah, her. She'd never let me go."

"How many times have you told me she literally
doesn't care what you do? She's such a baddie, I bet
she'd usher you out with a six-pack and a joint."

"Tattoos don't make her a baddie, but anyway,"
I grumbled, ignoring his protest. "I have to babysit
Willow!"

"Saige can do it."

I scoffed. As if Saige, *the* social butterfly of the freshman class, would agree to that.

"You need to come out, Rory. I'm saying this as your
friend. It's junior year. What's wrong with having *fun?*"

"My cats are more fun than most people our age."

He closed his eyes for an extended, annoyed blink.
"Okay. How about you pregame with me and then decide how you feel?"

I huffed out a sigh. "I need to ask you a question,
and you can't get mad at me or react loudly to it."

"What?" Stoff said, eyebrows raised.

"Never mind."

"*What?*"

"What—is *pregaming,* exactly?" I asked, trying to
untangle the cord to my headphones and act casual.

Stoff paused dramatically for a few moments with
his eyes closed, taking in the pleasure of my ignorance.
"Okay, Ror," he said, putting both hands on my shoulders and looking down at me. "You need to know this

before going out into the world. Pregaming is when you get drunk before the actual party. *I probably just saved your life.* Remember: Pregaming is what?"

"Drinking before the party."

"Correct. So that's what we'll be doing. And then can you drive us there?"

"Well, if I'm *drinking*," I said, "I probably shouldn't be *driving*."

Stoff looked as though it was the first time it had occurred to him that drinking and driving might be a bad combination. Like we didn't watch videos about it in health class, in driver's ed, in homeroom. Like we didn't have to wear "drunk goggles" last fall on Social Emotional Learning Day and walk in a straight line in front of our entire class, proving that it can't be done.

"We can Uber?" he suggested.

"I don't have an account," I said. "And if you do, I'm guessing your parents won't like seeing that charge."

But I knew that this party was important to him. Even if it hadn't been obvious in his face, just from having known Stoff for six months, I *knew* he'd never forgive himself for missing it. And he was genuinely trying to get me to come.

Almost like it wouldn't be the same without me.

But also, when I got home from school on Fridays, it was finally *over*. There was nothing better than shoving my dirty clothes in the hamper, pulling on flannel pajamas, and cocooning on the couch with my headphones and a book. Knowing that two full days lay ahead without a single hint of the outside world, and high school, and real life. Sleeping in, reading all day, helping Nonni make dinner.

Best of all, on Friday nights, I used to stay up with

Mom after everyone else went to bed. We'd listen to records, and I'd get her all to myself. I'd help her organize papers or water the plants, ask her about music, and get her to rant about the sleepless nights she spent dancing with Dad before I was born, blowing out her eardrums at concerts without a care in the world. She'd show me different albums, ask my thoughts on which were the best, and nod thoughtfully when I responded. On those nights, Mom lit up like a Christmas tree, and we could talk for hours. We hadn't done this since we'd moved to Clarksdale, because she'd been so stressed with her new teaching job, but I kept hoping we'd start again soon.

I obviously would've rather passed away than admit that I didn't want to go out on a weekend night because I wanted to hang out with my mom, but Stoff still seemed to read my mind, knowing I needed an extra push.

"Bagels on me Saturday morning," he said. "And Sunday. And all of next week." He blinked down at me, snow dotting his eyelashes. "Like deadass, I will bring you a bagel every morning for a week. Different kind, every day."

The bus sloshed up to us, spraying everyone's legs with dirty snow. My high-tops soaked slowly and steadily until my feet were weighed down with slush. Stoff exhaled a string of expletives, looking down at his pink pants, which were now splattered. Wrenching my feet out of the slush, I joined him and the throng of other kids who stood at varying levels of angst and disgust, pushing and sliding and bouncing off each other to line up for shelter. I could've hitched a ride with Mom, but she liked to stay and grade most afternoons, and I wanted to get out of there as soon as humanly possible. Most Telsey kids had a parent or nanny (or, in some cases—and I'm not exaggerating—a hired car) pick them up from school, especially on a day like this. When I told this to my mom last fall, asking if maybe Nonni could pick me up sometimes, she burst out laughing and couldn't stop for three minutes. *You,* she said, *are taking the bus,* hiccup, *until the day,* hiccup, *you buy your own,* hiccup, *motherfucking car.*

*I get it, Mom,* I said, as she shoved a dollar in the swear jar.

"Please," Stoff said now, one more time, once we were squeezed against a window at the back of the bus and it was bumping unpleasantly down Evergreen Lane. The air was like a thick, cold blanket woven entirely of high school BO. Stoff's bangs hung in dark upside-down triangles on his forehead. I read in his face how disgusting he felt, how much he wanted to leave this bus and extract every germ from his body. How much, despite his flawless Instagram and flourishing social life, he actually hated high school.

"Fine," I said, and his smile lit up his whole face.

## chapter five

At ten on Friday night, numb with social anxiety, I pulled up at Stoff's in our family minivan.

"Hey, bitch," he said cheerfully as he slid into the passenger seat. "Did your mom put up a fight?"

"She briefed me on the signs of alcohol poisoning and then pushed me out," I said shakily, pulling back onto the road.

"Aww. Baby Ror's growing up!"

I ignored him and twiddled with the stereo.

"Sorry, but *what* is this music right now?" Stoff asked, and I could smell the alcohol on his breath. His parents had a nice stock, apparently, and at this point he was an expert at breaking into their expensive scotch without their notice. He yanked the aux cord out of my phone, putting an abrupt end to the Velvet Underground, and plugged in his phone instead. Kendrick Lamar's "HUMBLE." exploded out of the speakers.

"Stoff," I said.

"Don't," he replied, as the car started jumping to the bass.

"It's just . . . we're in a minivan. In fucking *Clarksdale.*"

He pretended not to hear me.

Ten minutes later, we pulled up to the biggest house I had ever seen. People stared as we got out of the car, and I couldn't blame them: I'd just pulled a catastrophic parallel parking job, and Stoff was still shouting the lyrics to the song. When we walked down the dark path to the house, he noticed my backpack for the first time.

"Wait," he said. "Did you *bring* stuff?"

"Um, yeah," I said, trying to take in my surroundings. The giant house was pounding. People meandered around the porch like ants, holding red Solo cups (which I thought only existed in movies) and dressed impractically. I never knew what boys wore to parties, but now I saw that it was just the same stuff they wore to school, except a bit more plaid and less pastel. The girls, though, were in potentially the least logical clothes possible: everyone seemed to be wearing crop tops and miniskirts, and despite the fact that it was January, only about half of them wore tights. My legs prickled just looking at them, and I wondered what could ever be important enough to sacrifice the basic comfort of not freezing. Some girls were—I'm actually serious—plunking around the snow in heels. I mean, like, those types of heels that probably cost hundreds of dollars but can hardly be walked in on flat concrete, let alone in *snow*.

I was wearing—shocker—black jeans, a black shirt and coat, and Mom's old Docs.

"What did you take?" Stoff asked excitedly, looking at my backpack. I barely had time to figure out what he meant—what did I take *from my mom*, as in, what alcohol did I steal—when he wrenched open my backpack.

"Um, Ror?" He lifted a spiral notebook halfway out and started laughing. "Are you trying to do *homework*?"

"No," I said. My teeth were chattering; I wanted to go inside. "Yes. Sort of."

He looked at me blankly.

"It's my college essay, Stoff," I said. "My mom really wants me to get it done by this weekend. I need to brainstorm. I just thought, if I come up with any ideas here . . ."

He blinked down at me. I couldn't tell by his silence if he was shocked, frustrated, or just too drunk at this point to understand my dilemma.

"I'm driving, so I can't drink anyway," I said, trying to sound encouraging.

Stoff replaced the notebook and handed back my bag. I thought I was off the hook, but then he grabbed my arm and pulled me into the house, where the floor pounded with music. Bodies swarmed everywhere. The stench of alcohol and something else—*something skunky?*—filled my nose instantly.

I wasn't cold anymore, but I started shivering harder. I broke away from his grasp.

"Ror," he whined. "Just try. Can you just *try* to be normal?"

Everything around us seemed to muffle as I looked up at him.

*Normal.*

For a moment I was back at a sleepover party in eighth grade. Cassidy, my childhood friend, was cornering me near the bathroom. *What's wrong with you? Why are you being so weird and quiet? Just act normal!*

I was at Cassidy's house before the freshman dance, showing up late to find her and her soccer friends all dressed in similar mesh dresses and heels. I was looking down at my Converse, which had felt so right when I put them on earlier with my denim jumper and cotton shirt, and now suddenly felt so wrong. *Why didn't you dress normally for once, Rory? It's a school dance!*

I was in Cassidy's basement with her and two other boys, and the latest Star Wars was playing, but no one was paying attention. Cassidy and the first boy were glued to each other, and I was sitting a solid foot apart from the second boy, though his hand kept creeping toward me, and I kept scooting farther away. Cassidy, texting me later: *You know, he really likes you. Why were you so cold toward him? Why can't you just be NORMAL?*

I never could figure out what normal was. I only understood that it was something I wasn't.

"Put your bag upstairs," Stoff said, pulling me back to now. I shook my head, trying to clear it. "Then meet me in the kitchen. I have to introduce you to these other choir kids."

I took a step back from him, clenching my jaw tightly to stop shaking. I pushed Cassidy out of my mind. We hadn't talked in years.

*Go*, Mom had said earlier, wrapping an extra scarf around my neck. *I trust you to be smart. Just go.*

The music pounded.

"Okay," I said to Stoff. "Okay. I'll be right back."

\* \* \*

Wandering through the mansion, I stayed mostly invisible, except for the four times my backpack swung into another person, after which I frantically apologized. The music was so loud that most of what I heard was just the rattle of the floor, people shouting, and my heart at each rhythmic thud of the bass.

As I stumbled around the mass of bodies, I had one intense thought, like the words were written in neon letters in the middle of a pitch-black night: UPSTAIRS. FIND THE STAIRS.

I climbed a back staircase, dodging a couple making out in the process, trying not to recognize the girl as the one who sat behind me in APUSH. I came out into a hallway lined with doors, family portraits, and expensive-looking art. The twin hosts of the party, whoever they were, smiled at me from six or seven places on the wall.

I had basically no social life, but I still knew what happened in bedrooms at parties like this. Instead of barging into one of them to stow my backpack, I aimed for a glass door at the end of the hallway, which looked as though it led to an enclosed balcony. I strained my ears but couldn't hear any sound coming from behind the doors, nor could I make out any shapes in the darkness, so I decided to risk it.

At first, carefully twisting open the door, I felt relief flood my cheeks, sure that I was the only one there. A millisecond later, my heart jumped into my mouth.

"Hey," said Liv, as in *the* Liv with the colorful clothes and the gum and the Instagram that I'd stalked. She blew a stream of smoke out neatly in front of her, and the skunky smell intensified. "Do you mind shutting the door?"

She sat slumped on a nice-looking couch, feet crossed on top of a table that was littered with magazines. Her hair was tied into a flawless middle-part updo; she wore black high-waisted jeans, a shimmering long-sleeved top, and chunky boots.

I closed the door awkwardly behind myself and inhaled more of the thick, mossy air. With another jolt, I realized we weren't alone: there was a guy sort of draped over the couch in a wrinkly white shirt, with a head of messy black hair resting on part of Liv's leg.

"Sorry," I said. "I didn't mean to interrupt—"

"Who is that?" said the slumped human in a slurred voice.

"Shut up," Liv said to him, before turning to me. Her face lightened. "No need to say sorry, you're more than welcome to join us."

"Liv," the guy gargled. "We were talking."

"*You* were talking," Liv said. "I want to talk about something else now. Rory, you want a hit?"

Liv held out a glittering pipe to me. It looked like a thick spoon from one of Nonni's old antique collections, or maybe a piece of glass art. A small pile of what I quickly realized was weed—the first weed I'd ever seen—was packed neatly inside.

"I'm not done with our conversation," said the guy.

Liv raised her eyebrows at me, ignoring him, still holding out the pipe. I tried to look casual, tried to ignore how awkward I felt with my backpack over both shoulders.

"I'm good for now," I said. "Thanks."

She shrugged, and I sat gingerly down in the armchair diagonal from them.

"I want another drink," the guy said, raising his head. As soon as he did, Liv moved her legs away from him and folded them over the arm of the sofa.

"Great," she said, holding the pipe to her mouth and flicking the lighter.

The guy sat up all the way. "Can you, like, get a

drink *with* me?"

Liv rolled her eyes and expelled the smoke, not bothering to turn her head away from him, and he started to cough. "No," she said.

"Why?" the guy asked, rubbing his hands over his eyes and then through his hair. "I'm gonna get fucking lost."

"You'll figure it out," she said.

He stood for a few moments and then stumbled out the door, mumbling something.

"What?" Liv asked him.

"Nothing."

"Correct," she said.

As soon as the door slammed shut, she sank deeper into the couch. "Sorry about him," she said. "Harrison can be such an ass when he's faded."

"It's fine," I said.

"No, it really sucks. Every time he gets like this, we end up fighting."

I took a breath and asked, "How long have you guys been dating?"

Liv looked surprised for a moment and then started to laugh. "We aren't dating," she said. "I'd rather be burned at the stake than date that boy."

"Oh," I said. "Word."

"Have you noticed that about guys at Telsey?"

"Noticed what?"

"That every single one of them is a fuckboy with an inch-long dick?"

Now I coughed.

"My bad, I'm blowing this into your face," she said, changing positions. "I'm just *so* over them. I don't think there's one guy at our school I'd consider dating anymore."

"Okay," I said, finding something I could relate to. "Yes. Mood."

She raised her arm to brush some hair out of her face, and the sleeve of her wool sweater fell. I caught a glimpse of a small tattoo on the inside of her wrist.

"Is that . . ." I started, before I could catch myself.

She looked at me for a moment before flashing a slight smile and following my gaze to her wrist. She pulled her sleeve down and brought her arm closer. I saw her tattoo clearly now: the silhouette of two retro-looking bicycles, one following the other. "Do you know what it's from?" she asked, her eyes glinting.

I scooted to the edge of the chair. "Is it . . . *Stranger Things*?"

"But of course, milady," Liv said fancily.

I smiled, proud of myself for guessing right. Although I hated the gore in that show, Saige and I had binged every season as soon as it came out—her because of her massive crush on Steve, and me for the near-perfect soundtrack.

"I know it's kind of cheesy," Liv said, gazing down at the little bikes. "But I just thought, what the fuck. It's my body." Her mouth twisted into a bigger smile as she looked back at me. "Also, Eleven's a vibe. Like, I would absolutely love to throw buildings around when I'm mad."

I shrugged off my backpack and carefully placed it on the floor. "Eleven's the best character, hands down," I said, curling my arms around my legs. "My sister always says I'm like Will."

Liv looked at me for a moment. "No, definitely Max."

I gaped back. "*How*? She's a badass. I'm—"

She shrugged. "You're quiet, but I just get the feeling you have a majorly hardcore skater streak below your skin. You just choose when to show it."

She took another hit, and I lay back in my chair, wondering how on earth she had come to that conclusion.

When Liv had expelled the smoke from her mouth, she turned to me. "What did you think of the latest season?"

I started talking, and soon we were deep into an analysis of the show. Liv's twisty smile grew while I talked—again, like she knew something I didn't—and as we spiraled about Hopper/Joyce theories, eighties music, and the Mind Flayer, I felt a rush in my chest. I didn't know what it was, really. The scent of the weed, maybe, or the excitement of talking to someone who wasn't my family or Stoff. The tug of her smile that said, *I want to listen to you.*

I wanted to talk to her. I wanted to say everything at once, all the words in the English language at the same time.

I didn't know how to process that, so I just kept talking.

At one point, Liv abruptly narrowed her eyes and asked, "Who's your favorite random character?"

"Mr. Clarke," I responded immediately, the feeling in my chest settling to a nice warm buzz. "He could pull more than any other guy on the show, hands down."

Liv shouted in laughter, tipping her head to the ceiling and clapping.

"Dude's, like, a full ten," I said, encouraged by her reaction. "And he *knows it.*"

"Finally," she said. "Someone's *actually* on my level

of obsession." She lay back onto the cushions and curled up, facing me. "God, Rory, where the fuck have you been for three years?"

"Oh," I said. "I just moved here for my mom's job. She teaches at Telsey." I cleared my throat, not ready to switch topics. "Ms. Quinn?"

"Ms. Quinn, as in the badass new bio teacher with a British accent?"

"Yep."

"She's your *mom*?"

"Yeah," I said, trying to sound casual. "She's all right." Sometimes I got pissed at people idolizing my mom just because of an accent and some tattoos, but right now, I desperately wanted Liv to think she was cool.

Honestly, I desperately wanted Liv to think that *I* was cool.

"Holy shit," Liv said. "She's a *queen*."

I shrugged, trying not to grin.

"Well, welcome to Clarksdale," Liv said. "It's a shithole." She flicked her lighter again, and I laughed. "What?" she said in a compressed voice, a stream of smoke escaping from the corner of her mouth.

"This is the nicest, bougie-est town I've ever seen," I responded. "It's the opposite of a shithole."

She tipped her head back again, releasing the rest of her breath. "Most people living here are in the top one percent of our country, and they fucking act like it. Clarksdale's a rich, WASPy bubble. I mean, I'm half-Filipinx, and my dad and I are practically the only people of color here. And like, people grow up here, they go to a great school, and then eventually they come back and raise their own kids, and they never actually leave the bubble. It's disgusting."

"Oh," I said.

"Yeah."

We stayed quiet.

"Well, you'll leave," I finally said.

She looked at me, eyebrows raised. "How can you tell?"

I looked up at the ceiling, wondering if I was backing myself into a corner. "Just from the way you sit in choir. Or the way you walk down the hall with your headphones and everything. It's like . . . you're somewhere else. You're not here." I swallowed. "Not the way everybody else is."

She smiled, keeping her eyebrows raised. "Okay . . ."

"I didn't mean it in a bad way," I said quickly.

"No," she said. "You're right. I don't fit."

I shrugged. "I don't fit, either."

She surveyed me from her couch, looking up and down. And then she smiled again in a small, conclusive way.

"What do you think about choir?" she asked.

"I don't know," I said. "I just need an A in something."

"I feel that," she said, leaning back. "It's really funny how much people care about choir here. Actually? It's really funny how much people care about *everything* here."

"Yeah, I'm starting to notice that," I said.

"Like last year, in PE, my friend Natsuki—"

The balcony door opened suddenly, and Harrison with the greasy black hair staggered in. Invasively loud rap music pushed into the room with him.

"Yooooooo," he slurred, moving toward Liv as though about to lounge on her lap again.

"You smell like shit," she said sharply, and everything about her suddenly changed. She was back to the Liv I knew from choir, the one at school, the one who looked coolly through her dark eyes, refusing to crack.

This was why we hadn't talked until now. Because of her shell.

And I realized, as my body automatically went rigid and my arms and legs crossed in front of me, that I was not much different.

I watched from my crossed, guarded stance as she forced Harrison to leave.

"I don't want to talk to you," she said simply.

"Why?"

"Because you're too fucked up, and I don't talk to people who are too fucked up. I gain nothing from it."

"Sorry that not everyone wants to talk about pretentious shit all the time," Harrison said, running his fingers through his hair.

"Big words," Liv said, sounding bored. "Cool. I think you should go back downstairs now."

Harrison smiled and shook his head, laughing. "It's just funny," he said in response to our blank stares, "because you literally think you're so much better than everyone else."

Liv raised her eyebrows. "Keep talking."

"You know what I mean."

"I really don't," Liv said. "Is there a reason you're throwing shade at me right now, Harrison? Or is this just a super unattractive, misogynistic quality you have that only shows itself when you're drunk? Can you enlighten me?"

Harrison seemed lost for words, which was honestly an improvement. He shook his head, and Liv watched, eyes narrowed. He finally turned around, roughly pulling the door open and tumbling through.

He muttered, just loud enough for us to hear: "Selfish fucking bitch."

I don't know how Liv reacted, because suddenly I couldn't look at her. We sat in the cold silence for what seemed like years, and then she got up and slammed the door after him, muffling the music and voices again. For one moment, she stood there with her back to me, her shoulders rising and falling in a single, prolonged breath. My mouth felt as though it were wired shut.

She turned around and flopped back onto the couch.

"I—I'm sorry," I faltered. "I should have said something."

"Dude," Liv said, shaking her head. "One, don't apologize. We're taught to profusely apologize for just *existing* because we're girls. Don't subscribe to it."

"But—" The gravity of what she said hung confused in the air, and the floor beneath us pumped like a heartbeat.

"No buts. And two, he's not worth getting salty about." She slumped back into the pillows, flicking her lighter again. "I'm not upset, so you definitely shouldn't be."

I sat in silence, trying to figure out what to even say. "He was so *mean.*"

At first, I thought she wouldn't respond. She took another hit, releasing her breath slowly, and took out her phone. I tried to resist the urge to take out mine, too. Everything that felt warm and safe five minutes ago had ended.

Then, Liv suddenly said, "Homeboy wanted to hook up over winter break, and I refused. He's been a dick ever since. *Hilarious* if he thinks he's getting some now." She drew a deep breath and then sang, in a strangely clear, operatic trill, the entire pre-chorus of Beyoncé's "Sorry." I thought about that strange smile she'd flashed at me in choir, before straightening all her features again and turning back to stone. It was like a whole new person had emerged.

"*TELL HIM BOY, BYE!*" she shouted. And I couldn't help it; I was cackling. She kept going until I was curled on my side, begging her to stop.

"God," she said finally, throwing herself dramatically back onto the couch. "Why am I even *here?*"

"You're—" I hiccupped. "*Liv!* Don't say that! You're so special and cool! You have so many reasons to be here!"

She looked at me, startled. "No, I just meant at this party."

*Just absolutely killing it, Rory.*

"I mean, I don't even know these people." She twisted leisurely onto her side, stretching one leg straight in the air. "They're, like, my friend's boyfriend's friends or something. Do you know them?"

"No. My friend Stoff just really wanted to go. I don't know why I agreed," I said, suddenly feeling worked up. "It's miserable outside, and I want to be reading in my bed."

"Mood," she said. She inhaled from her pipe, reached her foot to the coffee table, and deliberately knocked a pile of home improvement magazines to the floor. "Fuck high school."

I stared at the mess for a moment, then leaned back into my chair, stretched my leg to the table, and knocked a few down myself.

chapter six

*T*he Monday after the Duvall twins' party, we woke up to a fresh blanket of snow and the temperature down to negative two.

"Rory, I'm dying," Stoff whimpered, as we sat in the hallway before school.

Despite having had two full days to recover, Stoff and the rest of the kids I knew who'd been at the Duvall twins' party looked terrible. The Telsey way of "looking terrible," I should add, might not be the typical way: instead of cashmere sweaters and designer jeans, there was an abundance of Lululemon "casual" apparel and designer sweatpants. The girls held venti Starbucks cups, and some wore their Ray-Bans all the way to first period.

I wore my maroon fleece pullover and sat munching on my third payback bagel with a still-hungover Stoff slumped beside me. Everything was normal and quiet.

Then, Liv walked by.

She wore a red turtleneck top and a fitted, nineties-era plaid jumper over black tights and combat boots. The wings lining her eyes were blue today, and thick as ever. Endless dark brown waves of hair flowed behind her as she sauntered by, seeming somehow weightless, but simultaneously taking up the entire hallway. It was like she existed in a layer of the atmosphere above everyone else. Her eyes pointed like lasers straight ahead, rising above our mere lockers and straightened hair and teenage drama. She had so little time and patience, I realized. For us. For the uncool.

My face mildly brightened in the way it does on the rare occasion that I see someone I like, but the next moment, I slumped back down: there was no way I could be friends with someone this cool, this ethereal.

I looked down at my bagel and focused on my very boringly human activity of eating it while keeping Stoff's head from dropping onto my shoulder. Staying invisible worked out for me until Stoff sat up straight and shouted, "O-*kay*, sis! Step on me with that jumper."

It was like someone pulled the plug out of the speakers in the middle of a party. Every head in the hallway turned.

Liv took her time to carefully remove her headphones and allow Stoff a cool half-smile. "Thanks, dude," she said, looking briefly at him, but then her eyes flickered to me, and her smile grew wider. "I forgot to tell you something, Rory," she said, walking over to us and kneeling beside me, as if it were the most casual thing in the world for someone dressed like her to interact with someone dressed like me. I could hear the music pounding out of her headphones and thought I recognized it from an old Tame Impala album, but I had no time to say so. She cupped her hands over my ear and whispered, "My favorite random character is Officer Callahan."

"Heavily underrated," I whispered back.

She dissolved into quiet, tiny giggles, stood up, replaced her headphones, and walked away.

Then we didn't talk for the entire week.

Everything became buried in snow, in history papers and TikTok challenges and some type of sinus-y plague that spread through the school like wildfire. Mom and I fought about homework and college; Stoff's parents discovered the missing scotch and took away his phone. Winter droned on. And Liv sat stoically beside me in choir, not saying a word.

Then, one day before ninth period, as I was grabbing my books for APUSH, I suddenly felt the presence of another human beside me. I whipped around, twisting my headphones haphazardly around my neck, and emitted a strange type of choking sound, trying to pull them loose. Liv was leaning casually against the locker next to me. Today she was wearing corduroy overalls, and her hair was woven tightly into Dutch braids. I wondered how she could look this cool and unapproachable while wearing literal overalls.

"Hey," I croaked.

She graciously ignored the fact that I was the most awkward human on earth and peered down at my phone, raising an eyebrow in mild interest. "What are you listening to?"

A wave of brand-new stress washed over me, and I tried in vain to push my phone between two books, but it was no use. She'd glanced at the screen, and she was smiling.

"'Test Drive,'" she read. "From . . . *How to Train Your Dragon?*"

She looked at me. I looked at her.

"Girl," she said.

"Yeah, I . . ." I brushed my hand through my unkempt hair. "I like to listen to movie soundtracks when I'm . . . overwhelmed."

*Why don't I just tell her now that I still sleep with a stuffed rabbit, have weird black hair on my left ankle that I pluck every week, and still have trouble with tampons?*

"Cool," Liv said, nodding.

I blinked, and around us, Telsey kids flurried past in their small bubbles, thinking their small thoughts.

"Better than the ear-splitting bullshit everyone listens to here," she continued, switching her bag to her other side. "If you like soundtracks, you should check out *Lord of the Rings*. I listen to it when I can't sleep."

"Oh," I said. "Bet."

She smiled again and pushed herself away from my locker, gliding back into her separate world.

* * *

Two more silent days passed. And then, in the middle of choir, Liv held her folder up in front of our faces and turned to me.

"I'm teaching myself a fourth language," she said.

I just stared back.

"My parents made sure I could speak Tagalog with my grandparents, and I've pretty much nailed Spanish, so I decided to challenge myself with something different."

Her eyes glinted. She wanted me to ask.

"What is it?" I obliged. "What language?"

"Swedish," she said, the word rolling delicately off her tongue. She brought down her folder, and we faced forward once again.

These tiny snippets of conversation began to occur more frequently: Once a week. Every other day. A few times per period. Sometimes, entire days would still pass where she wouldn't say a word, but then, two minutes before the bell, she'd turn to me and whisper, "Have you ever read *Siddhartha?*" or "My lower back is *murdering* me today. Fuck periods." She started telling me bits and pieces of her day, random observations. She'd wonder out loud about other people's personal hygiene habits, or show me her list of goals, which she frequently updated, because apparently going to a nationally ranked high school while researching colleges couldn't keep her busy enough. She'd say, "I think I'm gonna take a glass-blowing class" or "I'm bored with Bach, so I'm learning some Florence + The Machine on the cello instead."

I started telling her little things, too, though they didn't feel as interesting: the weird, funny thing that Willow said at dinner the previous night, or the latest book or album I was obsessed with. It became unbearably exciting, having someone who wanted to talk to me about things that weren't high school, college, or other people.

After each of these small conversations, she'd stiffen back into her shell, looking coolly over her music and chewing her gum, giving off a mildly irritated, bored vibe. But whenever we made eye contact, whenever one of us cracked to tell the other something, the ice seemed to melt a little.

One Thursday, I found myself chewing off my thumbnail and watching the clock as Liv railed on quietly next to me:

"—and my latest project is building a loft, so do you want to go to Michaels with me today to get supplies?"

Mr. Wong was working with the sopranos on a Handel piece, and Liv was smacking on her gum, balancing her choir folder on her knee, and editing an English paper with a purple pen.

"Can we rewind?" I said quietly. "You're building a loft? Like, physically?"

"Yes," Liv said, no longer bothering to lower her voice. "I need a new reading spot. My room's boring."

"Tenors!" Mr. Wong called. He was still very excited about us being part of the tenor section, finding an almost unhinged delight in us being "two of the guys." "How're my lady tenors doing?" he asked. After we gave him a noncommittal response and he moved on to the sopranos, Liv lifted her folder up in front of our faces and whispered, "Why does he think we automatically identify as ladies? I answer to *woman*, *queen*, or *witch*. Not *lady*. And like, what about the fact that there might be nonbinary people in choir? Any gender can sing any part." She rolled her eyes and blew a bubble.

"Measure twenty-four!" Mr. Wong shouted at us, before I had a chance to respond. Although my mind was spinning so fast, I hadn't even fathomed what I might reply. I was realizing that Liv was right: it *was* kind of shitty to trans and nonbinary kids to sort us like this. Why didn't I think about this stuff before?

I caught accidental eye contact with Stoff in the bass section. He narrowed his eyes and stuck his tongue out between his fingers. I flushed—as usual, his goal—and turned my eyes back to my sheet music, where I saw Liv writing a quick note to me on the upper corner, using my thigh as a platform.

"Liv, what are you doing?" Mr. Wong asked in the patient voice he seemed to reserve for her.

"Helping Rory with her measure numbers," Liv said

smoothly. "She got confused."

"Great!" Mr. Wong said, raising his baton. "Love the teamwork!"

Liv sat up, sticking her pen behind her ear, and we started to sing. I stole a glance at the corner of my music she'd been bent over. Directly under Handel's *Dank sei Dir, Herr*—"Thanks be to thee, God"—she'd drawn a stick figure and written, *Shut your whore mouth, George.*

"Awesome," I muttered. "This is rented music."

"You're *so* welcome."

When we finished with our section and Mr. Wong had moved on to the basses, I turned back to Liv. "I have to check that I'm not babysitting, but potentially yes to Michaels."

"You babysit a lot," she observed.

"Six-year-old sister."

"That's cool."

"Is it, though?"

"I'm an only child, and my parents are lawyers. So it's usually just me, alone at home, like—" She rolled her eyes back and shook her head, emitting a quiet, guttural groan.

"Hey, can you make that noise one more time?" I asked.

She did.

"Everything okay in the tenor section?" Mr. Wong said, raising his eyebrows.

"Golden," Liv said.

As he turned away from us again, Liv took her purple pen and wrote her number on my wrist. "Text me after school," she said casually, and then returned to her music.

\* \* \*

When I got home, I talked Saige into babysitting Willow. It wasn't easy: I had to offer to do her chores for two weeks and take a photoshoot of her in her new Lulus for her to even *consider* ditching the lacrosse girls for Willow. After that humbling exchange, I commenced my usual after-school routine of shoveling down three bowls of cereal while mindlessly scrolling through social media, retaining nothing from other people's posts except a mild feeling of my own inadequacy. Mom was getting ready to leave for some type of mega-nerd conference in Michigan for science teachers.

"How's the homework load, Ror?" she asked, stuffing a giant stack of papers into her briefcase.

"Good," I said in a muffled voice as some Honey Bunches of Oats fell out of my mouth.

Life at home was its usual tornado of the school year: Bologna sandwiches flew through the air. Nonni waged war against Saige's lacrosse uniform, which culminated in her throwing it out the laundry room window and blaming it on the wind. Mom's nightly glasses of wine inched subtly earlier each day as her patience with winter waned, which was agreeable for everyone, because it dramatically improved her mood. Thankfully, the routine chaos that transpired in a household of six people—Nonno's various health appointments, Willow's chorus rehearsals—kept Mom from breathing down my neck about studying and college scholarship research. It was one of the few parts of my life I wish Mom cared *less* about.

"I barely have anything," I told Mom for effect. "Couple of pages of French and a math quiz."

I also needed to read six chapters of *Jane Eyre*,

memorize the Civil War section of my history book, and learn the entire subjunctive mood of French verbs, but I just smiled.

Mom seemed mildly satisfied. She left the room, and I opened my phone to text Liv.

I spent fifteen minutes trying to sound casual, and not completely stoked, that we'd upgraded our friendship to texting. There's low-key a lot to worry about when texting someone for the first time: How many grammar rules do you follow without sounding like either a slob or a prude? You don't want to be like, *omg r u srsly 4realz cuz ily lolz!* But, on the other hand, you can't just be like, *Hey, girl! I write texts like I write my English papers; in other words, I'm a complete tool.*

Trying to text her the way I texted Stoff, I wrote: *Hey not bb-sitting tn. Still down for Michaels?*

I sent the text, realizing approximately one second later that she didn't yet have *my* number, and added choppily, *This is Rory*, and then a frail *Btw.*

*Triple texting*, I thought. *Rock on.*

I quickly learned that Liv, unlike Stoff, was *not* a rapid-fire texter. Probably, I reasoned with myself, because she was too busy being cool and nonconformist and teaching herself Swedish. When my phone chirped an hour later, I pulled off my headphones (nothing wrong with a little pre–*Jane Eyre* Joni Mitchell) and read her response:

*Actually change of plans*

*I just remembered there's a show I wanted to go to tonight in the city*

And then, a third gray bubble:

*Wanna come?*

My brain went into a mild panic. It was Thursday. A school night. People like me did not go to shows in the city on school nights.

A fourth gray bubble appeared:

*It's Problem Child*

Problem Child? What was Problem Child? Was that a person or a band? What were their pronouns? I rapidly Googled "problem child," and then "problem child music," and then "problem child music chicago." A few articles finally came up. It was a band, so *them*. Okay. That was a start.

*I've heard they're cool, let me check*, I texted, and then I crawled under the covers to come up with acceptable reasons to say *no*.

Of course, I had legitimate reasons. It was just that none of them counted as cool and casual things to say to Liv: *It's my night to feed the cats; my self-mandated bedtime is ten; I don't have a fake ID; I feel bad taking advantage of my non-English-speaking grandparents; I literally can't afford the Metra round trip downtown; and mostly, I'm scared.*

I had decided on a very boring *Ugh fuck my mom wants me to babysit after all* when I checked my phone again and saw that she'd already texted me twice more.

*They're playing at Dreamtown which is a pretty chill venue, they never check ID*

*I have 2 round trips left on my metra card*

I panicked as my excuses evaporated one after the other.

Then she sent: *We can pick up Chipotle on the way?*

*Fuck*, I thought.

Mom poked her head into my room. "Leaving," she

said. "I'll be back Saturday afternoon. Don't drop acid while I'm gone, yeah?"

"I'll try not to," I said, and she smiled briefly before shutting the door.

I watched the little blinker on my phone. *Type message here*, the blank space told me tantalizingly.

Liv sent me the burrito emoji, three exclamation points, and a question mark.

I thought of all the things she'd shared with me in the last few weeks: Her projects. Her observations. Her thoughts.

I wondered why she had picked me.

I swallowed twice and then typed: *Ok*.

*I*t was a good thing that Liv hadn't casually mentioned that the show started at ten. And that there were two opening bands. And, also, that she'd bring along four friends from school.

If she *had* mentioned these things, I would have bailed faster than you could say *peace*. But she hadn't, so three hours later I found myself sitting between two strangers on the Metra, wearing tights, and feeling a bit sick.

I'd told Nonni I was going to study with friends. For continuity's sake, instead of bringing a purse, I took along my backpack, complete with two books. Thankfully, Nonni's English vocabulary and my Italian vocabulary didn't intersect enough for an argument, so Nonni ended up sending me on my way with a silent frown and a small Tupperware of leftover lasagna instead. I tried to push down my guilty conscience. *People sneak out all the time in high school. Breaking some casual rules is healthy.*

*One might even say . . . normal.*

"Is girls only?" Nonni had asked, eyeing me suspiciously as I clamored down the stairs. The goal was to wear Saige's plaid skirt and prove that, in fact, I *could* dress like I understood fashion—but she didn't let me, so instead I sported the retro (but not cool-retro) style

of shorts on tights with a denim jacket and Mom's
Docs. Nonni had tugged down at the hem of my shorts,
as though hoping that passionate wishing alone would
increase their length.

"*Sì*, Nonni," I'd said, kissing her on the cheek. "*Solo
ragazze.*" Only girls.

Now that I was on the train, I regretted everything,
from the lie to my innocent grandmother to the weird
trying-to-nonchalantly-resemble-a-teen-who-goes-out-
on-Thursday-nights-and-doesn't-have-lasagna-in-her-
bag outfit.

"So, this is Rory," Liv said.

"Hi, Rory," her friends chorused around me.

"I'm Jem," said the guy right next to me, awkwardly
extracting an arm from between us to shake my hand.

"Like in *To Kill a Mockingbird!*" I shouted rather
than asked, as the train rumbled below us. My stomach
churned. Trying to ignore the burrito jostling around
inside me, I continued, "Jem and Scout are an underrated brother-sister team."

"Uh—yeah," said Jem. "Not named after him, but
still cool."

"Rory loves to read, too," Liv explained.

"Thank god," said the girl to my right. "Someone'll
finally know what you're talking about half the time,
Liv."

The girl introduced herself as Grace. The other
friends were Natsuki and Milo. I studied their features
while still trying to follow the conversation. Grace's hair
was wavy and aggressively, perfectly golden. Natsuki
wore a choker and had purple-streaked hair. Milo was
wearing one flannel on top of another and had a scruffy
beard, and Jem's braids were tied into a top knot even

bigger than Liv's. Everyone looked cool, no one looked like they attended Telsey, and yet I recognized some of them from the halls. I wondered how these kids came to be who they were while coexisting with golf-obsessed, pastel-wearing Clarksdale-ites. I had only lived in this town for six months, but I already felt the preppiness creeping toward me.

"What're your favorite bands, Rory?" Natsuki asked suddenly.

I tore my eyes away from Natsuki's hair and saw them all, including Liv, staring at me.

"Yeah, I don't know why we haven't talked about this until now," Liv said, sounding genuinely curious. "What do you listen to? Besides David Bowie?" I flushed, and she added hastily, "I mean, I just assumed Bowie was a given. Because of your shirts."

She meant the five T-shirts I wore to school, basically in diligent rotation: one for every Bowie concert Mom had attended.

"Yo, Bowie's a king," said Jem, giving me a fist bump, which was tiny, since we were squashed together.

I was painfully aware of everyone's eyes still resting on my face. I took a breath. *NO PRESSURE, BUT THE TIME IS NIGH TO BE COOL*, my brain bellowed. *DON'T JUST SAY THE FIRST THING THAT POPS INTO YOUR HEAD. DO NOT.*

"I really like . . . Fleetwood Mac?"

*Cool.*

Liv's friends all did the thing you do when you need to refrain from wrinkling your nose: they looked down, sniffed, frowned, and nodded a bit. Liv cleared her throat.

Because I was unfamiliar with the custom of not

beating a dead horse, I continued. "My mom listens to, like, oldies and rock and sad-boy punk. Eighties and nineties. And I use her Apple Music account, since we don't have Spotify. So, yeah . . . I'm really into Britpop, just because it's all *she* listens to, like the Stone Roses and Blur. But I can also get down with more eighties rock, like Springsteen and Guns N' Roses, and Prince, who I basically consider rock even though he could also be described as pop or R&B, so . . ."

"Dude, *yes*," Jem said, while everyone else gaped at me. "Prince is all genres. He's a god. Do you listen to any seventies funk?"

"Stevie Wonder," I said immediately. "I can get with Commodores and Curtis Mayfield, too—"

"Fuck yeah!"

"But I'm much more into the eighties these days. Anything you hear on *Stranger Things*, honestly. The Police, New Order . . ."

I looked around at the rest of the group and quickly realized that I was digging myself into a grave. Continuing to spout old bands wasn't generating the effect I needed—which was for everyone to break out into relatable smiles and say, "Oh, yeah! Same!"—so I tried a new, more modern direction.

"But I also love Beyoncé," I said, aware that my eyes were probably popping out of my head. "She can literally do no wrong. Lizzo's amazing, too. And Billie Eilish. And I know this is random, but Amy Winehouse." I folded my hands over my chest in prayer and said, "Rest in peace, Amy."

*Why are you like this?*

Just when I thought it might be time to jump ship— or jump train, more likely, by saying, "I forgot I already had plans!" and hitchhiking to Alaska—Liv came to my rescue. She grabbed my arm and looked me dead in the eye.

"Amy Winehouse," she said, the wings over her eyelids almost quivering, "is my *queen*."

Politely deciding to ignore the first 97 percent of my speech, her friends all assumed casual positions again and Grace said, "Yeah, Liv's not over Amy's death yet. It's been, like, over a decade."

Liv rolled her eyes back and said, very dramatically, "Time has no meaning when the heart truly grieves, Grace. You wouldn't *understand*."

\* \* \*

The venue, Dreamtown, was a fifteen-minute walk from the train station. I tried to look casual while also struggling to find the warmest position inside my jacket.

When we finally got inside, a gush of warm air greeted us. I'd never been in a bar before, and it wasn't exactly what I'd been expecting, but as Liv later clarified to me, it was more of a *lounge*. The lights were dimmed to a reddish glow, soul music played out of a jukebox, and there was a musty smell about the place. Not exactly the stench of hard alcohol that soaked the air at the party last month at the Duvall twins' house, but more of a smell that said, *We're adults, so we can drink and be casual about it, without anyone projectile vomiting.* It was a true miracle that no one checked our IDs, or simply just held out an arm to prevent me alone from following the crowd inside. I looked like a fourteen-year-old who'd swallowed the grungy section of Forever 21 and then barfed on myself.

"Want a drink?" Natsuki asked, hitting me in the

face with her hair. I saw Liv up ahead. There she went: to the bar, to order a beer. I looked at her and felt very, very young.

"Uh, sure," I said to Natsuki.

"What kind?"

*Fuck.* I looked around and saw a Heineken glinting in a guy's hand.

"Heineken," I blurted.

A few minutes later, Liv came back with a Blue Moon in one hand and a Heineken in the other. I watched the other kids crowd around Milo, who seemed to be the only one besides Liv with a fake ID, and took a sip of my beer. Sawdust filled my mouth, with a tinge of wet sand.

"You don't have to drink," Liv said, watching my face. "You really don't. Want me to take it?"

"I'm fine," I said in a gravelly voice.

"You sure? Come with me, I see a table."

We sat at a "table" the size of a pancake. There was no way a single person could comfortably sit there without spilling. I must have been blushing, because she continued, although without any sense of urgency, "It's not a bad thing to not drink, you know. It's your choice."

"Yeah," I said. "I know."

"Cool."

We sipped our beers in silence.

"You guys wanna go to the back?" Natsuki asked, weaving through the crowd up to us. "I think the Bumfucks are about to go on."

I followed them to the back of the venue, my beer warming in my hand, and I whispered into Liv's ear, "Sorry, but like, is that a band? Or is she just calling them bumfucks because they suck?"

Liv swigged down her beer, taking time to swallow. "Every time you unnecessarily say 'I'm sorry,' you have to pay me a dollar."

I stared at her, thinking of Willow and the swear jar. Willow's earnest, toothy smile as she held out a hand to me after I let an f-bomb slip, compared to the fierce look Liv was giving me now, her hand similarly outstretched for my money. I couldn't help it; I scoffed.

"No, really," she said, a glint shining in her eyes. "And yes, by the way, the Bumfucks are a band. But we should do this, Rory." She took my arm and led me to the back of the lounge. "I'll pay you whenever I apologize, too. It'll make us more *aware*."

"Aware of what?"

"Of how much we're subscribing to bullshit." She let go as a few flamboyantly dressed musicians filled the tiny stage, tweaking their guitars and synths. I breathed in the smoky air, closing my eyes, trying not to worry about how many people were crowded into this one tiny space. Trying to be seventeen, and not twelve or eighty-five. I thought of my parents, briefly—the stories Mom told me of the two of them jumping around at shows back in the nineties. Maybe I'd finally understand what she felt back then, why she missed it so much.

Liv spun me around to face her, bringing me back. "No more apologizing," she declared, and the gleam in her eyes had turned into a fire. She brought up her right fist, level to her mouth, and looked me dead in the eye.

Around us, a pulsing beat filled the air, and the people began swimming in a thick wall of bright blue sound, arms and teeth flashing under the moving lights, the brightness pushing against the walls. I felt the bass in my heart. The band had started, but Liv remained facing me, waiting.

I raised my left fist, my knuckles bumping hers. "No apologizing."

* * *

It turned out that all four of Liv's friends were there because of the second band, Mindless, which, coincidentally, I hated. Something about hairy men romping around and spraying sweat on your face while emitting piercing screams made me really wish I were eating Coco Puffs in my bed with the lights off.

*Is this what cool people listen to all the time?* I thought, trying to identify a beat to nonchalantly nod my head to, while everyone else threw themselves around. Next to me, Liv wasn't exactly losing her shit, but her eyes were closed, and a look of bliss had spread across her face as she shook and swayed.

When Mindless finally finished, Jem and Natsuki extracted themselves from the mob of flannels and body odor and bounced up to Liv and me. Jem was jogging in place, and Natsuki moved her mouth expressively, which I realized meant that she was talking. I tried to mentally unstick my eardrums from the walls of my brain.

"LIKE, WE WERE THINKING OF GOING?" she shouted, even though the music was no longer playing.

"PROBLEM CHILD HASN'T COME ON YET," Liv shouted back. I was glad that everyone else's temporary loss of hearing pretty much equated to mine.

Milo and Grace found us.

"READY TO BOUNCE?" Milo asked, shaking out

his hair, showering us all in sweat.

"PROBLEM CHILD!" Liv roared, tapping her watch.

Grace inched a bit closer. "WE HAVE THAT TEST TOMORROW," she shouted in response. "SO WE WERE THINKING OF TAKING THE 11:35 TRAIN!"

Liv rolled her eyes and grabbed our arms, pulling us out of the throng.

"*I* came here to see Problem Child," she said without preamble, once we were at the other side of the lounge. "So you guys can go, but I'm staying."

"Don't you have the same test as Grace?" Milo asked, grinning. Jem was still bouncing up and down.

Liv shrugged. "I already studied."

"What about you, Rory?" Natsuki asked.

"Um—" I said. Nonni and Nonno were already asleep, there was no question about it, and Mom was away at her conference. I could stay out.

But also, that bowl of Coco Puffs. And my bed.

Liv looked at me and blinked. Her friends looked at me and blinked. Natsuki and Grace, I noted, had both winged their eyeliner, but neither's looked as cool as Liv's.

"I'm fine staying," I said.

Liv linked her arm into mine. "We'll take the 12:35 train," she said, dragging me away. I waved and gave a weak "Bye!" to her friends, who had already started to walk toward the door.

I thought we'd stop at the back of the venue near the stage, but she led me to a back door.

"Are you afraid of heights?" she asked suddenly.

"No," I lied.

"Cool," she said. And then we climbed four flights of stairs to the roof of the building.

We stepped out onto the cold, flat roof, and the walls around us disappeared. The yellow and orange lights of Chicago fanned around us, blinking underneath the inky black sky.

Liv wrenched an apple out from the bottom of her bag. "Hold this," she said, placing it in my hand and continuing to rummage. I stood with my mouth slightly open as she handed me a pencil, a lighter, and a very tiny canister.

"Have you ever smoked out of an apple?" she asked, in the same way that you would ask, *Do you know if it's going to rain tomorrow?*

"Um, no," I said, becoming aware that I was holding drugs. Drugs! In the canister!

I had never smoked, period.

"It's easier using apples when you're not at home," Liv explained, and I watched—my mouth still just a *tiny* bit open—as she transformed the apple into a pipe. "They can pass off as snacks." She held the apple to her lips, flicked the lighter, and inhaled, eyes pointed toward the sky.

*Like the movies*, I thought. *My life is like the movies now.*

While she held her breath, I took a 360 of the rooftop. It was vast, plain, and very dirty, with a brick wall probably less than a foot high on all sides. I could see the headlines of the *Clarksdale Gazette* now: *LOCAL TEEN, RORY QUINN-MORELLI, FALLS OFF ROOF WHILE ILLEGALLY AT BAR ON SCHOOL NIGHT. "I really thought I could trust her to be responsible," says Eve Quinn, mother of the deceased.*

*"Now I know I was wrong."*

"Do you want a hit?" Liv asked.

I didn't, but also, I did. I could not describe the feeling. I wanted to be this person. The girl who went out on school nights and danced to sweaty bands and smoked out of apples and stood at the edges of tall buildings without being scared.

I wanted—*Fuck*, I thought. *I think I want to be her.*

So, for the second time that day, when my first instinct said, *Hmm, probably not*, I said, "Yes."

* * *

A few minutes later, feeling very warm, I followed Liv back downstairs. She had been a wonderful teacher: "Don't cough. *Don't* tip the apple. Here—let me just—can I help you?"

On our way down, she said, "A lot of people don't get high their first time. So don't freak out if nothing happens."

I wanted to tell her that things were already happening, but by the time I reached the end of the thought, the beginning of it had started to slip away. *How lovely is this*, my brain told me sleepily. *You can't stress out if you can't form complex . . .*

I ordered cheesy fries from the bar, and we found another tiny table. As soon as we sat down, a guy swaggered up to us and plopped down backward on the third seat, draping his arms over the top. He looked like he was in his mid-twenties, scruffy and ginger-haired. A well-fit flannel stretched across his obviously muscular chest. I was about to ask Liv if she knew this man when he smiled and extended a red, hairy arm to her. "Hey, I'm Finn," he said.

Instead of taking his hand, Liv dug into my fries. "Liv," she said.

"What are you drinking, Liv?"

She swallowed, looking at him. "Beer."

"I mean, what kind? I'd love to buy you a—"

"I have a boyfriend," she said evenly.

There was an uncomfortable pause, and to keep myself from suddenly breaking into a sweat, I tried to focus on the song that was playing and realized it was an oldie: Solomon Burke, "Cry to Me."

"So," said Finn, placing his untaken hand on the table in the space between them. Liv eyed it with distaste. "I won't tell him if you don't." He smiled.

"Fuck off," Liv said, her voice calm.

"Yeah," Finn said quietly, standing up and heading away.

Liv looked at me and then rolled her eyes.

"I didn't know you had a boyfriend," I said.

"I don't. That just makes them go away."

I cleared my throat. "You mean . . . guys who hit on you?"

"Yeah. Usually, they don't keep trying after I tell them I'm seeing someone. That was a new level of disgusting." She took another handful of my fries. "That's why I want to go to Blackwell. I can't fucking deal with men."

I'd heard Mom talk about Blackwell, that tiny all-girls college in Vermont. *The best of the best go there*, she'd always said. *First woman president? She'll be straight out of Blackwell.*

I watched Liv as she chewed, staring off into space, nodding vaguely to the music. She swallowed and caught me staring again. Before my body could react by flushing—like, *Jesus*, Rory—she smiled and jerked her head to the music even more, looking silly and dramatic, mouthing the words to me. Fleetwood Mac's "Dreams" was ending, Stevie Nicks's voice floating sleepily away.

"I've never been hit on," I blurted. "By anyone."

"Lucky," she said, continuing to dance.

"I mean . . ." I motioned to my angular body, to my square shoulders and flat chest. "There's not much for guys to hit on, anyway."

Liv leaned back in her chair with her eyes blissfully half-shut, humming. Now the jukebox started blaring some sentimental ballad from when my grandparents were growing up—Sam Cooke, or maybe it was Otis Redding. Soft boys with big hearts.

"I'm envious of you," Liv said out of nowhere, and then took a sip of her beer.

I swallowed too hard, and my throat seared. "Pause," I said. "Rewind. *You're* envious of *me?*"

"Yes," said Liv. I vaguely wondered how she could seem so sober when she'd consumed twice the alcohol and weed that I had.

"*Why?*"

She shrugged, playing with her bracelets.

"You're small," she finally said.

I looked down at my small chest, my knobby knees. "You don't want this."

Her eyes narrowed the slightest bit. "You don't know what I want, Rory."

Normally, I would have balked. But maybe because I was high, or maybe because I was *really* passionate about it—I just kept going.

"I mean, I'm seventeen," I said, "and I could pass for twelve. My mom and sister have an inside joke where they sing 'Someday My Prince Will Come' from *Snow White* but exchange 'my prince' with 'Rory's boobs.' When Stoff elbows me and it actually hurts, he laughs at me for being weak. Nothing fits me right. Nothing *ever* fits me right." I took a deep breath. I was still high, and the words were slipping out of me like melted candle wax, so why not keep going? "Only one guy has ever called me cute, the guy my friend tried to set me up with freshman year, and he was gross, so it doesn't count. My mom and sisters are all beautiful. *You* are beautiful. I'm just . . . weird. I don't know what's wrong with me."

Liv stared at me. Perfect lines of makeup, glowing under the blue light. The sad song, tumbling from the jukebox.

"I'm sorry," she finally said.

"No apologies, remember?" I said. "Cough up."

"I'm sorry you feel that way about your body." She drummed her fingers on the table between us, playing an invisible piano. "But there's nothing *wrong* with you."

I gazed down at my fries, no longer hungry.

"Hey," Liv said. "Look at me."

It took everything I had, but I did.

Liv pursed her lips, making a funny face. "I think you look fabulous," she said, making me laugh.

"Well," I said. "I think you look even more fabulous. Period."

She smiled, and I wondered how she could keep her lipstick so perfect for so long. "Should we just start dating now? Or . . . ?"

"*Mademoiselle*," I said, offering her my hand.

Then, an amplified voice rang through the bar, coming from a microphone somewhere in the back near the stage.

"Good evening, folks," it said. "Many regrets, but Problem Child has to—"

"Don't you *dare*," Liv hissed.

"—cancel this gig, on account of—"

"*NO!*"

"—a drummer with a stomach bug, so if everyone could—"

"This is *bullshit*."

"—just sit tight, and we'll see what awesome playlists we can pull up for you guys—"

"UGH!"

"—and again, we apologize profusely for the inconvenience."

Liv looked at me so murderously that I threw my hands up in the air. "Not my fault!"

"This fucking *blows*. This happened last time I tried to see them, too. They keep bailing!"

"At least they caught it now," I said brightly, trying to cheer her up. "What if they started their set, and then the drummer started blowing chunks on us?"

Liv continued to look as though she'd spit venom for approximately three seconds, and then she burst out laughing. "Blowing chunks?" she said. "That is *heinous*, Rory."

* * *

We stayed at the lounge to complain a bit with everyone else—"Just because he's vomming doesn't mean he can't still play the drums," Liv snarled, to a chorus of, "Fuck yeah!"—and then we realized our train was leaving in fifteen minutes.

The run from Dreamtown to Union Station was one of the most adrenaline-ridden and silently painful experiences of my life. There wasn't time to say, "I actually can't run, funnily enough—never have, never will—" before Liv was a blur of burgundy wool and flying dark hair, so I just took off behind her, deciding at the last minute to try and abandon my body and fly with my mind instead. We skidded into the station and bounded down the stairs, each of us tripping, and then literally slid onto the platform as the conductors stepped onto the train. At exactly 12:35 a.m., we collapsed, freezing and gasping for air, onto the seats.

"That was close," I rasped, when what I really meant was, *I can't feel my legs. Do you think that's okay?*

Liv said nothing for five breaths. I noted that the few other people on the train were staring at us under the fluorescent lights as if we were a two-headed dragon, or maybe a giant glob of mucus. Her lipstick had smeared, her coat hung off her shoulder, and I had a gaping hole in the left knee of my tights. We looked like we'd been in a brawl.

The train lurched.

"God, I could eat a horse," Liv huffed, ignoring everyone's stares.

"I have lasagna!" I cried, and Liv's eyes widened. She watched as I dug around in my backpack and pulled out the Tupperware and fork Nonni had packed for me.

"Sorry," I said. "I mean—not sorry, but like—I know it's—it's weird to have lasagna in my bag."

"Fuck weird," Liv said, taking the fork out of my hand. "You're a miracle, Rory."

We were halfway through the lasagna before Liv suddenly dug into her bag and extracted her big headphones and an adapter. She pulled out a vintage silver iPod from deep in her burgundy jacket and, like it was the most normal process in the world—like everyone on earth didn't just own AirPods—she plugged the adapter into her iPod and the headphones into the adapter. I stared.

"I know," she said, reading my expression and gesturing to the iPod. "It's so old. I've had it since I was eight, but it still works like a fucking charm. Give me yours."

"I don't have an iPod."

She grinned. "Your *headphones,* Roo. Does anyone call you Roo? You're such a Roo."

I reached into my backpack and handed her my beloved headphones, unsure of her plan. "No, I don't think Roo is a very intuitive nickname for Rory."

"Hm," Liv said, plugging my headphones into the adapter, too. "I think it is." She started scrolling her iPod, her eyes narrowed in focus. "Bowie and Fleetwood Mac are great, but you need some of this century in your life, too." She slid her own headphones over her ears, and I did, too, and everything around me muffled.

Then a strange, stirring mix of sounds filled my ears, growing in volume. Something rising, expanding. I met her eyes and realized that we were listening to the same song.

"This is Mitski," Liv said, overarticulating so I could still hear her. The music hummed on, waking me up. From her bag she pulled out a tiny notebook, flipping to a new page. She wrote MUSIC WE LISTENED TO ON THE TRAIN and, underneath, *Mitski / "Pink in the Night."*

\* \* \*

When I crawled into my room at 2:14 in the morning, I did not swan dive into my bed, as I had been planning on doing for so many hours. Instead, I sat down at my desk. Just sat, stared at nothing.

After a few minutes, I taped Liv's list to the wall right above my computer, directly in my line of vision, right below the poster of the Beatles crossing Abbey Road.

MUSIC WE LISTENED TO ON THE TRAIN
Mitski / "Pink in the Night"
Bon Iver / "AUATC"
Angel Olsen / "Spring"
ABRA / "Human"
Childish Gambino / "Redbone"
Solange / "Don't Wish Me Well"
y La Bamba / "Ojos Del Sol"
HAIM / "Gasoline"
James Blake / "I Need a Forest Fire"
Lucy Dacus / "Direct Address"
Sufjan Stevens / "Death with Dignity"
Kelsey Lu / "I'm Not in Love (cover)"
Florence + The Machine / "Sky Full of Song"
Maggie Rogers / "Symphony"

I took the laptop to my bed and crawled under the tunnel of covers. I found the artists, most of whom I'd never heard of, on YouTube—sitting there patiently waiting to be discovered, on this winter night when I was seventeen.

I closed my eyes and listened to all the songs, beginning to end, three times through. I couldn't stop.

*T*he next morning, I woke up to my blaring alarm to find myself wedged between my bed and my floor, the half-open laptop on its side at my knee. The inside of my mouth seemed to have rusted over like an old car stuck in someone's dead grandpa's garage, and I thought sluggishly of water, of the sheer blessing of toothpaste. There was a strange feeling behind my closed eyes, like a layer of felt had embedded in my frontal lobe. My ears rang.

I patted around the bed until my fingers closed around my phone. I'd gotten two texts from Liv.

The first, at 6:45 a.m.: *I still have your fork from last night, should I bring it to choir?*

The second, at 6:49 a.m.: *Also when r we gonna make my LOFT*

I maneuvered back onto my bed with a hand on the laptop, which had died. My legs shifted underneath the uncomfortably starchy tights that I hadn't bothered to take off. Every bleat of my alarm punctured my skull like a dart, and I fumbled around to turn it off.

A third text: *R u awake? Tell me you're not hungover*

Before I could even begin to form a plan on how I'd manage to get up, eat, dress, go to school, and make it through nine periods, I heard footsteps clamoring up the stairs. In a split second of panic, I threw the duvet over my clothes. Nonni burst into my room.

"Is breakfast!" she shouted, before looking down at me. I prayed that the denim jacket wasn't showing, that her vision problems would—just this once—come to my advantage.

"Rory," she said in a different tone, and my heart began to sink. I inched my head out of my comforter cocoon, blinking in the sunlight. I looked into the dark eyes of my grandmother, holding my breath, and she looked back, a vein ticking in her cheek.

We stared at each other for a bit.

And then she placed her warm hands on my cheeks and said, "You are sick." She brought her lips to my forehead and backed out of the room, saying, "I am call the school. You sleep, yes?"

I tried to clear my throat. "*Ti amo*, Nonni," I gurgled.

"Okay," she said, pulling the door closed. "I make you something to eat."

Knowing it was stupid, that I wouldn't get away with this in the future, and feeling guilty as hell, I went back to sleep until eleven.

* * *

*Rory you did NOT stay home today*, Liv texted me around noon, when it must have become clear that I wasn't coming to choir.

*...Lol*, I texted back. After convincing Nonni I was well enough to come with her to CVS, I was wandering among the hygiene aisles while she picked up Nonno's prescriptions.

*NO! Are you seriously hungover?* Liv texted back.

*You're not?* I responded.

*Bitch you had like 1.5 beers. If that.*

*Whatever. Nonni came in, saw that I looked like a zombie, and made me stay home.* I sent her the angel emoji.

She sent back about twelve rows of the smiley-face emoji, followed by *I hate u.*

I looked up from my phone and found myself in the makeup aisle. The pounding in my head had gone down since that morning, but the fluorescent lights weren't doing me any good. My phone buzzed again.

*Even though I'm mad at you, Problem Child is playing again in 2 weeks so ur coming*

I smiled.

*Also come over tomorrow, we gotta make that loft*

I shuffled closer to a row of eyeliner. Just out of curiosity.

*Also, everyone who goes to Telsey is preppy and annoying and I hate everyone except you.*

I walked up to the cash register, my phone continuing to buzz in the pocket of my jacket. Looking over my shoulder, I made sure Nonni's back was still turned. I pulled out a wad of babysitting cash and watched the cashier place my items into a plastic bag: eyeliner, mascara, deep-red lipstick.

"Sixteen forty-nine," the cashier said, although I'd already pushed the money eagerly toward him, away from myself.

chapter nine

*nine months after*

*T*hat whole spiel people feed you about how time heals grief is bullshit.

It's when the thoughts and prayers *stop*, when people start living their regular lives again. Finding time to laugh. Pretending that the world didn't already end. *That's* when it hits you.

You wake up in the middle of the night and can't breathe. You're sitting on the Metra watching kids play with their siblings, businessmen sleeping against the windows, and for absolutely no reason, it becomes fully clear to you: She died. She's dead. She's not coming back.

Thankfully, when these moments have happened to me in the past nine months, I've always been within twenty feet of a trash can. I'm terrified for the day when I'm not, when I'll have to just throw up on the floor.

"It gets better with time," says Mom, says April, says Telsey's principal and Stoff's mom and the neighbors and my dentist and the reporter from the *Clarksdale Gazette.* "You might not believe it right now, but it does."

It gets worse with time.

These days, I'm home alone often, because Mom works and my sisters go to school and Nonni and Nonno run errands. And when I am, I close my eyes very tightly shut. And I walk backward. I try, with every cell in my body, to go back. To take back the breaths I've taken, the heartbeats I've used, since she left. To walk backward until I reach the night of January 4th, until we're laughing under the bluish lights of Dreamtown, until she's facing me with her red lipstick stretched into the largest smile I've ever seen. Until we're about to get into the car.

When I get there, I'll say, "Wait."

When I get there, I'll hug her. I won't let go.

I'll make us sleep on the floor of that fucking club, until the sun starts to peek through the next morning and she sees January 5th. And then, only when the sun starts to rise, only when no one else is on the road—when all the possible reckless, texting drivers are asleep in their beds—then, we can go home. And start the rest of our lives.

* * *

"It would have been *so* easy," I say.

April is trying to do something with her face that I can't figure out. I don't know if she's trying not to smile, yawn, or cry. I want to be mad, but I understand.

"What would have been easy?" she says, cocking her head. "Keeping Liv safe?"

"I could have made us take the train."

"How could you have known?" she asks. "How could you know that *specific* driver would run that *specific* red light and hit you?"

My stomach lurches at these words, and I curl forward, but she keeps talking.

"How could you know that some irresponsible person

was texting at the wheel, right at that moment in time?" April asks.

"It was a Friday night," I manage. "Everyone drives recklessly on Friday nights."

To my surprise, April leans back and cocks an eyebrow. "Well, I don't."

I stare at her for a moment, wondering if it's a joke or if she's actually pissed at my assumption. "Well, I didn't mean that *you* do. Necessarily."

She raises both eyebrows. "Good. Because I'm *very* responsible." Seeing that I'm still lost, April smiles. "Relax, Rory. I'm teasing."

For some reason, I find myself smiling slightly, some tension easing out of my muscles. Liv used to tease me, breaking character just when I started to panic. It never made me upset. I like when someone feels comfortable enough to joke around me. Like, they know I can take it.

April shakes her head, still smiling, before she sighs and recrosses her legs. "Anyway, Rory. I really want you to get it into your head that this *wasn't* your fault."

Just like that, the light feeling dissipates. My muscles seize, and I shut down.

"No," I say.

"It was unpreventable."

I shake my head.

"You were both sober and alert," April says softly. "It was pure random—"

"No."

April leans forward, looking me in the eyes, a crease forming between her brows. "Hon. You couldn't have saved her."

"No," I say once again. "I could have."

"Why do you say that?"

"Because," I say. "If you told me right then and there, I would have pulled us off the road into a ditch. I would have made her switch seats with me. I would have—"

"Rory," April says, and I realize that my hands are purple, that it's been too long since I last took a breath.

"I would have done anything," I tell her.

"I know. But Rory," she says, and she leans over the table and stares at me. *"You couldn't have known."*

It's our sixth appointment, and I still haven't been able to say the last part of our mantra: "It's not my fault for being the one who survived." I just shake my head until our time runs out, and April has to let me go home.

\* \* \*

The next day, I'm prowling through the Ancient Egypt wing of the Art Institute when they find me.

You aren't supposed to touch the glass in front of the sculptures, but I can't help myself. Ancient Egypt was the shit. They actually had female pharaohs, like Hatshepsut, who had men bowing down to her, worshipping her every move. And don't even get me started on the mummification process; it's *sick*. My forehead and left hand are pressed against the glass encasing a golden tomb, my mind lost somewhere around 1450 B.C.E., when someone rests their hand on my shoulder. I jump and jerkily pull my headphones down, the right side snagging on the collar of my shirt. "Sorry," I gulp to the museum guard, before realizing that he is not a museum guard.

"No, *I'm* sorry," the not-museum-guard says, stepping

backward. "Didn't mean to frighten you, Rory."

My heart jumps out of my mouth and rests on the floor between us.

"We just saw you looking around and wanted to say hello," says the woman with him, who is Liv's mom, Eleanor. She joins the not-museum-guard, who is Liv's dad, Ramil.

I try to find my breath. Try to pretend that my heart isn't pounding in panic, that this moment hasn't almost pulled me out of my skin, like every other sudden noise or movement since the Worst Night.

" . . . Hello," I say, when what I really mean is, *There's blatantly a scar on my cheek from the time your daughter died right next to me and there's absolutely nothing else I can think about in this moment, so if you could please step away and we could all pretend that we didn't see each other, that would be golden.*

Because I'm still working on speaking my mind, five minutes later, I am in the Art Institute Café, allowing Eleanor and Ramil to buy me coffee.

During our year of friendship, Liv became a part of my family. Mom told science jokes to her and asked about her music taste, and Saige started copying her eyeliner (meaning that the entire lacrosse team did, too), and Nonni called her *mia quarta bellissima nipote* (my fourth beautiful granddaughter) and fretted over her not eating enough bread. Nonno beamed whenever she entered the room, and Willow trod silently about six feet behind her at all times, watching her with starry eyes.

On the other hand, I did *not* become a part of Liv's family. Her parents were rarely home when we were, which allowed us to blast music and yell "FUCK!" at the top of our lungs with liberty whenever we felt the need to. They're lawyers, and they've always been kind, but completely unrelatable. Ramil is dark and handsome, distant and polite, and Eleanor is small, cheerful, and pristinely put-together.

"So, how've you been?" Eleanor asks, setting a small cappuccino down in front of me and an extra-large one in front of herself.

"I've been great—good," I say. "Very . . . cold."

*Did you do this on purpose?* I ask Liv. *Are you just sitting in heaven right now, laughing your ass off?*

"Hard to believe winter's coming again, isn't it?" asks Ramil.

"Totally."

*I'm glad you can laugh at something, at least,* I tell Liv. *Sorry that I can't make you laugh more. I mean . . . not sorry. But it sucks.*

"And you're taking a gap year, right?" Eleanor asks.

"Mm-hmm. Yeah."

"I think that was really smart, Rory," says Eleanor, stirring sugar into her coffee. "What happened—it's just so much for such a young person to bear." She says it softly, looking down into her coffee, before rising to meet my eyes again. I don't know how she could possibly muster it, but she gives me a small smile. "I'm glad you're taking a break."

The thing about Liv's parents is that they don't cry.

I don't need April to explain why: When you are this sad, there are no tears at all. Just white, blinding pain. A silent nightmare that becomes reality. A reality so unspeakably bad that it actually allows you to smile, and speak English, and buy your dead child's friend a coffee when you run into her at an art exhibit.

"So, how've you been keeping busy?" Ramil asks kindly, folding his hands on the table. My heart pounds. He looks exactly like Liv, and it makes me hurt.

"Yeah," I say. "I'm, uh . . . working at the music school in town. My sister sings in the chorus."

"That sounds nice," says Eleanor. "A time filler till you go to school next year, something to keep you busy?"

*Actually, all I do there is hope the phone doesn't ring and think about death while being forced to listen to Christmas carols on repeat.*

"Definitely," I say.

"And how's your recovery going?" Eleanor asks, sipping her coffee, a crease forming between her eyebrows.

For a moment, my heart falls into my stomach in panic. But then I take a relieved breath because she means the Worst Night. She doesn't mean the Xanax Incident.

She doesn't *know* about the Xanax Incident.

"Recovery's going well. See?" I flex my left hand and fingers for them, as if my reinstated dexterity will somehow make up for the fact that I'm sitting here, breathing, while Liv is not.

"A lefty, right?" Ramil asks, smiling. "Liv told us you were. She was so jealous."

"What? Really?"

"She'd say, 'Lefties are unique.'" Eleanor lifts her eyes and does a surprisingly accurate imitation of Liv. "'Only, like, fifteen percent of the world is left-handed, Mom!'"

"Twelve, actually," I say quietly.

"She was always looking for ways to be different,"

says Ramil.

"She *was* different," I say, and then realize that this could be interpreted in a variety of ways. "She was *cool*-different. She was unique. I mean, she didn't even have to try. She *didn't* try."

The sadness in Eleanor's smile makes me want to tear my heart out.

"She did try," Liv's mother says, her voice far away. "She did."

Her eyes travel to somewhere over my shoulder. I read once that mothers who have lost a child have a biological instinct to look for them forever, even when they know that they're gone. When her eyes find mine again, I have to look down, because the hurt is actually blinding.

"Liv was so lucky to have you, Rory," she says. "I know she may have shown her love in confusing ways, but . . ." She looks down again, and a hundred different memories flash before me: Liv nudging her head away when Eleanor tried to kiss her cheek. Liv furrowing her brow when Eleanor gushed about a cello competition she'd won. My phone lighting up constantly with Liv's complaints of being smothered by her mother, when I just wanted mine to smother me more.

Eleanor quietly shreds her napkin in front of me.

I don't know why it's so hard to give people the love they need.

"She was," says Ramil. "Extremely lucky."

"We've been thinking about you a lot, actually," Eleanor says, lifting her eyes to me again.

My phone starts to buzz in my pocket, and underneath the pounding in my chest, I think, *Thank god.*

"We hope you haven't been feeling guil—"

"Oh, my mom's calling me," I say, cutting her off.

Because I can't hear that. Not from her.

Mom is already in the middle of her sentence by the time I pick up, and I wonder when she last took a breath.

"—grab Willow from chorus on your way home? I have to take Nonno to the doctor and I've got conferences after—"

"Uh, yeah, I guess . . ."

I watch Ramil and Eleanor quietly converse with each other. She won't look him in the eye. I wonder how they live, how they even interact, if they just prowl silently around their house filled with flowers and condolence cards, refusing to look at each other.

When I'm off the phone, Eleanor brings her gaze back to me and says, "Got to head out?"

"Unfortunately, yes. I have to pick up my sister."

"Well, before you go, we wanted to tell you—" Eleanor begins, and I pray that she won't pick up where she left off, because I don't know how much more of this I can stand. But she goes somewhere far different. "We're moving."

Ramil nods. "We've decided to sell the house. We don't need all the extra space, now that—"

*Don't say it.*

"Well, we both work downtown," Eleanor says. "So we just thought we'd—"

"For sure," I say.

"The house sold faster than we'd hoped," Ramil says. "We need to be out a week after the New Year. We're trying to get everything packed and ready before the holidays, so we've got a busy six weeks ahead of us."

"It should be easy," Eleanor adds, wiping an invisible

spot of coffee off the table. "But, as you can imagine, we have a lot of trouble with Liv's room."

I swallow. My heart is pounding so hard that it hurts, like someone is throwing a rock at the base of my throat, and my vision is clouding. I feel tremors deep in my chest, and I know what's coming: an avalanche. My avalanches have been coming, sporadically, since the Worst Night. Even though they happen inside my body, it feels like the whole world shuts down around me. I look through the windows of the Art Institute Café and imagine a gray mountain of snow crushing the streets of Chicago, darkening the sky, pressing in on all sides. The glass, about to shatter. Me, about to shatter.

"Realistically, we'll need to get rid of a lot of her belongings," Eleanor continues.

*Stay calm. You're fine.*

"Give her clothes and books to charity, throw away her school supplies. I know she'd want her stuffed animals to go to children in need."

"I can help," someone says.

Eleanor and Ramil look at me with raised eyebrows. I realize that someone was me.

"With . . . ?"

"Liv's room," says my mouth, and I listen in wonder. "I can help with Liv's room, if you don't want to do it."

I can almost *see* April sitting at the next table over, staring me down. *This is a very bad idea*, she tells me, as the sky turns to ash.

"Well, if you're not . . ." Ramil says. "If it's not too . . ."

"That would be *lovely*, Rory," Eleanor says. "If you're truly up to it, that is." She leans across the table and takes my hand.

My last thought as I'm pushing through the glass doors of the Art Institute, smiling and waving to Liv's parents, is this:

*Mom and April cannot know.*

Trying to clear my mind and failing, I begin power walking down the sidewalk. I run into the first café I see, beeline to the bathroom, and throw up. I flush, turn around, and bury my head in my knees, letting the tremors ride out in big, slow waves.

We sat side by side on the bus, shoulders bumping carelessly, our headphones secure over our ears. We were listening to Bon Iver's *22, A Million* from beginning to end, which Liv said was necessary for my "becoming a human."

"This is the best track on the album," she whispered in my ear. Three minutes later: "No . . . this one." And again: "No. *This* is the *best* one."

"I feel like I'm floating," I said, as "666 ʇ" started.

"Remember when you were an uneducated heathen and didn't listen to any of this music?" Liv said, cracking a smile.

"Remember when you farted in choir yesterday?"

She shoved me into the window.

\* \* \*

Life felt very different in March.

Mostly because Liv, with her new music and winged eyeliner and silly, twisted smiles, was now my best friend.

In the past month, she'd spent more time at my house than her own. Nonni set an extra plate at the dinner table; Mom quizzed her over spaghetti the night before a bio test. We'd stay up for hours lying on our stomachs, half-bullshitting through homework and half-gurgling out inappropriate jokes and weird thoughts. In the mornings, we'd silently and grumpily sit in the hallway before school, our headphones plugged into her old iPod. We didn't talk; we just sat stoically, like icicles. And no one bothered us.

The music wrapped around us, engulfed us, separated us from everyone. We made endless, chaotic playlists, combining the new names she brought to me with the old ones I brought to her: Joni Mitchell twining with Mitski and Solange; Britpop and eighties rock thrown into sad, folky voices of the 2010s. We didn't have a genre or a pattern, we just listened to everyone we could, as much as we could: Maggie Rogers, Nina Simone, Billie Eilish, Amy Winehouse, Stevie Wonder, Lizzy McAlpine, ABRA, Phoebe Bridgers. We'd talk about the songs for hours, and we'd never get to the end of one before one of us frantically changed the track to show the other that no, you need to listen to *this. Now.*

In choir, we whispered and smacked our gum and made other people laugh and, probably, feel uncomfortable. When Mr. Wong cared enough to separate us, we made weird faces at each other across the room. The other kids' heads would turn back and forth like at a tennis match, seeing who had the gall to be the most obnoxious. Mr. Wong mostly gave up on telling us to be quiet, sing along, and spit out the gum. One time he even stopped class to see how big Liv's bubble could grow before it popped.

In the middle of March, Liv went on a trip to visit Blackwell College with her parents. She came back glowing.

"How was it?" I asked, as we sat down with our choir folders.

"Amazing."

"Why?"

"Because," she said, her eyes glinting. "No one irritated the shit out of me like they do here."

I choked back a laugh as the piano started playing.

As winter finally melted away, for the first time in my life, I walked through high school without staring obsessively at my feet. Nothing had changed about the way others perceived me—I still got those scandalized up-and-downs from girls sauntering by in their designer clothing, the snickers from guys in their preppy ensembles. But now, I was a different Rory. The one from Liv-and-Rory. The one who went to shows and smoked weed and didn't care whether people laughed at her vulgar jokes. The one who dressed in high-waisted skirts over dark tights and band T-shirts, Doc Martens, and overlarge retro sweaters. Who knotted her hair at the crown of her head and kept eyeliner and lipstick in her pocket, applying it thickly in the girls' bathroom every morning while listening to MUNA or Robyn.

This was us. We were this, together. And I loved every inch of us.

Even when Liv wasn't swaying through the crowded halls beside me, pushing my headphone aside to mutter observations into my ear, I felt the constant layer of her presence. And that presence said:

*We are the only ones who matter.*

*They couldn't* dream *of touching us.*

* * *

We paused Bon Iver to get off the bus and walk down the snowy sidewalk of my block. Inside, we greeted Nonni and Nonno, then trudged up the stairs to my room, peeled off our many layers of outerwear, and collapsed on the floor. Two hours of "studying" later, most of which involved YouTube videos of goats, Liv teaching me yoga poses, and a strangely deep talk about lingerie, I crawled to the bathroom to pee. I came back and flopped down next to her, and Liv said, without looking up from her laptop screen, "Fell asleep on the shitter?"

"Sorry, what?"

Liv typed some more; she was writing an important paper for AP English entirely from scratch. It was due the day after tomorrow. She didn't seem stressed.

"I could've given birth during the time you were in the bathroom," she said after a few moments. "And you owe me a buck for that 'sorry.'"

I rolled onto my back and away from her. "I was just staring at my hag self in the mirror."

"Mood," Liv said, still typing.

"But Liv," I said, looking at the ceiling. "I'm like, *ugly.*"

She closed her laptop immediately. "Okay, Roo." At this point, she refused to call me anything else. "Say that again and I'll kill you."

We talked over each other, me deflating in argument as she progressed.

"You and I both know that you're not ugly."

"It's not, like, *that*—"

"I mean, first of all, you have traits that are biologically considered attractive. Long eyelashes, facial symmetry—"

"That's not what I meant."

"Big eyes, smooth skin—"

"Okay, just stop. I don't want to do this."

"When we see ugliness in the mirror, I feel like it's

never what everyone else sees," Liv said, sitting up on her knees. "Like, okay. Sometimes, I think I look like a horse."

"*What?*"

"Exactly," Liv said. "*You* don't think I look like a horse. But I can't help it, it's just what my brain tells me sometimes."

"But there's literally *no* basis—"

"I could say the same thing about you." She lay back on her side, folding her knees into her chest. "Usually when I don't like what I see in the mirror, I need to change."

"Change clothes?"

"Change *something.*"

I thought, staring up at the ceiling. And then I sat up.

"I really fucking hate my hair."

Liv raised her eyebrows at me.

"It just hangs there limply and it's been the same since I was four and—"

"So change it."

I stared at the ceiling again.

"Liv," I said.

"What?"

"You need to tell me the truth."

"I'd never *not* tell you the truth."

"Would I look completely heinous if I got bangs?"

Liv sat up again, even quicker than the last time. "No. I think they would look cool. Like, Joni Mitchell cool."

We faced each other for a long time. And then she started to smile. "Are we about to cut your bangs, Roo?"

"Liv," I said.

She screamed.

"Oh my god," I said.

"Give me scissors."

"We need to at least look at a tutorial—"

"Dude, I've been cutting my own hair since I was eleven."

"You don't have *bangs*!"

The shrillness in my voice seemed to convince her to wait while I scrolled through social media trying to find advice. An hour later, I was sitting in a chair we'd dragged into the bathroom and she was hovering over me, a pair of kitchen scissors glinting in her right hand, a comb in her left. Surprisingly, I had become calm. Maybe numb, but completely calm. I wanted it done. I wanted bangs.

Liv, on the other hand, had started uncontrollably giggling.

"You're not making a good case for yourself," I said. We'd combed a front portion of my hair straight in front of my face, and I watched between two strands as the scissors loomed nearer.

"I don't know what's going on with me," she panted between laughs. "I'm, like, sweaty and shaking."

"You said you cut hair all the time."

"I cut *my* hair all the time."

"So are you saying *I* should do it?"

The scissors floated between us, quivering in Liv's hand.

"I don't know," she said. "But I'm about to pee my pants." She placed the scissors on the counter and bounded around me to the toilet.

And while she peed, I snipped.

It was over before I realized it had started. My hair looked strange, just sitting there in my lap, ten inches of detached strands still damp and frizzy from the rain. I lifted a hand tentatively to my forehead, felt the rough edges above my brow.

"I did it," I said shakily, as Liv flushed the toilet.

She hurried back around my chair and faced me.

I watched her lips fold into themselves, her mouth becoming the tiniest line.

"Okay," she said.

"Okay what?"

"Okay."

"Okay or not okay? Liv. You're scaring me. You told me I should do it myself."

"I said *I didn't know.* Okay, it's not that bad, though." Her mouth quivered.

"*Stop!* I don't want to look in the mirror now."

"You have to," she said. "We'll fix—I mean, we just—you have to."

I stood up and turned around. Took it all in.

For a while, I just stared at my reflection—at the jagged edges of hair framing my face—and so did Liv. When I met her eyes, I started to tear up.

"Okay," she said more securely. She brought her hands to my shoulders. "Roo. No big deal. We just need to get those tiny scissors to even it out, and then buy some product—"

"I look like a mop," I wept, hiding my face.

"I'll drive us to CVS—no, you have to drive us, we're at your house—"

"I'm not going out in public!"

Liv's hands tightened on my shoulders. "Okay. Repeat after me," she said, and her mouth was twitching again. "I, Rory Quinn-Morelli, am a fucking badass queen. I *will* survive this haircut."

\* \* \*

Before we left the minivan, I pulled the hoodie so tight around my face that my sunglasses popped off. It took a while to fit everything back on—the glasses, the headband, the scarf, and the hoodie—but in a loyal move, Liv, usually impatient, waited in the passenger seat until I was ready.

We teetered through CVS under the harsh fluorescent lights—me behind my layers, bumping into shelves because I couldn't see, Liv acting like everything was normal. An older employee kept looking darkly at us, as if we were about to shoplift or start vaping in the middle of an aisle. Liv got into a minor fight with the cashier—the same one who checked out my eyeliner the month before, in fact, so I had to hide behind another shelf—and then we were back outside.

"See? Not so bad," Liv said, swinging the passenger door open.

I collapsed into the driver's seat and pulled off the layers around my head. "I don't think I can cut it again," I said. "I don't trust myself with scissors. I should just go to a salon."

"*No*," Liv barked as we pulled out of the lot. The rain had turned, once again, into snow. "Don't pay for something you can do yourself."

"But I clearly can't do it myself."

"I can," she said. "I'll fix it. I swear." I heard her shift in her seat so she was facing me. "Do you trust me?"

I stole a sideways glance at her, saw her waiting,

leaning forward. The impeccable lines of makeup. The silky brown hair wrapped at her crown, a few wavy strands falling out. The intensity in her dark eyes. I noticed for the first time that they weren't just brown: a few specks of green exploded outward like fireworks, changing the tone of her face. Changing everything.

"I don't know," I said truthfully.

She turned back to the front, and so did I.

"Okay," she said.

I didn't realize I was holding my breath until I released it. "Just . . ." I started, and then tried again. "Just don't make it worse."

"Okay," she said again, and I wasn't looking at her, but I could hear the smile in her voice.

*   *   *

A few days and many hair compliments later—including one from Stoff, who pretended to faint when he saw me—Liv and I sat listening to HAIM together in the library, "studying" but actually sending each other memes. After I sent her a particularly great picture of a swamp monster, with the caption "how'd they get this pic of u," Liv checked her phone and sniggered so loud that it sounded like she threw up. She turned away from me and hid her head, bobbing up and down, which set me off. When we emerged, wiping our eyes, Grace was standing over our table, smiling and shaking her head.

"You guys are literal children," she said, looking down at Liv's phone screen. "Okay, so next Tuesday, over break. My parents are leaving town at six, so come over at nine. Liv, are you still getting that eighth tomorrow?"

"Eighth of what?" I asked. They shushed me. Grace spun her head around, her blond waves hitting us.

"Yeah, unless Harrison's bitch-ass bails on me again," Liv said under her breath.

"Perfect," Grace said. "Milo's bringing the alc." She turned to me. "See you there, Rory?"

Liv also turned to me, and I faltered. She must have seen it in my eyes. "You don't have to," she said.

I met Grace's eyes instead of Liv's. "I'll come. It's not a problem."

Grace smiled and flounced away just as the bell rang. Liv and I gathered up our stuff, and she leaned in close to my ear. "An eighth of *weed*, by the way," she whispered.

I tried to push down the flush spreading across my cheeks.

* * *

A few days later, as we stood in the dark of Liv's hallway before Grace's party, I felt safe saying it for the first time: "I'm stressed."

Liv didn't stop in her tracks; she kept her hold on my arm as we made our way through her empty house, but I saw her turn around briefly.

"Why?"

"Parties—are not, um . . ."

"Not your thing?"

Liv pulled me into her room and tugged on the lamp, and her green walls glowed around us. Famous women stared down at us from posters lining each wall. The first time I'd been up here, I thought it was creepy, but now I liked it. My favorite was one of Billie Holiday right above Liv's bed, singing in what looked like orgasmic happiness mixed with unbearable rage.

"Are you, like, shy or something?" Liv asked, and it took me a few seconds to realize she was being sarcastic, at which point I threw my jacket at her face.

"Listen," she said, when she had finished laughing and turned to face the mirror on her dresser. "Let's stay at Grace's for a half hour. If you're not having a good time, we'll leave."

"I don't want to drag you down with me," I said automatically. "They're your friends."

She made eye contact with me through the mirror. "Bitch, *you're* my friend."

Warmth spread through my chest, and I pressed my lips together. For some reason, I didn't want her to see me smile. So instead, I cleared my throat and played with my nails, and Liv disappeared into her closet, violently rifling through clothes. Not knowing how to respond, I eventually muttered, "Okay, bitch."

"Okay, slut."

"Whore."

"Wait, which shirt?" she said, emerging from the depths of her closet in her black, lacy bra. She held two—one a collared button-down with vibrant patterns, the other an olive-green tank top.

I tried to focus on the shirts, and not on her bra. I didn't even know bras could fit that perfectly. Where did people even *get* stuff like that? What would Nonni say if she found one of those in my laundry?

Liv turned around to throw the shirts across her bed. "Help me, Roo. I need guidance!"

That's when I saw it for the first time: the plant tattooed against her side, on the smooth plane at the top of her ribs. She saw me staring and raised her arm so I could have a clearer view.

"It's a lilac branch. I got it last summer," she said, answering my unasked questions. "Same day I got the *Stranger Things* tattoo."

"What, is there some place in the city that specializes in underage tattoos?"

She smiled. "I was in France with my parents. The age there is sixteen, so I told them I wanted to spend a day shopping on my own. They never found out."

"Did it . . . hurt?" I said, intrigued.

"Like a mother*fucker*," she said. "Way more than the first. But I love it."

I wanted so badly to ask why she got it. What it meant. How she was only seventeen, but already so layered with thoughts and memories that she'd get some of them printed on her body, like Mom.

Instead, I said, "I love it, too."

She smiled, picking the button-down.

\* \* \*

When Liv and I walked up the steps to Grace's house, Natsuki opened the door. She didn't seem to notice that there was a gaping hole under the armpit of my sweater, or comment on the raggedness of my shoes. She didn't force a drink into my hands, and she didn't just breeze past me and on to Liv.

She said, "Hi, queen! I'm so glad you came!" and gave me a hug.

Then she let go and said, "Guys! Liv brought Rory!"

And everyone cheered.

And I tried to be chill about it, but I think I beamed anyway.

\* \* \*

By midnight, I was on my third beer. My sweater was long gone, and my faded T-shirt, one of Mom's from the nineties, stuck uncomfortably to my armpits, and I could feel my hair frizz around me. Next to me, Liv inhaled deeply from her blunt and blew it into my face.

It was the best party I'd ever been to.

Liv's friends kept asking me questions. They asked about my favorite Bowie album (I cheated and said *Legacy*, a compilation, because it had everything I loved); what my mom thought of teaching high school (she drank a lot of wine when she got home); and if I'd been to another country (Italy, once, when Saige and I were little. Mom got wine-drunk and cried and decided to never travel with kids again).

"What's it like living with a six-year-old sister?" Natsuki asked, sipping on her Sprite. She was the only one who'd driven to Grace's, so she was automatically on DD duty for the rest of us. "I feel like I would die."

"Oh," I said. "It's nothing compared to living with two seventy-year-olds."

I could see the change in their faces, the confusion. Most people in Clarksdale, I reminded myself too late, had grandparents who lived in mansions in Florida. Not down the hall.

"Rory's grandparents are the best," Liv said from beside me, as I stiffened. "They're Italian, and she calls them Nonni and Nonno, and they are the purest human beings I've ever met."

I privately considered that to be an overstatement, since the first time Nonni met Liv, she thought Liv was a door-to-door saleswoman and then, upon realizing that Liv was my friend, dug her nails into Liv's wrists and pulled her in through the screen door, insistent on feeding her, while Liv tried to cover up the fact that she was bleeding.

"Yeah, they're . . . they're keepers," I said.

"I want to meet them," Natsuki said. "Your life is so cool, Rory." They started talking about something else, and I sat there, bathing in it.

\* \* \*

A few hours later, we were comfortably very far gone. I'd stopped drinking after my three beers, but for some reason, I still felt as though I was getting progressively drunker and higher with everyone else. And in, like, the best possible way. We sat around the firepit in Grace's backyard, listening to a never-ending playlist, talking about never-ending things in never-ending sentences.

"I mean, functionally, capitalism has been a complete disaster for us," Milo was saying, stretched back in his chair, creaking his fifth empty beer can with the edge of his thumb.

"Well, that's a little extreme," countered Jem. "It's not like going totally socialist would . . . I mean . . . Bernie, like—"

"Yeah, but essentially, like . . ."

I sat there vaguely pretending to follow the conversation, but I didn't worry about it too much, because the smoke from the fire and the warmth in my stomach made everything softer. I watched Liv across the fire as her face swam in the smoke, her catlike eyes flicking to whoever was talking, and I briefly wondered how she could always act soberer than the rest of us. Why she always sat there sharply, looking ready to pounce.

Finally, Grace's boyfriend, Devon, cleared his throat and stood up, stretching.

"Not that this spontaneous weed-induced econ debate hasn't been enjoyable as *fuck*," he said, "but I'm killing it now. Let's do something."

Two minutes later, we were on the roof of Grace's house.

"Hey," Liv breathed in my ear, while the rest of them blundered around, laughing. "You okay?"

The beer hadn't hit her as strongly as it hit everyone else, but she was still giggling a little.

"I'm fine," I said.

I was trying to be.

Grace had one of those modern, split-level houses with a flat roof, easy to climb up to from her bedroom window. The roof jutted out over a shimmering, turquoise pool.

"I do my homework up here, like, every day," Grace said casually as we spread out, looking at the starry sky.

"That's literally false," Jem said.

"Well, like, sometimes."

It had been one of those oddly hot days in early spring, and we were all sweating heavily by the time we sat down on the dusty roof, stretching our feet in the center like a weird amoeba. We talked some more, laughed a lot. Listened to Frank Ocean and Lizzo and Labrinth. Told embarrassing stories until everything hurt, but in a good way.

At some point, Liv stretched out with a groan, peeled her flannel away, and said, "I'm having the biggest fucking hot flash."

"Menopause looks good on you," Natsuki commented, and Liv threw the flannel at her, laughing.

"Yeah, I'm soaked," Milo said, shaking his shirt.

"The pool's freezing, otherwise I'd make you jump in," Grace said, scooping her hair into a knot at the top of her head.

"Well, now that you mentioned it . . ." Milo said. A huge smile started to spread beneath his dark stubble.

"I mean, you *can*," Grace said. "If you want to. You're just going to be cold as fuck."

Milo stood up slowly, and everyone groaned and laughed and drummed their hands against the roof. He peeled off his shirt, and in the turquoise light rising from the pool, I caught a quick glimpse of a tattoo spreading across his chest. A bear.

"I guess he went to France, too," I whispered to Liv. But she didn't hear me. Her eyes were glued to Milo, narrowed, and a smile was spreading across her face.

Milo walked to the edge of the roof confidently, and then looked down.

"Shit," he said, stepping back, and we all laughed.

"You don't have to," Natsuki said. "We're all very impressed—"

I was the first one to notice Liv's dark shape gliding past me, kicking her shoes to the side, unbuttoning her shirt and throwing it down. Before anyone could react, Liv was approaching the edge of the roof in her lacy bra and underwear. She briefly turned to smirk at Milo, and in the shimmering blue light, I saw the tattoo of the lilacs snaking down her side.

"No—" Grace had time to say, before Liv was a silhouette suspended in the air, her hair flying around her. As though in slow motion, her two middle fingers glided toward the sky, and she twirled, happily flipping us all off, before she fell.

By the time she hit the water, we were all at the

edge of the roof. I watched as she splashed, creating a dark flower of swirling brown hair and limbs in the blue light. How the water rushed away from her to the edges of the pool as if in shock. She emerged, pushing hair out of her eyes, her mouth stretched into her mischievous smile, and threw herself into a back float to look at us.

"*What the fuck, Liv!*" shouted Natsuki. "Aren't you *cold*?"

"I'm fine," she said, kicking her feet. "You guys are weak as hell."

We stared down at Liv swimming around, and I heard a sound next to me: Natsuki throwing off her shoes, giggling.

"You're ridiculous, Liv," Jem said, laughing, ripping off his shirt and jumping in.

\* \* \*

The next morning, I woke up feeling like a rat had crawled in between my ears and lay down to die, but I had become an expert in shielding morning-after headaches from my family. I perched at the end of the breakfast table, sipping my coffee casually as if I didn't want to inject it directly into my eyes, and scrolled through my phone as Nonni, Nonno, and my sisters bustled around.

Mom trudged into the kitchen in her flannel pajamas, pausing to kiss the top of my head grumpily. Her hand rested on my head for an awkwardly long time after the kiss, and she bent over again to sniff.

"What?" I asked quickly, pulling away.

"Your hair smells different," she said.

She stared at me, and I stared at the wall.

"New shampoo," I said.

"Ah." Mom moved away, and I released my breath.

*Did ur parents catch u coming in last night?* I texted Liv.

She responded by seemingly hitting her keyboard at random, followed by a simple, *RORY.*

I quietly excused myself and left the room. Burrowed under my covers, which still smelled like chlorine, I responded.

Me: *What??*

Liv: *OMG*

Me: *Stop just tell me.*

I realized, suddenly, that my stomach had started to knot up. I curled onto my side and tucked my knees up, wondering if maybe I did drink too much last night.

Liv: *remember when we got out of the pool...and i went to borrow one of grace's shirts...and didn't come downstairs for a hot sec...*

Me: *Yeah, Natsuki drove me home after u went upstairs. Sorry I didn't say bye*

Liv: *did u see who went up with me?*

Me: *No...who?*

Liv: *...Milo.*

The tug in my stomach, right under my diaphragm. There was a knot deep inside me, squeezing itself together. I closed my eyes, trying to concentrate, wondering if I needed to bolt to the bathroom. My phone buzzed again.

Liv: *...*

Me: *Wait u hooked up with Milo??*

Liv: *...lol*

Me: *omfg I'm like shook*

Me: *him??!?!!?*

Liv: *what's wrong with him?*

I uncurled with difficulty and stared at the ceiling, trying to imagine it, wondering how I'd never thought of it before. Milo's luscious hair and dark stubble and square hands. The way he wore cardigans and talked about great authors and always seemed to be right. How all the girls melted a little when he looked at them. All except Liv, of course, who stayed cool as ice.

*God*, I thought, blinking at my sudden realization. *He's kind of annoying.*

Liv was waiting. I racked my brain hard, but I couldn't come up with anything bad to say about Milo, anything to justify my sudden angst. Nothing. Not even that he had a strange smell or chewed loudly. So I said it: *Nothing. Lol. Was it good??*

Liv: *Rory. It was amazing.*

My stomach twisted again, and I rolled back into a cocoon under my covers.

Liv, after a few minutes: *U still there?*

Me: *Ya sorry I feel like sick lol. Gonna sleep it off.*

Liv: *K come over later bitch*

Me: *Obv*

*nine months after*

*T*he leaves have all turned. I hate being cold, but I love fall. I love sweaters and hot coffee and having an excuse to cancel plans because you can see your breath, and you don't have the right coat yet, and it would be so much better to just rewatch John Hughes movies with your cats.

"How are things at home?" April asks today, like she always does, as the sky darkens outside. As usual, I have to grudgingly admit that I really like how she's dressed: baggy, light-colored jeans and a rustic, autumnal sweater, her braids swept over one shoulder. I wonder if there's anyone she's dressing to impress. A boyfriend. A girlfriend.

"Home's fine," I say.

April smiles but doesn't talk, which makes me feel the need to keep going. I hate this trick, and I hate that I fall for it every time.

"Um," I say. "Well, Saige is taking the SAT on Saturday. And since I'm hopeless at science, Mom's fixed on *her* going pre-med. Willow's working on a book report on Helen Keller. And Nonno's chugging along. It feels like he's had a cold for the past six years, but I think it's just because he's super old. And Nonni's being annoying and trying to distract everyone with food. And the cats are . . . well, cats."

"I see," April says. "Yeah, my mom tries to fix everything with food, too. I'm like, you do understand that homemade mac and cheese isn't a solution to every single problem, right?"

"Well, my Nonni's mac probably comes close," I say, quirking a small smile.

"Oh, I bet," she says.

I look out the window at the leaves. Golden, deep red, burnt orange. I know the perfect soundtrack to this weather; I can almost hear it. I wish fall lasted forever.

"How about that tension you were experiencing with your mom?" April asks, drawing my focus back in. "You know. Regarding the pills. I remember that your mom was finding it difficult to be . . . *empathetic* about the mistake you made back in August."

We are finally referring to the Xanax Incident as a "mistake." I think April still believes it was an attempt to harm myself, but it seems like she's given up on this particular battle.

Which is good, because it wasn't.

"Empathy isn't my mom's strong suit," I say, twirling my hair. I think about last night, sprawled across the couch with the whole family after dinner, watching *E.T.* with Italian subtitles when Mom nudged me with her foot.

"Homecoming game on Friday," she said, spooning ice cream directly from the carton into her mouth.

"And?"

She flipped her hands out, as if it were obvious, and some ice cream flew off her spoon and onto Nonno's forehead.

"I think you should go," she said. "Might be fun."

Saige, who was half watching the movie from the

floor and half scrolling TikTok, looked up at Mom and me in disbelief.

"Rory's not a Telsey student anymore," she said to Mom, looking scandalized.

"So? I've never been a Telsey student," Mom responded.

"You've also never been to a homecoming game."

"I'm just saying," Mom said, readjusting her feet, while Nonni turned up the volume—pointless, because she was reading the subtitles— "It might be nice for Rory to spend a bit of time with friends."

"Friends?" I asked.

"Isn't Jem going to school in the city? Or Stoff? What about Stoff? They're just thirty minutes away, yeah?"

*There's no way Stoff would ever want to talk to me again,* I thought, and had to cut myself off from saying.

Before this year, Mom had rarely concerned herself with my social life. She barely knew where I was last summer when I spent every waking minute with Liv. And all the years before that, when I spent every weekend night at home with her, she equally didn't care. It would have been funny, her suddenly running herself into the ground trying to make me go out and have fun, if it weren't so infuriating.

"They're busy," I said, grabbing my popcorn and stepping over Willow to leave.

"You can't stay cooped up in this house forever," Mom called after me, ignoring Nonni's frantic shushes.

"According to Ridgewood College, I guess I can," I retorted, and I could practically *hear* her eyes roll.

"Rory?" April says now, and it breaks me out of my reverie.

"Sorry," I automatically say. "Zoned out."

"You don't have to apologize to me," April says, smiling softly.

My whole body is made up of apologies, though. Apologies for getting in the way, for taking too long, for not responding. Apologies to Saige for traumatizing her when she found me. Apologies to Mom for scaring her. Apologies to Stoff. Apologies to Jem. Apologies to Eleanor and Ramil. Apologies to Liv.

*I am sorry I survived and not you. It should have been me. It should have been me.*

"Rory," April says again. "There's actually something else I wanted to bring up with you today."

I look up at her, wondering how she has enough will-power to get dressed every morning. How she has the audacity to sleep and breathe normally when the world has disintegrated.

"I thought we'd cover this by now in our meetings," April continues, "but it hasn't come up yet." She cocks her head. "Romantic or sexual feelings? Sexuality? Lack of sexuality?"

God. Hearing a therapist say the word *sexuality* is my new least-favorite thing.

"Uh," I say.

"I just mean, you haven't brought it up once during our sessions. And I know it has to be on your mind in some way, right? Whether you're feeling unfulfilled in that area, or someone's making you nervous, or you're actively avoiding thinking about it . . ." She trails off, and then finishes, "I just want to see if we can explore that."

"Oh," I say. I don't know what this feeling is, bubbling up in my chest.

I just know that I want it gone.

"I . . . I haven't felt anything," I say. "I mean, in that department . . . since the Worst Night."

"That makes sense," says April. "It was such a huge shock to your system. Sometimes, when someone experiences a traumatic event, sex drive will disappear for a little."

I release my breath.

"What about before the accident, though? Did you have any sexual feelings or experiences before it happened?"

I hold my breath again.

April definitely notices.

She goes on a tangent, then, about different words that end with "-sexuality," and what they all mean: bi, demi, pan, omni, poly. She talks about things I'm already familiar with, stuff we talked about in school, online, everywhere. She talks about resources and community. She is listening to herself speak.

I am not really listening. My mind is wandering again. I'm thinking about them: Liv. Jem. Milo. Grace. Natsuki. Devon. Hearts beating, too loud. And it's all swirling around in my mind, and I'm embarrassed but I don't know why, and it's getting harder to hear myself think. Is an avalanche coming? At first, I can't tell, but the snow swirls louder and April's voice hums quieter and I am starting to see spots again.

*I will not go away*, I try to tell myself firmly. *I will not go away.*

The cold doesn't listen. It never does.

*J*unior year was over.
Liv and Milo were dating.

The summer was a fever dream, days and nights fused together, stretches of Grace's pool and Jem's basement, flashes of Liv's white teeth as she whispered observations and secrets to me under dark ceilings and skies. It was a blur of sparkly eyeliner and vaping and marshmallows and music and conversations that didn't make sense, but they did. Our time moved in infinite circles: Shows at Dreamtown. Bike rides home. Sleeping in the basement. Bagels frying under the sun, pounding headaches, screenshots from last night, high-pitched cackles, stares from old ladies, dirty flip-flops. The beach: Listening to music on the beach. Falling over each other on the beach. Liv and Milo kissing on the beach.

Liv, after: "There's sand *everywhere*, Roo. Even in places where—"

Me, sunburnt: "No, Liv. Nope. No."

Liv's giggle in my ear, her hair brushing my neck as she biked us home in the weak hours of the morning, me sitting behind her, my arms looped too tight around her waist, the lights blurring past us one by one.

No one put their foot down. No one stopped us.

The best part was Grace's pool. We'd jump off the

roof and pound into the water, night after night, sinking in slow motion. Even though I was starting to get comfortable, I still liked my alone time, and my favorite part of the night would be the jump: sinking underwater, everything suddenly quiet and blue and slow. I never wanted to come up for air. I sat underwater, my back scratching against the rough white wall, observing everyone's blurry legs interweaving. Liv came down to sit with me one time, and then pulled me up again.

"I don't know how you stay underwater for so long," she gasped, flipping her heavy dark hair out of her face, rubbing her eyes. Streaks of makeup, but she didn't care.

"I like watching," I said. Milo came up to us, sneaking his arms around Liv's waist, and she smiled into his neck.

\* \* \*

Mom seemed to know about my new, suddenly thriving social life. She seemed to know and subsequently tune it out. As it always was at my house, too many lives were bursting with too many details and needs: Willow got bronchitis, and Saige needed an English tutor, and my grandparents were getting old, and Mom was responsible for all of it. I was allowed to sink below the surface.

One time, I came home at six in the morning, the latest I'd been out, and although I felt like cocooning myself in the cloud of my bed for fifteen hours, I forced myself to shower instead. When I was leaving the bathroom, I ran into Mom in the hallway.

"Nice night?" she asked, passing me on her way to the stairs.

"Yes."

"Eggs?"

My stomach lurched. "Maybe later," I mumbled. "Just going to—"

I went to bed.

\* \* \*

Liv's parents definitely *wouldn't* have been chill about it if they had known anything.

We slipped in and out of her house like water, Liv saying something to them about a sleepover, a movie, a birthday, no boys, just us and popcorn and pedicures.

"Can you distract her?" Liv asked one morning from the cocoon of her blankets, when Eleanor's chirpy voice flew up the stairs. So I went with Liv's mom to Starbucks, Walgreens, and the dry cleaner's, and she asked me questions about my life the whole time. When we came home, Liv was freshly showered and functioning.

"Hi," Liv said to us, taking my arm and steering me out of the house again. "Bye."

"Do you two want to come back for lunch?" Eleanor asked, and for a moment, I wanted to stay in the air-conditioning and keep listening to her soft voice, rest my head for a little while. But Liv rolled her eyes and pulled me harder, so I just waved.

"I don't know why she needs to *know* everything," Liv said to me as we approached her bike. "I wish she was more like your mom. She's so dope. You can do whatever you want."

"My mom can't even remember my middle name," I scoffed, joking, but then wondering if she really couldn't.

"Exactly," Liv responded, giving me her twisty grin.

*I wish* my *mom was nosy,* I thought, hopping onto the back of her bike, wrapping my arms around her waist. I pushed down that thought, just like I'd started pushing down the others: That college apps were approaching like a huge black cloud. That I needed to get a second summer job. That I was scared that if we got caught drinking, Eleanor wouldn't smile so brightly when she saw me; she wouldn't ask about my life anymore.

We made our way to the next person's house.

* * *

At the end of June, the status of my virginity started coming into question.

"No, but Roo," Liv said one night as we rode in the back of Devon's Nissan. "You've never even *kissed*?"

Devon and Milo were in the front seat, and Natsuki, Jem, Liv, and I were in the back. Everyone except us was pounding their fists to the Labrinth song blaring through Devon's speakers, screaming along to the lyrics. We'd just danced for hours to a DJ at Dreamtown who went by RosyCheeks, and the world was now spinning.

"Not even a kiss," I said quietly. Liv and I sat squashed into one seat, her sitting on my lap, our heads glued together as we thumbed through her Instagram. "I have virgin lips."

She laughed, and I felt the rhythm of it against my body. My left arm kind of had no choice except to sit around her waist, and I was so high that I could feel everything, I was aware of *everything*: the texture of her jean cutoffs under my palm, the sliver of warm skin that my thumb kept accidentally brushing when we hit a bump or turned a corner. Every time she breathed, I breathed.

"We're going to fix that," Liv said, clicking off her

phone as Devon pulled onto the highway.

"What?" I said distractedly, as lights buzzed past our windows like tiny, bright flowers. Devon hit a crack in the road, and we lurched—and, without knowing what I was doing or why, I tightened my arms around Liv's waist, pulling her in closer.

Liv responded, pressing her cheek against mine. "Your virginity. We're fixing it," she whispered straight into my ear, and I could hear every single lilt and breath in her voice. The vibration of her words, tickling my ear.

*Damn, I really am high.*

"Does it *need* to be fixed?" I asked, or maybe I just thought it, because Liv didn't answer. Instead, she reached up and opened the sunroof of Devon's car. Wind rushed in, biting, and everyone yelled at her over the music to close it.

"One *sec*," she told them, and she lifted herself off me. "I just want to feel it."

She stood up, her head and arms disappearing through the sunroof. Before I could make my own decision, she reached back in, found my arm, and yanked me up with her.

Wind punched through my chest, splitting my bangs and throwing my hair cleanly behind me. At first, I panicked, because you *definitely* weren't supposed to stand through a sunroof, and I was *definitely* going to fly out like a Dunkin' Donuts napkin, never to be seen again. But then I turned to Liv and saw the smile stretched wide across her face, the colorful makeup smudging down her cheeks after hours of dancing, the way she closed her eyes against the wind and laughed, yelled, shouted words that I couldn't hear. The joy sparkled and popped away from her, seeping into me, and then I was laughing harder than I ever had, and her hand was clasping mine. It was a Tuesday night, and we were seventeen, and we were listening to every single song at once.

* * *

Liv wasn't the only one who started trying to get me laid, although she was the most direct. More than once, Grace sidled drunkenly up to me at a party or a show, saying point-blank, "Who do you like?"

To be truly honest, I'd never really thought about dating at my old school. Mostly because I was a quiet, angular weirdo who listened to old music and couldn't look anywhere except at my feet, but also because dating, to fifteen-year-old me, had still seemed gross. My friend Cassidy would always try to push me toward the few skinny, nerdy boys she visualized me with, inviting me on double dates, but I'd always back away. When I saw my classmates making out behind auditorium doors and clumsily pawing at each other in Cassidy's basement, I'd literally feel nauseous.

*Late bloomer*, I kept thinking, repeating the words of some Judy Blume or American Girl book to myself. No boobs yet? No boys yet. *I'm a late bloomer. Someday, someone will come along.*

But now, Liv and Milo were everywhere—kissing, spooning, holding hands under the table—and it was all suddenly different. Here, now, in my face. And I was seventeen, and I was comfortable.

And, okay, my boobs had *kind of* started coming in.

And Jem had been looking at me recently, sitting next to me in the car, splashing me with water, finding any excuse to touch my shoulder or my hair. So, right before the Fourth of July, when we were all lounging in his basement after another show at Dreamtown, I decided I would try.

I got up and sat next to him.

"Hey," he said, stretching his neck to blow out smoke.

He turned to me and smiled, scooting closer. His braids were longer now, and he'd started doing the half-up half-down bun, which we all loved.

"Hey," I said.

"What did you think?" he asked.

I coughed. "What?"

"About the show."

"Oh," I said. "It was awesome."

"Yeah?"

"Yeah. I loved the lead singer."

"She was fire," Jem agreed. "Kind of like . . . HAIM, Tegan and Sara–type sound, but so much more . . . like . . . what's the word I'm trying to find?"

"Uh . . . light?"

"*Crunch*," said Jem, slicing his hand down in front of him. "So much more *crunch*."

"For sure," I said.

"Anyway," Jem said, but it seemed like he was done talking. We sat in a soft silence, looking around the basement. Christmas lights outlined the walls of the low-ceilinged room, bathing people's faces in a dim reddish glow, and huge posters of Jem's favorite bands lined every inch of the walls. The whole friend group was here, plus some extras. Liv and Milo had "gone on a walk," and I was trying not to think about it. Trying to be casual about everything.

I felt Jem moving next to me, slowly breathing,

soft and relaxed, like he had nowhere to go. My phone buzzed under my thigh, and I checked it: Stoff. After briefly wondering why he'd call so late at night, I clicked it off and took a breath. I'd call him back later. There was something I needed to take care of, *right now*.

"Where are the rest of your records?" I asked Jem, twisting toward him. I already knew the answer.

"Oh, they're actually in my room," he said, and then he twisted toward me.

The earth silently rotated around us.

"Can I see them?" I asked.

\* \* \*

The stairs creaked, but Jem's parents were out of town visiting his sister, and so we hopped up carelessly, laughing for no reason except that it was two in the morning, and we were high, and we both knew what was about to happen. Strange bubbles rose from my stomach to my chest, expanding and popping, one by one. I had never felt this way before. I could not believe I was doing it: Going upstairs. With a guy. To his room.

*Look at me, Six-Months-Ago Rory! Look at how BraveCoolRelaxed I am! It was this easy, all along!*

We tripped into his room, still giggling, and I flopped on the floor as he turned on the lamp. The records were scattered across the carpet in no apparent order.

"Uh, I was trying to sort them," he said, sitting down next to me.

"By what?" I asked.

"Still figuring that out."

I laughed, running my hands across them, spreading them out to see them all. "These are incredible," I said, and I meant it. He had everything, from Bob Marley to the Smiths to Prince, and everyone in between. *Mom would be impressed*, I thought, briefly remembering the countless hours we used to spend talking about music. Wondering how many months it had been since the last time we did that.

"Let it fill you up, love," she'd say, as we watered houseplants or sorted spices or just lay like starfish in the middle of the living room of our old house, late on a Friday night.

I tried to push Mom out of my mind as Jem moved closer, his body still parallel to mine, facing the records. He pointed out his favorites (pretty predictable: *Purple Rain, Roots*, and *Currents*). I pointed out mine (also pretty predictable: *Abbey Road, Legacy*, and *Blue*). We kept pointing over each other—this one, no *this* one, no *this one*—and the room felt hotter, and my heart rate felt faster, and my stomach started churning, so eventually, I faced him.

"Jem?" I said.

He turned to me, raising his eyebrows, and I saw it clearly: the brightest hope in his deep brown eyes, the question on his face. We looked at each other for a moment, and then we both leaned in, and his lips were on mine.

My brain took a moment to process it, firing small fragments of thoughts: *Soft lips. Where to put the nose? Eyelashes, fluttering. Wet lips. His mouth is open. Mine is not. Should I open? Oh, teeth. Hi. I've never touched someone else's teeth.*

I got used to it after a few moments, my mouth settling into his, noting the different things he was doing: Hand on neck. Other hand on neck. Tongue.

I settled, and I started waiting.

Waiting to feel.

I'd read so many books, I'd watched so many movies, and I'd seen how this went: fireworks, butterflies, pounding heart, warm bodies glued together, fingers through hair, chills up the spine. I waited for those things, for any of those things. And in some parts of my body, I wondered if they might be happening: My heart was definitely beating faster than normal. My hand was crawling up his shoulder. The hair on the back of my neck was standing up.

*This is what you do*, my brain kept instructing me. *This is what Liv and Milo do. This is what everyone does.*

*This is you, being seventeen. This is you, being* normal.

But his tongue was in my mouth. In my *mouth*.

And I wasn't feeling fireworks or butterflies. I was feeling gross.

With that thought, I stiffened, and my head pulled back, and then my body pulled back, and I was just looking at Jem, my kind, music-loving, currently surprised friend, with spit down his chin and a bit of my lipstick on his cheek.

"I—" I faltered.

"You okay?" he breathed.

"Uh. Yeah. I just."

"Totally."

"I didn't . . ."

"No worries."

"Yeah. It's just."

"You don't need to explain, Ror," he said softly. He smiled and nodded, showing me it was okay.

We sat there.

"You—you wanna go back downstairs?" he finally asked, wiping his mouth on his shoulder. I watched the little stain it created—my spit? his spit?—on the shoulder of his worn T-shirt, and I nodded.

\* \* \*

The basement was how we left it: Christmas lights, smoky air, Billie Eilish humming out of the speakers. Grace and Devon cuddled in a corner; across the room, Natsuki looked at me with a sly grin. We sat back down on the couch, my body feeling more and more like I was made out of wood. A puppet, a doll.

Then the door swung open, and Liv glided in, pulling Milo behind her by the hand. He was rubbing his eyes and smiling.

I wanted to stand up and say, "I did it, Liv. I kissed Jem. Look. I can do it, too."

Unlike the rest of us, Liv did *not* look like it was almost three in the morning and she'd ridden two sticky buses and eaten Jimmy Johns and danced in a sweaty throng of people at Dreamtown before taking another two buses back. She looked quietly radiant, unbothered. Not exactly happy, but content.

There was only one small detail, which probably no one noticed except me: one of the buttons on her shirt was buttoned into the wrong hole.

"How was your *walk*?" Devon asked Liv and Milo, failing to keep down the sarcasm in his voice. Milo punched him in the arm. Liv ignored him, plopping down next to me, trying to hide her smile. We made eye contact for a split second, and she started to laugh.

"Let's go home," she said quietly, looping her arm through mine.

* * *

I didn't know why, but I couldn't tell her about Jem. Not yet.

We biked the twelve blocks back to my house, sticky with sweat. We barely talked until we had traipsed all the way upstairs, peeled off our dresses, stepped into large T-shirts and boxers, and fallen onto the mess of sheets on my bed.

Then, slow and quiet with sleepiness, she asked if I was okay.

"What?" I said, twisting around to get comfortable.

"You looked weird," Liv said. "When Milo and I got back."

"Oh," I said. "I . . . I kissed Jem."

Liv contracted into herself, squealing into my pillow, the tiredness draining out of her.

"Shut up!" I said. "You're going to wake up Nonni and—"

"*Finally*," she whispered, hitting my pillow. "We've been waiting for so long."

"We?"

"How was it?"

"It was . . . I don't know."

"How far did you guys go?"

"Just kissing . . ."

Her voice lowered. "Was your shirt on?"

"Liv."

"Okay, I'm just—"

"Liv," I said again. I faced the wall, not her, so she wouldn't see my eyes. But my voice cracked, and she sucked in her breath.

"Roo?"

Her hand on my arm. I felt so stiff, and she must

have felt it, too, because she quickly took it off again.

"What happened?" she said, her voice suddenly, completely different. Hard. Urgent.

"Nothing, I . . ." I swallowed hard, but the lump wouldn't go away.

"Did he ask? Rory, did he ask first?"

I finally turned a little, rolling to my back. "It wasn't like that," I said.

"Are you sure?"

"*I* started it," I said, facing the ceiling, pressing the edges of my palms against my eyes. "I thought I wanted to. But . . . something happened."

"What? What happened?" Her hand was back on my arm, warm. She lay on her side, just inches away. I knew if I looked at her I would melt even more, so I stayed on my back.

"Well, it's more like . . . *nothing* happened," I said, after many shaky breaths. "We were kissing, and I kept waiting to feel something, but . . . just . . . I thought I liked him, but I wanted him to stop touching me. I felt gross. And cold." I swallowed. "I felt like ice."

"That's okay," Liv said, her hand heavy on my arm.

"But . . . it's just Jem. He's cute, and there's no guy I feel safer with. I *initiated*."

"So? You can change your mind."

"But what if there's something wrong with me? What if I can never do it?"

"Roo, that doesn't need to be a bad thing. Maybe you get some experience and then figure out hooking up's just not for you. So what?"

"It's not that," I said. "I . . . I *want* to hook up. Or . . . to feel that closeness, you know? It's almost like I crave it. But with Jem it just . . . felt . . ." I couldn't find the right words. "You make it look so easy. You and Milo. It's perfect."

"It's not," she said. "Not even close."

"But—"

"Listen." Liv took her hand off my arm, also rolling to her back. "Rory, you don't have to be ready to do shit yet. I know it seems like everyone is doing it, but they're not—"

"They are," I said. "We're almost seniors. I should have some type of . . . *experience* by now. What the fuck am I *missing* that everyone else has?"

Liv stayed quiet, breathing steadily. When she spoke, her voice was softer. "There's nothing wrong with you," she said.

"But I don't . . . *feel* that," I said. I took a breath, feeling my heart pound against my chest. "I don't think I . . . feel it for boys."

The air hung heavy between us. Liv squeezed my arm.

"What about people who aren't boys?" she whispered.

I listened to my heart beating in my ears, trying not to feel so tense. Wondering why my arm clenched so tightly under her hand. Probably sensing it, Liv let go, but she stayed just as close to me.

"You know I don't care what you are," she said. "Right? You're my Roo."

She said it lightly, playfully, and a soft, achy feeling filled my chest. I couldn't tell if it was hope or longing or a combination of both.

"Right," I whispered.

"And also, like, sexuality is fluid," she said, yawning. "And girls are fucking *hot*. I definitely want to hook up with other people besides men. Probably in college."

"Yeah," I said, my voice getting stronger. College. A place to be . . . different. *Actually me.* But still a safe distance away, so I didn't have to think about it too hard. "Me, too."

"Girls are just *better*," Liv added, making me snicker. "It's honestly almost embarrassing how attracted I am to Milo."

Just like that, the hopeful feeling in my chest evaporated.

"It's not embarrassing," I told her.

"I know. But I literally think about him all the time," she said sleepily, smiling. "Like, it's barely even his personality. I mean, he's great, but it's also just his *body*. It's like, ridiculously primal and shallow, and I know it won't last forever, but at least right now I just want him *with* me. You know?"

"Mm-hmm."

Liv was quiet for a long time, her breathing steady. So steady that I thought she'd fallen asleep, so I rolled away from her, hugging my knees, trying to silence my thoughts.

Then she whispered, "Hey, Roo. Guess how many guys I've kissed?"

I closed my eyes tight, wishing she *would* fall asleep and forget this conversation. "Five?"

"Twelve."

*Why are you doing this to me?* I wanted to ask her.

"Guess how many of those guys gave me butterflies?" she continued, her voice now inches behind me.

I stayed silent.

"One," she said. "Milo."

Her hand on my arm, one last time.

"Stay cold for now," she whispered. "I think it's easier, sometimes, if you don't feel."

She turned around, and within moments, she was asleep.

*T*he week after I run into Liv's parents, I walk into their house for the first time since the Worst Night. Liv's house has always been immaculate; it's all angles and shiny marble and simple pastel colors. No flowered wallpaper or scattered science papers, no mismatched cushions, no cat hair or overflowing spice cabinets. The Martinez family is neat and clean.

"Rory," Eleanor says, opening her arms for a hug. I let her steer me into the kitchen, trying to pretend that I'm not in a complete daze, that I don't expect Liv to come thumping down the stairs at any moment.

The whole time we're at the kitchen table, and Eleanor and Ramil are asking me about my family while feeding me cheese and crackers, I cannot shake off Liv. She's standing in the corner, pouring herself a glass of orange juice, still in her going-out clothes. It's three a.m. We just got back from Dreamtown.

When I finally accept that Liv is *not* in the room, I convince myself that the shower is running upstairs, and I wonder why her parents haven't set another place at the table, knowing she'll come down any moment with her hair wrapped in a towel. They know how hangry she can get. How wildly hilarious will she find these boxes of cards filling the dining room table? And all the flowers, which, after nine months, are still being sent?

*I'm right here, you fucking weirdos*, she will say, before nudging me and making a joke about choir.

When it must become obvious that I'm incapable of functioning in a normal conversation, Eleanor sighs and smiles. "So. Are you ready to go up to Liv's room?"

*No*, I think.

"Sure," I say.

The stairs creak as they always have, and I flush with a wave of second-degree anxiety from the memory of sneaking up them last summer, trying not to wake her parents. When I reach the first room to the right of the staircase and see the rainbow letters across the door spelling OLIVIA, I abruptly turn to Eleanor.

"Sorry, but . . . is it okay if I . . . do you mind if I just . . ."

"Go in by yourself? Absolutely." She's already backing away, retreating into the shadows of the landing. "Ramil and I are going to counseling, but we'll keep our phones on. Call us if you need anything, all right?"

I nod.

I walk in.

The first thing I notice is a book lying under the lamp on her bedside table, a ribbon sticking out near the beginning. Unfinished. Less than halfway through.

I close my eyes, and then open them and try again.

Then I see a half-built loft, and my chest caves into itself as a flurry of memories rushes through: Liv and me, one Saturday last fall, running through Home Depot to grab building supplies. Liv shutting down the two separate men who tried to explain hardware to us, insisting she could do it herself. The way we worked earnestly in her room for three hours before collapsing into an exhausted fit of hangry, hysterical laughter, promising each other we'd finish the loft another day soon.

*It's okay. It doesn't matter. Stay cold.*

I turn away from the loft to face her bed and realize it's the first time I've seen it made. I wonder why, and when, Eleanor decided to make it, fluffing the pillows and smoothing down the duvet. Was it right after she heard? Or did she wait a while, staring at the last imprint of Liv's head on the pillows?

*Stop. Start again.*

I stand alone in her room, the door closed, green curtains drawn, and try to get my bearings. Everything except the bed is the way it was when we left on the Worst Night: the top of her wooden dresser overflowing with earrings and bracelets, books haphazardly stacked in piles around her desk. A guitar, a cello, and a keyboard stuffed in the corner. Earrings and necklaces draping from pins stuck into the wall at random.

From each wall, famous women stare down at me, each more magnificent and powerful than the rest: Frida Kahlo, Maya Angelou, Lea Salonga.

Angela Davis, Michelle Obama, Alexandria Ocasio-Cortez.

Solange, Amy Winehouse.

And, largest and most radiant of them all, Billie Holiday singing above the bed frame, the velvet blue notes of misery and quiet survival floating from her ruby-red lips.

I breathe in until my body is filled with their words, their sorrows, their joys, and I beg them all: *Tell me how to make it stop. Tell me your secrets. Tell me how you breathe.*

They don't. They look down at me, stoic and silent.

\* \* \*

Eleanor said to start with the clothes. Anything Liv made or really loved, put in a pile to keep. Everything else—charity. *Socks can go away,* Eleanor said, but I brought my backpack, and Liv had great taste in socks, and I can see her *fuming* at me for throwing some of these fuckers in the trash. Burgundy fishnet stockings? Hot pink ones that say, *Would you kindly go fuck yourself?* In flowery, curly writing?

"I've got you," I tell Liv, stuffing the good pairs into my backpack.

I'm dropping pair after pair of untouched athletic socks into a trash bag when I find a metal sandwich box featuring Elsa and Anna from *Frozen*. Sucking in my breath, I pop it open and find more weed than I've ever seen in my life.

I slam it shut quickly and look up at the poster that rests above Liv's dresser: Michelle Obama, looking sternly down at me.

*Do your parents know you smoke?* I asked Liv once, and she laughed like a hyena.

*They'd probably send me to a fucking boarding school if they had the slightest clue.*

I grab the box. It's not light. "Jesus, Liv," I whisper, stuffing it in my backpack.

I move on to her bedside table. A half-filled glass of water: I scan the rim for lipstick marks and find them, but instead of feeling satisfied, I feel like I've been punched in the chest.

Then there's a crooked pile of books leaning toward the bed, all looking very old, with multiple pages dogeared, some overflowing with colorful notes. I scan the titles:

*The House of the Spirits, Isabel Allende*
*The Awakening, Kate Chopin*
*I Know Why the Caged Bird Sings, Maya Angelou*
*Christmas Thoughts About Love, Donald E. Saunders Jr.*
*Percy Jackson and the Lightning Thief, Rick Riordan*

I realize, my heart tightening, that these are her comfort books. The ones she would grab and thumb through when she felt scared, sad, angry. She never explained this to me, but I understand it at once. I remember asking her once about *Christmas Thoughts About Love*, and how she flushed, hugging it.

"I'm *not* sappy," she said. "Love sucks. Whatever. But I found this at a garage sale, and it's like . . . this cardiologist used to write an essay about love every year, and when I read them I feel *so* warm."

"You're sappy," I teased, and she flipped me off.

I run my thumb over the spine of each book, and then, feeling slightly stupid, I smell them. I'm trying to find her, of course, but I can't bring myself to touch her bed. Not yet. So I smell the books for a while, and that's when I first see the black notebook.

I watch, wishing I could stop but unable to do so, as my hands lift the five books and carefully place them on Liv's pristine bed. I brush dust off the spine of the notebook and thumb the peeling sticker on its cover. *Fuck This!* ☺ it says in a flouncy, pretentious font, surrounded by flowers and stars. I bought this sticker for her, for her eighteenth birthday. A week before Christmas, when we caroled to rich old people and cried about college and convinced each other we were better than we were, stronger, braver. When we drove through the snowy streets of Clarksdale, listening to the radio. This sticker was the only present I gave her. I knew there would be countless more Christmases and birthdays and celebrations. I didn't think twice about it.

The sticker is now peeling off this tiny black notebook, which I know was her diary.

For hours, maybe years, the diary and I stare at each other. My mind, for the first time potentially ever, is silent.

And then, the tiniest voice: *What if they read it?*

I swallow, looking at Billie Holiday singing her heart out over the bed frame. Liv saw a strange, powerful beauty in Billie. She called her one of her "soul people." I blur my eyes, so that Billie's dark curls, olive gold skin, and painted red lips could be Liv's.

"What do you want me to do?" I whisper to her, my hand resting on the journal.

*I don't talk to my parents,* Liv said one day, early in our friendship. *I mean,* talk-*talk. I love them, but we just don't have that kind of relationship. It's better if they don't know.*

*Don't know what?* I asked.

*Anything,* Liv responded, smoke spiraling from her mouth.

"Okay," I whisper, closing my eyes tightly. I lift her diary, weigh it in my hands for just a moment, and then pocket it.

I scan her room, as if I'm expecting the FBI to pop out of her closet or from underneath her bed, yelling, "Put the diary down!" Although what I do end up seeing is far less dramatic, it still brings my heart to a full stop. Right there, sitting intrusively at the edge of her dresser, is a graying plastic bag. Something that doesn't belong. Something from After.

I cross the room in giant steps that take forever and pick up the bag, slowly turning it.

Through its cloudy lens of worn plastic, I see a tube of wine-red lipstick, a tiny coin purse, a pack of gum. An ID. The grainy photo of Liv smiling the cold, polite smile that didn't spread to her eyes, a backpack slung around her shoulder, a faint glisten of sweat over her left brow. *Olivia Smith*, the ID reads, showing a date of birth that put Liv in her twenties.

I feel my insides hardening.

*"WAIT!" Liv shouts, her eyes sparkling under the greenish light of her room, hair pulled into a magnificent bun. "I need this," she says, grabbing the fake ID.*

*"I thought we weren't drinking," I respond, trying to perfect the pattern and balance of rings on my right hand.*

*"We're not, but Dreamtown cards now. We just have to get in."*

*She stuffs her ID into a pocket of her high-waisted, below-the-knee skirt.*

*"I fucking love this skirt," she says, twirling around, and we're in the sixties, not some cold night in the present, and I watch as the light catches the sparkle in her eyes. "It's like a cave. I don't have to bring an actual bag, I can just keep all my shit in here."*

*I watch as she fixes her makeup in the mirror one more time. Erasing the smudges. Erasing the last hour, or maybe the last week, or maybe the last four months.*

*She takes a tube of lipstick—wine red, her favor-*

*ite—and stuffs it into another pocket. She grabs her gum and her coin purse. Then she looks up at me and grabs my arms, spinning me around, her eyes bright. And it's as if the vase never broke at all.*

*Don't think about it,* I tell myself. *Stop.*

I continue to turn the plastic bag in the air, taking it in, knowing it's too late, knowing I've already burned myself, that I cannot turn back now. I don't want to know what this bag is, but I do. It's what they gave back to Eleanor and Ramil, in the blank stretch of time during After.

The *Personal Belongings.*

I try to convince myself it isn't real. This doesn't mean it necessarily happened. Nothing *looks* as though it's been through a car accident; if I focus hard enough, this can just be a normal compilation of Liv's shit, something she'll grab on her way out next time, unable to care enough to have an actual purse.

But then I rotate the bag fully, and behind the coin purse, I find it. I find the evidence. Five inches of shattered black glass.

It used to be an iPhone.

And I drop the bag. I'm done.

I start to feel cold in my chest, my breath quickening. I need to be doing something with my hands. *Now.* I start to twist the skin around my arms, teeth chattering. The tremors are back. Everything is so loud, and I can't stand the screeching in my ears, so I pull the headphones out of my bag with effort and shuffle a playlist, curling into a ball on the ground.

The song: Andrew Bird, "Ethio Invention No. 1."

One of my earliest memories from After is lying in the dark, phone clenched in my fist, listening to this track on repeat. Most songs, that early on in After, made me throw up. That's not an exaggeration: I would literally hear the opening notes to a song and heave out what little food I'd been able to consume that day. I brought bags with me everywhere.

The songs came back to me, then, very slowly. One at a time. The first one was "Blackbird," and the second was "God Bless the Child." This piece, the one I'm listening to now, was third. No voices, just the plucking and weaving of Andrew Bird on strings.

I silently thank Liv for giving me this song in this moment. And then I start to speak out loud.

"I miss you," I start. "ImissyouImissyouImissyouI missyouImissyou," until I'm out of breath, until I'm hunched over and gulping. "I miss you." Breath. "I miss you." Breath. "Are you okay?" Breath. "I miss you."

Big breath.

"I'm not okay, Liv," I say, and then, just to make sure she hears me, I say it another ten thousand times. "I'm not okay I'm not okay I'm not okay I'm not okay. You need to help me. Where are you? Where did you *go*? Tell me where to go. Tell me what to do. Just . . . help me. Please. *Please.*"

After that, I can't breathe for a while, so I have to stop talking. Andrew Bird's violin sways, wrapping me in a thick wool blanket, too thick, too tight. I close my eyes so I don't have to see her, her brow furrowed in sorrow, in disappointment, in *anger*. Her lips shut into a thin red line. Because she knows.

She knows that I took up less space, that I had fewer words. That there was less of me to lose. If I died, the hole in the world could be stitched up fast. Nothing like the gaping trench she left.

It should have been me.

*Here, bitch!* Stoff texted me. *Let's hustle!*

It was the Fourth of July, and I was squinting in the bathroom mirror, halfway through my eyeliner, winging each end. Nonni, Nonno, Mom, and my sisters bustled around downstairs loudly, home from the fireworks, a delicious late-dinner smell rising through the floorboards.

*One sec*, I texted him, hoping he'd understand that it meant *five minutes.*

When I finally got into Stoff's mom's Mercedes, ignoring the six more texts I'd gotten from him and the eight I had from Liv, he groaned, "Oh my *god.*"

"I know I just took, like, a million years," I said, but then I realized he wasn't shouting at me.

"Devon just texted me. They're already running out of alcohol!" he said, not waiting for my seat belt to click before speeding down the road.

"Fuck," I said instinctively, although I didn't really care.

"Anyway." Stoff twisted the wheel like his life depended on it. "Nice to see you still exist."

"Nice to see *you* still exist," I said, checking my reflection in my phone. "How's choir camp?"

*"Drama* camp," he said. "I mean, it's fine. I guess."

*Which eyeliner,* Liv texted me, before sending a

picture of one eye in blue sparkles, another in green.

*Green*, I replied. *It's gorg.*

*Thanks mama!*

"Cool," I told Stoff, clicking my phone off. "Why is it just fine? Did something happen?"

"No," he replied. "Just vibes." He sighed huffily.

"What?"

"I *need* to get drunk tonight," Stoff said, changing the subject. "You don't have a fake ID, Ror, do you?"

"I look like I'm twelve," I said, laughing. "A fake would never work for me. You should get one."

"I'm too poor," he whined.

"Says the boy who owns six pairs of Oxfords."

"Most of them were on clearance," he said. "J. Crew doesn't pay *that* well, you know."

I laughed harder, but it wasn't my usual laugh; something felt different. Harsher. And before I could catch myself, I said, "Don't your parents just buy them for you? I know you have an allowance. I know you could get a fake, if you really wanted to."

Stoff said nothing. He just turned up the volume on the radio. It was some Top 40 song that made me suddenly want to claw my ears off.

I should have said something polite, taken it back. Instead, I said, "Own it. Own your privilege."

I could feel Stoff bristle next to me, but when he spoke, he sounded confident. In fact, I could hear a laugh in his voice. "Okay, Rory. Okay."

"What?"

"It's just funny because *you're* telling *me* to own it. Check yourself."

Steam rose into my ears. "What are you talking about?"

"This?" He took his eyes off the road to wave at me, my outfit, my makeup. "This isn't *you*. This is you trying to be Liv. You're trying to talk like her and look like her and *be* her." He shrugged. "Everyone can tell."

Heat rushed to my face.

I said, very quietly: "That's not true."

"I don't know," he said. "The real Rory would never wear makeup. And she would *never* act like such a bitch. Especially to her only friend from last fall."

A screaming silence pounded in my ears, in my throat.

I wanted to say so many things.

I said none of them.

I recovered in silence, counting my breaths until my body had settled down, and when he spoke again— "Did you hear that Natsuki hooked up with that guy on the lacrosse team?"—I played into it, ignoring the pounding in my head, until I had pushed myself back to the surface.

※ ※ ※

When we arrived at Grace's house for the post-fireworks party, I immediately went to the bathroom and scrubbed my face, erasing the eyeliner.

*It's too hot for it anyway,* I thought.

Then I quietly left the bathroom and joined the throng of warm bodies in Grace's basement. It was a cave of red, white, blue, and beer. Liv and Milo were late, but as soon as I started fretting about what I would do if she didn't come soon—everyone seemed somehow scarier when she wasn't around, a fact that I always tried to ignore—Liv snuck up behind me, snaking her arms around my waist.

"Hello, queen girl," she said, leaning her chin on my shoulder. I turned to face her, and she let go. Of *course* she was wearing all black today, the only minimalist in a sea of drunken patriotism: black overalls, black T-shirt, black scrunchie, black boots. The only color came from rows of rhinestones lining her eyes, and the green sparkly eyeliner across her lids.

"Where's Milo?" I asked, as she grabbed a beer.

Liv shook her head. "He'll be back soon. Bitch can't go a single night without getting high. I know he'll come back, though," she said, rolling her eyes to the ceiling. "His favorite homeboy came through." She nodded toward the corner, where Harrison was talking to someone, a blunt in his hand.

Harrison. From the Duvall twins' party. The one who called her a "selfish fucking bitch."

"Milo and Harrison are friends?"

"They're tight," Liv said. "Like, my-vagina-when-I-see-Harrison tight."

"Oh, bitch," I said, as she started cracking up at herself. "Oh wow. Okay."

I looked back at the crowd, and rap music roared from the speakers behind us.

"What?" Liv said suddenly, as she caught her breath again.

"What-what?"

"You. What."

She looked me in the eye, and in one millisecond, I knew she could tell I was upset. I shook my head. "Stoff. Just being kind of a dick on the way here. It doesn't matter."

"Yes, it does. What did he say?"

"I don't want—"

Jem descended on us, holding two mismatched shot glasses filled with something clear. He held them out to both of us, smiling. Liv looked at him—literally just looked—and he shrugged, taking both himself instead.

"He knows I can't. I'm driving," Liv said, as he walked away. "So? What did Stoff say?"

I took a deep breath. "I just—"

Then the music was cut off midbeat, and someone yelled, "HOT SEAT!"

Liv rolled her eyes to the ceiling again and groaned. "This is literally the worst game of all time."

But for some reason—probably because it was the Fourth of July, and it was super hot, and it was easier to just go with the group on super-hot nights—we both sat down and played.

\* \* \*

As usual, the Hot Seat questions were exclusively about sex. With every bit of information released, no matter how boring, the crowd would shout "OOOOHH!" or some other unintelligent monosyllabic word, and fist bumps would swim across the sea of kids trying to one-up each other, and flecks of beer would rain down, and the sacrificial lamb on the Hot Seat would blush and giggle and say, "Whatever, guys," even when it was very far from *whatever*.

"What's your number!" someone shouted at Natsuki, as soon as she sat down. I noticed how her lavender-dyed hair looked silver under the light, how her sparkly makeup was smearing off.

"Six," she said, smiling and shrugging.

Everyone except Liv and me screamed.

I whispered in Liv's ear, "Sorry, but what . . . what's someone's 'number'?"

"It's how many people you've had sex with," Liv said quietly. "And you owe me a dollar."

I grumpily fished in the pocket of my dress until I found a crumpled dollar bill, then pushed it into her expectant hand.

Natsuki smiled through her questions, tossing her shimmering hair behind her, flushing but never flinching. Yes, this rumor was true; no, that one was not; here's what really happened over spring break. About eight inches. No, that wasn't the biggest.

"Who hasn't gone yet?" said Stoff's friend, a bossy soprano from choir, once Natsuki had sat back down.

There was a chorus of "*Liiiiiiiiiiv.*"

Liv rolled her eyes at me and stood up, tossed her phone in my lap, and glided to the stool at the front as if weightless.

"What's your number?" Stoff asked, before she even sat down.

"Two," she said flatly, folding her arms. "Next?"

"Try not to sound so excited about it, Liv," said Harrison, and next to him, Stoff turned his head away. I realized he was laughing.

More people laughed, too, and I suddenly felt myself deflating the tiniest bit. Liv had been in my life for six months, and until now, I'd just been under the impression that she'd landed like a balloon from outer space, nonexistent until the day in January when she gave me gum in choir. For the first time, it occurred to me that Liv had been a person before then. Here. In Clarksdale. With these people.

"Shut up and ask another question!" Grace said,

sounding annoyed, but also so drunk she couldn't sit up straight.

"When's the last time you gave head?" Harrison shouted, earning himself a soft slap from Natsuki.

Liv's stare bored into his eyes, and her lips curled. I felt the same weird, uncomfortable tug in my stomach, but this time it wasn't because of anything I drank. I wanted to stand up, to march right into Harrison's face and—

"I don't keep track," Liv said, not breaking her gaze.

"You have to remember," said Harrison.

"Well, I don't," said Liv.

"It was *that* boring?" asked Stoff, and everyone laughed again.

"It truly was," Liv sighed, and they laughed harder.

"Milo won't be happy to hear—" Harrison began, but Natsuki cut him off.

"What's the worst thing you've ever done?" she asked, sounding eager.

Liv's brow furrowed. "Legal-wise?"

"Anything-wise."

She thought briefly. "I got really high before my grandpa's funeral."

"Oh my god, *tea*," said Grace.

"I have one!" Stoff said cheerfully. He crossed one leg over the other and folded his hands in his lap, cocking his head. "Why do you hate everyone?"

The earth took a giant breath and held it.

During the one million years of silence that followed Stoff's question, my brain shouted, *SAY SOMETHING. CALL HIM OUT. SAY, "THAT WAS RUDE." DO ANYTHING.*

But I did nothing except wilt. I stared at Liv. And

Liv stared at me, for the tiniest fraction of a moment. Nothing in her face had changed the entire time she'd been sitting up there; she was fearless, emotionless. Her eyes left mine and returned to Stoff's.

"I don't," she said softly, and she rose from the stool, floated back to me, and sank down to the floor.

I felt her breathing beside me and wanted to turn, but I didn't. Everyone was chatting and laughing, but the sounds were melting together into a muffled buzzing, and I thought bizarrely of beehives, dark and sweet and loud.

"*Rory's turn,*" came a voice, and I felt myself shrink even more.

"Hey, man," Jem said from behind me. "Don't make her. She clearly doesn't want to."

"Everyone has to go, Jem," Harrison said. "Don't be gay."

Liv's head snapped around. "First of all. Did you seriously just use the word 'gay' as an insult? Grow up, asshole. And second of all, Rory's not doing jack shit if she doesn't want to."

Jem smiled at her appreciatively, but Liv was fuming too hard to see.

"Fuck off, Liv," Harrison said loudly.

"Tell me that one more time," Liv said, starting to rise from her seat, and without knowing what I was doing, I placed my hands on her shoulders and pushed down. I was irritated as hell at Harrison, but if I didn't stop Liv, she would start a fight. As in a physical fight. And he deserved it, but—

Conflict. It stressed me out.

So, I tried to defuse it by walking up to the Hot Seat instead.

*Bitch, sit down*, my brain warned as I stepped between bodies up to the stool. Bodies that were swiveling in slow motion between me and Liv. Turning to Harrison, who was trying to say that it was just a joke. To Liv, who was ignoring him, staring at me fixedly. To Milo, who had just walked down the stairs, who climbed through everyone until he found Liv. He sat down behind her and pulled her into his lap, and she entwined her fingers with his but didn't look away from me.

Her eyes said, *I'll kill them, Rory. Just say the word, and I'll kill them all.*

I sat down on the stool, and everyone looked at me. It occurred to me, for the first time in my seventeen-year-long life, that I had four limbs. I immediately didn't know what to do with them. I wondered vaguely if I still had makeup smeared on my eyelids. Wondered if someone would be willing to throw a bucket of water on me, and then if everyone else would kindly turn their backs to give me privacy as I sank through the floor like the Wicked Witch.

"What's your number?" asked Stoff, and although I'd known it was coming, I felt my insides disappear.

I wanted to run. Instead, I looked him in the eye and said, "Zero."

Silence.

"Good for you, girl," said Natsuki. "We love a modest queen."

When I looked at Liv, sitting in Milo's lap, her hands were balled into fists.

"Do you like anyone right now?" Jem asked.

It was still so quiet. No one was laughing, like they had for everyone else. I tried to breathe normally.

"Not really, no," I said, taking the liberty of a long blink.

"What's your sexual fantasy?" Grace slurred.

"Okay, you're done," Liv cut in. "These questions are bullshit."

"She has to answer, babe," Milo said.

I kept my eyes closed this time. Not seeing them was helping just the slightest bit. "I don't . . . I don't know. Timothée Chalamet?"

"What's your biggest insecurity?" someone else asked.

"My body," I whispered.

"*Why?*" Natsuki asked.

"Yeah, honestly, I'd kill to be as skinny as you," said Grace.

*Don't*, I wanted to say, and couldn't.

"If you could have anything in the world right now," said Liv, and I felt her eyes burning into my forehead as I watched my own hands trembling in my lap, "what would it be?"

*My bed*, I thought. *And Coco Puffs.*

"World peace," I said instead.

"*Booooorrrrrriiing*," droned Stoff, and then he laughed. "I'm kidding, queen. Love you."

"Okay, that's finally over. Someone turn the music back on," said Harrison, standing up. "Time to *actually* get drunk."

Everyone stood up around me and started talking. But when I tried to do the same, my legs felt like jelly, and my throat glued shut.

*RelaxRelaxRelaxRelax*, my brain told me. *It's just a party. They're your friends. That wasn't embarrassing to anyone except you.*

Liv and Milo were a few feet in front of me. Him kissing her. His hands all over her. Hers down by her sides.

*You're fine*, said my brain, but my body was screaming against it. I took Liv's arm, and she turned toward me, her lipstick smeared.

"I want to go home," I said.

Milo raised his eyebrows at me and smiled, then looked back at Liv. I knew that look. He'd been giving it to her all summer. The look that said, *Is she serious? Come on. Really?*

Liv didn't look back at him; she just kept her eyes on me. "Okay. Now?"

I swallowed. "Yeah."

She tried to step away from Milo, but he said, "Stay." He tightened his arms around her from behind and kissed her neck.

And suddenly, her whole body tensed. She pushed him away, hard, and he stumbled into the cooler, throwing his hands back into the wall to catch himself, shoving them straight into a framed school picture of Grace. The frame fell to the floor with a crash.

The room filled with palpable silence.

Milo looked at his hand, which was bleeding.

"Oh-my-god-it's-totally-fine," Grace sang from across the basement, her words knit together with beer.

"Drunk much, Milo?" Harrison snickered, and people started talking again.

Milo stared at Liv.

"I didn't mean to," she whispered.

"What the fuck?" he whispered back.

"That picture's ugly anyway," Grace said, her voice coming closer to us. "I'll clean it up, hold on."

"Let's go," Liv muttered, pulling me toward the stairs. Milo followed, clutching his bleeding hand.

"Liv, hold on, I wasn't trying to—"

"Come on, Rory," she said, without looking back.

*H*olidays. Stupid shit always happens on holidays. I don't know why I need to watch the Macy's Thanksgiving Day Parade every year. It completely doesn't fit into my aesthetic: I hate corporate America, large crowds, colors, and loud noises. But . . . I don't know. Every time we sit on the couch at eight in the morning, drinking bad coffee, and Willow loses her shit over a cool new balloon, it feels kind of worth it.

Besides, no one in my family would dream of letting me skip it.

"GET UP, RORY!" Willow shouts, climbing on top of my warm ball of blankets, bouncing up and down. "GET UP GET UP GET UP! TIME FOR THE PARADE!"

I roll around for a bit, groaning, but when the smell of toasted bagels wafts up the stairs and into my room, I'm up and prancing toward the landing. Saige is already downstairs, her hair sticking out in all directions and one eye flattened closed with makeup.

"Don't talk to me," she orders, holding a coffee mug under Mom's no-one-fucking-touch-this espresso machine, a little too far to the left.

"Since when do you get hangovers?" I whisper to her, as Nonni flings nine bagels onto a large plate, humming.

"Saige has hangovers all the time now," Willow says

cheerfully, gluing herself to my side and taking my hand. "Which bagel do you want, Rory? Want me to put cream cheese on it for you?"

Nonno walks in, holding the iPad we all share in his wizened hands, looking bemused. My grandparents proceed to have their normal morning conversation in Italian, wherein Nonni says 100 percent of the words and Nonno nods. By the end of it, I vaguely understand that he's done at least six things wrong but that she loves him. Saige coughs and swallows largely, closes her eyes, and forces herself to take another bite of bagel.

"I'm good, Wills," I say, noticing that Willow is still holding my hand. "Thanks for offering."

She looks up at me for a moment before shrugging, gently taking the iPad out of Nonno's hands and beginning to play *Minecraft* with the volume all the way up. She misses a hit and whispers, "Crap!" Nonni lightly whacks her across the back of the head, still talking to Nonno.

"Everyone except Rory, get out," comes Mom's voice from the doorway. Saige immediately exits the room before Mom can sniff out her hangover, and my grandparents start grumbling. Willow misses another hit and says, "Shit!"

"Did you hear me?" Mom says, stealing Willow's untouched bagel off her plate and taking a bite. "I need the kitchen. Rory's helping me with dinner this year."

Nonni protests a bit before she leaves, dragging Nonno and Willow out by their sleeves.

"I am?" I ask, refusing to get up from the table.

Instead of dragging me up to help, Mom comes and sits down next to me, and that's when I realize I'm even more fucked.

"So. Tell me how it's going, yeah?" She takes another bite out of Willow's bagel. She's in her usual morning apparel: loose tank top and boxers, not bothering to cover up anything—side boob, stretch marks, fading tattoos from the nineties. She's wrapped an old scarf around her hair, but she doesn't look elegant like Liv used to; she looks like Professor Trelawney's weird aunt.

"What do you mean?" I ask.

"You know. How's it going with the shrink?"

I deliberately take a very long swig of coffee, and Mom watches me, annoyed. One of the cats jumps into my lap.

"I can see your boobs," I comment.

"You also used to suck them."

"Ew, *Mom!*"

"Just saying. Someday you'll also have a tiny monster biting down on your—"

"Shrink's great," I say. She smiles.

"So," she says again. "Feeling better?"

I close my eyes. "It doesn't work like that."

"You know what I mean, Rory."

"I don't know what you want me to say. April can't just *fix* me."

"I just need to know," Mom says, and the sudden roughness in her voice makes me open my eyes again. "I need to know you're not . . . you know, not about to . . ."

"What? What, Mom?" I lower my voice, although I feel like yelling. "*You're* the one who called it self-harm and made me go to April. Not me."

"*Don't.*" Mom runs her hand through her hair, pulling out the scarf. "Do not use that tone with me, Rory. *You* took my Xanax without asking. You think Saige would find you unconscious on the floor and I'd say, *Oh, that's just a normal mood swing. No therapy for her!*"

"*It was an accident,*" I seethe. "And now you're sending me to this fake bitch—"

"You just said April was great. And d'you know what? I actually think so, too. Even though I'm paying my own fucking bone marrow for her to spend forty-five minutes with you a week, I like her. I picked her because she gets results."

I feel like projectile vomiting in her face.

"*Results?*" I whisper, because Nonni and Willow choose that moment to barge back into the kitchen, talking loudly, although not really to each other.

"Oh, don't be sensitive," Mom whispers back. "You know what I mean."

"Stop making me go to therapy," I tell her.

"Not until you're better."

It's so hard to restrain myself from rolling my eyes, I end up putting my forehead on the table so she won't see.

\* \* \*

By the time we actually sit down for dinner—which was made 10 percent by Mom, 90 percent by Nonni, and 0 percent by me—it's almost nine. Willow's nodding off over her food but pretending that she's not. Saige is devouring the mounds of stuffing on her plate, hangover apparently cured. Mom helps Nonno tuck his napkin into his collar. Nonni makes us say grace, because it's one of the few nights per year that Mom allows it.

"And we say thank you, God," she says in her thick accent, "for to allow bread on the table."

Willow stifles a yawn. Mom stifles an eye roll.

"And this year, we thank God even more," Nonni continues, "for to keep our Rory safe."

I feel my insides freeze. Next to me, Saige flinches. Mom's mouth has formed a thin line.

"Because this year, our Rory suffers." Nonni's voice goes suddenly higher, and I close my eyes and think, *Please, no.* "God almost takes our Rory away."

"Elsa," my mom mutters to Nonni, trying to subtly shake her head, but Nonni doesn't see, because she's now wiping her eyes with her cloth napkin.

"When we find out a car crash into our Rory, we pray to God, 'Please, Rory is safe. Please, Rory survive.'" Nonni heaves a great sniffle. "And God is good. Rory is safe."

Willow's eyes are all the way open now, and her hands on the table are shaking. Her eyes dart between Nonni, Mom, and me.

"Thank you to God for our Rory," Nonni says, her voice quivering. "*Grazie per Rory.*"

"*Grazie,*" Nonno says, and I look at him for the first time. To my horror, his eyes are shining.

"Right," says Mom, and I see tears in her eyes, too.

Saige rubs her nose. Willow's hands tremble harder, and so does her bottom lip. She's just looking at me now.

Nonni takes my cold hand across the table in both of her small, papery ones. "*Sei molto fortunata,*" she says. *You are very lucky.*

I stare at her. I stare at all of them.

And then I scrape back my chair and run up the stairs.

\* \* \*

I barrel into the bathroom, lock the door, and kneel just in time. A horrible flow of vomit falls into the toilet, expelling everything I've ever eaten or drunk, everything in my body, and then I collapse onto the ground.

*When we find out a car crash into our Rory . . .*

I'm shaking so hard that my head bumps into the wooden counter supporting the sink, and stars erupt in front of my eyes.

*Don't remember don't remember don't remember don't remember,* I tell myself. I start saying it out loud, over and over again, until the words are the only thing I see and hear, until there is no room left and I've pushed out anything dangerous, anything that could possibly make me retch again.

I think of Liv, alive. Laughing. The chaotic symphony of the Liv Laugh, how it went up and down and filled the room, how she would throw her head back and fall over and convulse, how we would lie together on the floor, choking with mirth. How it was just like crying, the way she laughed, but worlds better, and how tears would sparkle in her eyes and she would gasp for breath, control herself for a moment before falling over again.

I have nothing but this memory. This memory is mine.

\* \* \*

"Rory? You okay?"

Saige. At the door. Of the bathroom. Where I just vommed.

"Yeah," I say, flushing.

"Why are the lights out? Can I come in?"

"No."

Unlike previous moments of breached privacy—a.k.a. Saige barging into my room an infinite amount of times to get my opinion on an outfit, or two slightly different photos she wants to post—this time, my sister actually listens to me and stays outside.

"I'm fine," I say, feeling bad. "Go back downstairs."

"The food's getting cold," she says quietly.

"I'll be down in a sec." I turn on the sink.

"Are you, like, hurting yourself?" Saige blurts.

I ball my fists against my eyes.

"I'm fine," I tell her, and I can hear her staggered breathing from behind the thin door. I fill my lungs with air, expel it as slowly as I can. When I open the door, she's standing there, the uncontrollable mess of being sixteen, hungover, and stressed: knots of hair cascading down her back, nails chewed and scabbing, mascara lodged in the corners of her shining red eyes. I wonder when we last tried to make each other laugh at the table. She hasn't sent me a silly selfie in months.

*She's the one who found me,* I think blankly.

Not knowing what I'm doing, I step closer to Saige, placing a hand on each of her shoulders.

"I'm fine," I repeat, in the most silly, nasal voice I can make, trying to make her smile.

She won't.

I let go of her shoulders and sigh. "You going Black Friday shopping tonight?"

Saige leans on one foot and crosses her arms, trying to look bored. "Whatever, yeah."

I fold my arms, too, attempting to speak her language. "So, like, can I come?" I swallow. "I want my little sister to drive me somewhere. Mom says you're crap behind the wheel, but I trust you. When are you leaving? Eleven?"

And, finally, the corners of her mouth start to slide up. "You can pick the music," she says, looping her arm through mine and pulling me back toward the stairs.

\* \* \*

Three hours later, regretting it, I jerkily force one arm in front of the other, pulling the passenger door open. This minivan is our replacement car from after the Worst Night—used and extremely old, an expense Mom never talks about, but that tears me apart whenever I see it. I've never ridden in it after dark.

I haven't been in any cars after dark since the Worst Night.

Once Saige is settled into the driver's seat, adjusting the mirrors, she says, "We're just gonna pick up a couple girls from the team, okay?"

I want to say, "No," but my mouth is clamped shut, because now I feel the engine humming underneath my legs, and my muscles have seized. Every inch of me, from now until I get out of the car, must be focused on keeping my mouth shut. On not throwing up my heart onto the dashboard and dying.

Last year, I brought up the idea of Black Friday shopping *very* casually and hypothetically to Liv. I'd never gone at midnight, and I thought maybe it would be worth it for the deals. "I have a big-ass family," I tried to explain, "and all of them want big-ass presents."

She looked me in the eye and said, "I'd rather be impaled in the ovary by Poseidon's trident than spend fifteen minutes at the mall on Black Friday."

At the time, I thought it was a bit dramatic. But

when I'm standing with Saige and four of her friends in the freezing cold—and when the clock strikes midnight, and the humans around me transform into rampaging rhinoceroses whose calves have just been threatened—I understand, for the very first time, that Liv had not been exaggerating.

I immediately lose Saige and her friends to the bloodbath that is Lululemon, but we have a deal: meet at the Macy's entrance at one thirty, and then we're booking the fuck out of here. I don't even entertain the thought of trying to buy anything. Crowds of people swarm around me, yanking at blouses and screaming across the room to their kin like fucking orangutans: *"GET OVER HERE, I'VE GOT THE LAST ONE," "WHERE'S BENNY? OH, FOR HEAVEN'S SAKE," "DON'T LET THAT BITCH TAKE MY JUMPSUIT, JESSIE!"*

*I just need to get to one thirty*, I think to myself over and over again. Ninety minutes. Forty-five times two.

True to Clarksdale, our mall goes above and beyond for the holidays. I wander aimlessly through Macy's, weaving among the brightly lit counters full of jewelry and perfume, draped in tinseled wreaths and red ribbons and sparkling golden lights. Twice, I choke on the scent of cinnamon and pine. Andy Williams blares aggressively through the speakers with his trumpets and his bells and his deep, echoing voice that seems to have been made for Christmas.

I'm loitering near the Converse section, trying not to wistfully stare at a pair of all-black high-tops, when I hear someone say my name. I turn, shocked, and my heart falls into the pit of my stomach. It's Stoff.

His brown hair is combed sleekly back, and his face is longer, smoother, somehow freed of tension. He looks taller. Of course, being Stoff, he's dressed superbly well: long, neatly cut pants and boots, a knee-length overcoat, a cashmere scarf tied loosely around his neck.

"Rory!" he says again.

I briefly smile and nod, and then I look down.

But he walks toward me. And he's smiling, for real.

"How are you?" he asks, putting a hand on my arm.

Two-years-ago Stoff would have screamed my name and run, limbs flailing, to throw himself on me and embarrass me as much as possible. He would have shouted, "Fancy seeing you here, BITCH!" and taken me on a stroll, his arm clamped around my neck. I didn't know Stoff was even capable of asking the simple words "How are you?"

"Uh, you know," I say, tipping my head back to look into his clean-shaven face. I try to smile politely, try to imitate him, but I can't.

He *squeezes my arm.*

"Bad question to ask," says the alien who invaded my old friend's body, actually sounding humble. "World's shittiest year, right? Who are you here with? I never thought I'd run into you at the mall of all places."

"Um, Saige and her friends," I say. "They're—somewhere. What about you?"

"Just some people from school," Stoff says, shrugging. "I'm already done shopping." A plump paper bag hangs from the crook of his elbow.

"You really—got a head start, then." *Why is it so hard to speak English right now?*

"I know. Now I have to *wait* for them," he says, rolling his eyes, and a bit of the old Stoff comes back.

"Hey—do you want to get some hot chocolate?"

For some reason, my heart pounds uncomfortably. It's my first social interaction with someone my age, I realize, in almost six months.

"I . . ."

"I know the barista working the café tonight," Stoff says. "He'll give us a discount. It's right around the corner."

My mouth is doing what it does on those rare occasions when I try to socially function: open and close, but without words or sounds.

"You don't have to," Stoff says. "But I'd love to catch up soon, okay?"

"Yarm," I say.

"Uh—what?"

"I meant, yes."

"Okay, see you—"

"Yes, for hot chocolate, now." I swallow. *Please don't make me use any more words.*

Stoff's eyes brighten. He takes my arm gently, and we weave between counters of perfume and Frango mints and ornaments, until our two arms consolidate to become one, until I finally stop shivering and let go of my breath.

\* \* \*

"It's like, if the benefits of the product outweigh the cost it takes to make it, then it's efficient, and if the costs outweigh the benefits, then it's inefficient," Stoff says, dropping three cubes of sugar into his hot chocolate and focusing on the swirling motion of his spoon. "That's the basic idea behind econ."

"I thought you hated math," I say, joining him in

staring at his drink.

"Econ is different. The math actually makes sense. It just all *makes sense*," Stoff says, now looking at a spot over my shoulder, and I can see a clarity in his face that makes my heart, underneath the thick layers of metal that it's accumulated in the past ten months, soften just the tiniest amount. "Everything fits," Stoff continues, placing his hands perfectly parallel on the table, palms facing each other. "And Northwestern's econ program is great. I might even be able to study abroad next year."

"That's awesome, Stoff," I tell him.

He smiles and then chuckles.

"What?"

"Nothing. It's just funny because I haven't been called that since high school." He clears his throat. "In college, um . . . I just go by Christopher."

I feel like I've been punched in the chest, because of course I don't know this. Because I don't know Stoff at all anymore. Because the last text from him, besides the obligatory condolences after the Worst Night, is from around midnight on July 5th, six months earlier: *idk, can we hang soon and i can tell u about it?*

And I never responded. I'm so ashamed.

"Listen, Stoff," I tell him, and my voice feels thick. "I . . . I need to apologize."

He shakes his head shortly. "Don't worry about it."

"No . . . I was horrible," I mumble. Tears fill my eyes. "I *dropped* you. I got caught up in all this stuff with Liv, and I dropped you. When you needed me, too." I try not to let my face crumple. I don't want him to feel like he has to comfort *me*.

"Listen." He takes my hand. "I genuinely want you

to forget about it, okay? Believe me when I tell you: I truly don't care. Everything that happened in high school is in the past. All right?"

I know I can't be let off the hook that easily, but the tears are threatening to spill, and this mall is so crowded, and I don't know how I'd survive an avalanche here. After what feels like a hundred years, I nod quickly, and he graciously ignores me as I blow my nose.

"So, anyway," Stoff says, now watching me stir my hot chocolate mindlessly, recovering. "What've you been up to? You haven't posted on anything in, like, six months. How's school?"

"Um, I . . . I'm taking a gap year." I swallow nervously, looking to his left, shaking my leg.

Stoff's eyes widen in comprehension. "Oh. Gotcha. Duh," he says. "Just, like, to reset?"

"Yeah," I say, wiping my nose again, although there hasn't been much resetting happening. "Working. Reading. Going to free museums."

"That sounds great, honestly," says Stoff. "Self-care is *so* crucial. I wish I could just take a semester off like that."

"You can," I say.

He shrugs, and in the silence, I realize that it's the tail end of that Andy Williams song "It's the Most Wonderful Time of the Year."

"Oh my god," Stoff says, starting to laugh. "This fucking *song*."

When we were caroling last Christmas for choir, we sang this in our rep. At the last minute, Mr. Wong had assigned Liv to sing an awkward "bum-bum" beat below the rest of our voices.

"She fucking loved doing those beats," I say, and I

feel a smile growing on my lips before I can hide it with my mug.

"I remember," says Stoff. He raises his hands and straightens his back importantly, and despite their obvious difference in gender and size, I see Liv in front of me, stern and prepared. "She'd sit there next to you, just, like . . . 'Bum-*bum*! Bum-*bum*!' . . . just *right* in your ear."

I start to laugh. "Oh my god," I say. "She's always trying to drive me insane."

He laughs, too, nodding, putting his elbows on the table. I appreciate that he doesn't correct my tense. Lets me just have this one.

"I miss her," he says eventually. "And I didn't know her half as well as you did."

I want to do what I usually do when people bring up Liv without my consent: tell him, in body language, to fuck off.

Instead, I swallow. "It's like . . . a limb," I say. "I lost a limb, Stoff."

He says nothing, doesn't move or look at me. Judy Garland is singing to us now, softly filling the café with her deep voice.

Finally, Stoff speaks. "I didn't mean to, like, make you sad."

"I'm always thinking about her," I tell him. "Whether we're talking about her or not. So, you can't make me sad."

Stoff gives a small smile. Suddenly, the barista scoots his way around the counter and comes up behind him.

"Can I get you guys anything else?" he asks. He's tall, dark-skinned with light-brown eyes, and he's currently beaming down at Stoff.

Stoff turns and smiles at him, and the barista puts a hand on his shoulder.

"Rory, this is Karim. From DePaul."

"Hey," I grunt.

"And Karim, this is my future wife, Rory." Stoff bats his eyelashes up at him.

"I'm sure it'll work out *fabulously* between you two," says Karim smoothly, giving Stoff's shoulder a squeeze. "Rory, can I get you something? Warmed cinnamon scone? Everything's on the house."

"I'm . . . good," I say, my voice coming out in a weird, gravelly crunch. *Talking to two people at once is hard*, I think, trying to mentally pat myself on the back.

"Well, if you need anything, I'm lucky enough to be here till four," Karim says, showing about forty-five sparkling white teeth when he smiles.

"Are you fucking kidding me?" Stoff asks, but with something other than the usual sassy twinge in his voice. It takes me a minute to realize what it is: care.

It sounds weird, new, and good.

"I'm getting time and a half," Karim replies, starting to walk away, his hand lingering on Stoff's shoulder before sliding off. "Maybe I can actually afford to get you a Christmas present."

After he leaves, there is about a minute of silence where Stoff and I look into each other's eyes. His cheeks are pink. Scratch that—magenta. And he's smiling.

Surprising myself, I start to laugh with joy. Stoff, with someone. Stoff, being himself.

"Shut up," he says eventually, shaking his head and looking down, waves of heat rising from his cheeks into the air between us.

*six months before*

We left Milo tending to his hand in Grace's basement and ran out of there like it was on fire. For the first time, Liv started driving without turning on music.

"I—"

"It's fine," Liv said.

"I didn't mean to start a whole . . . thing," I said.

"You didn't."

"But—"

"*Drop it*, Rory."

I felt that one in my chest, hard and cold. Like ice.

I took a deep breath, then another one, like I did sometimes when one of my family members was on my nerves. It didn't push away the anger at her shortness. I wanted to say something petty, something with no purpose except to bite her back, to make her feel a little dismissed, too. Because I had just been humiliated on the Hot Seat, and I was a virgin, and I was uncool, and I didn't feel like a bigger person just then.

I said: "Just drop me off at home and go back to the party. Go back to your boyfriend." I swallowed. "I'm clearly the weird girl that you took under your wing to be the hero."

It worked.

"Fuck *off*," she snarled.

"I *will*," I retorted, embarrassed at how my eyes were starting to prickle. "Just fucking pull over."

She did, shifting into park, and I unbuckled my seat belt.

Then she started hyperventilating.

I froze, my hand on the door, and looked at her. Everything that had just hung in the air between us—all the tension, the anger, the pettiness—had dissolved. She was still clutching the steering wheel, but her head had dropped, and her body was heaving with each breath. Each high-pitched, raspy breath.

I knew I should say something, but my throat had buckled itself shut, and all I could do was watch. She lifted her head and stared straight ahead, a look of existential dread in her eyes, the blood drained from her face. She let go of the steering wheel and placed her hands under her chin, her whole body shaking. The weird, raspy breaths kept coming, jagged, like a knife cutting clumsily through paper.

"*I . . . can't . . .*" she kept saying, over and over again, shaking her head, closing her eyes. "*I . . . can't . . .*"

"You're scaring me," I whispered.

She shook her head again, trying to say something. She was so pale. "*N . . . nor . . . normal,*" she choked out.

"Normal?"

She motioned to her chest, which was heaving. Each breath cut through the air sharply, puncturing the warm, stale haze in the car. She took five breaths before speaking again, and when she did, the words tumbled out, strained, as if it was costing her every effort she could muster.

"*Panic attack*," she breathed.

I blinked. I thought I knew what panic attacks were. This didn't seem like that. This seemed like a *heart* attack.

I fumbled around, realizing that I was shaking, too. "Should I call someone?"

She shook her head, eyes closed, face twisted. She took a deep breath, and then another. "*Had . . . them*," she choked out. "*Since . . . I was . . . twelve.*"

I stared at Liv, curled over the wheel. Vulnerable. Breakable. A weird jolt surged in my chest—at first, I thought it was pain from seeing her like this, but then I realized it was more than that. I wanted to say sorry, over and over again. *I'm sorry I snapped. Let me take your pain. Stay with me.*

I put my hand on her shoulder, but she twisted away so hard that I flinched.

"Don't touch me," she whispered.

"Okay," I whispered back.

And we sat there for minutes, days, years.

When her breathing finally slowed, she dropped her hands from her neck and slumped against the window, shivering slightly.

"I'm sorry," I said, finally, when I couldn't hold it in anymore. "I didn't mean to say that about you taking me under your wing. It was shitty. I felt like a joke at that party, and you're so cool and perfect and every-thing, and I . . . I got embarrassed, and I took it out on you." I took a breath. "Not because you're cool, or any of that. Because . . . because you're my best friend."

She stayed against the window, not looking at me.

"I don't know why we take shit out on the people we love," I said. "Everyone in my family does it. I'm trying not to be like that, but—"

She said, "I don't hate everyone."

It took me a minute, but then I remembered Stoff's last question to Liv, the one that had made me wilt.

"I know," I said, resisting the urge to touch her arm again. "I told you. Stoff's being a dick tonight—"

"They don't know," Liv said, her face muffled against the window, every part of her turning away from me. "No one knows."

I stared at her, holding my breath. Something horrible was snaking into my mouth, my nose, the air around us. Sinister, like a ghost. I waited for as long as I could, and when I finally spoke, my voice came out small. "No one knows what, Liv?"

She took a few more shaky breaths. Then she sat up in her seat, refusing to look at me, and pulled out her iPod. She connected it to the aux cord and fumbled around a bit, until Bon Iver started floating from the speakers. Then she leaned back and closed her eyes.

"When I was twelve," she said, her voice sinking into a monotone, "I was reading off Evergreen Lane, by the pond. You know, the one kind of by your house. I was sitting there, minding my own business, and a group of three guys came down to play Frisbee. Late teens, maybe early twenties. They were drunk and fooling around and making a lot of noise, and I was getting pissed off, so I rolled my eyes at them. And one of them said, 'What's the matter?' And I went back to reading, but he came up to me, and the rest of them followed.

"He was like, 'I said what's the matter, bitch?' and his friends started laughing. And then they basically started talking about my body. My boobs, whatever. They thought I was older than I was. They were getting closer to me, and I got scared, so I told them to go away. And then it was, you know. 'Take a joke, you fucking slut.'"

I could tell that she was fighting, forcing herself to keep talking.

"And I hadn't noticed, but . . . one of them kind of pinched my waist. Just to fuck with me, I guess, and he let go pretty quickly, but . . . he'd . . . *touched* me, you know? And I was so fucking *scared.*"

I was facing her in the passenger seat, my knees drawn up to my chest, shaking. My nose itched, my eyes blurred, and my heart pounded. Nothing inside me could move.

"They were laughing, but then we heard voices," Liv said. "There was a family at the pond, and they couldn't see us, but they were getting closer. The guys all decided to go. The one who grabbed me bent down to my ear and said, 'Learn to take a joke, babe.' And they left, and I just lay down. And the family came up and asked me if I was okay, because I'd wet my pants, and they called my mom and said that I'd fainted, and my parents came and took me home. I had a cello competition the next day. I got last place, and they kept asking where my head was, but I—I couldn't tell them."

The silence after her story drowned me. We sat there, not moving.

"Look at me," I finally said, and she did, her lips quivering.

And I knew.

"This is the first time you've said it out loud," I whispered, and she nodded, closing her eyes.

*Normal. Panic attacks. Since I was twelve.*

"You got scared," I said slowly, "when Milo wouldn't

let go of you."

Beneath the glittering rhinestones, two huge tears slid down Liv's cheeks.

I shook my head, trying to push the image away. Twelve-year-old Liv, losing her voice. Losing control.

*This is why*, I kept thinking.

Liv is one thousand warm and beautiful things, but this is why she's cold sometimes. Untouchable.

This is why—only sometimes—she feels so far away.

"Liv," I said blankly, my brain full of white fog.

"All the guys I've been with—every single one, until Milo . . . it hasn't been about attraction." She swallowed. "It's about getting some of that back."

"Some of what?"

"I don't know," she said. Her mouth twisted. "Myself."

I stared ahead, the world pounding around me, pressing on my ears.

"Let me kill them," I said numbly.

"No."

"But—"

"Rory," she said, grabbing my hands suddenly, scaring me with her urgency. "Please, just . . . *please*. Don't tell."

She stared at me until I said that I wouldn't.

"Promise," she said.

She had stopped crying. I had started.

"It's your story," I said, when I found my breath again. "Not mine."

She let go of me and turned back to the road, gripping the steering wheel with both hands.

* * *

We traipsed up the stairs to my room and shrugged into fresh T-shirts and boxers, not talking. I kept taking a breath to speak, but Liv seemed so far away, so exhausted, and I honestly didn't know what to say. While she was in the bathroom taking off her makeup, I sat at the edge of my bed in the dark, heart still racing, trying to distract myself with my phone.

Stoff: *you still up? can we talk?*

Stoff*: sorry im drunk but ik i was an asshole earlier, no excuse. i'm really sorry*

Stoff: *the truth is that this summer fucking sucks, i hate drama camp*

Stoff: *and shit kind of hit the fan with this guy i like*

Stoff: *idk, can we hang soon and i can tell u about it?*

The bathroom door closed softly down the hall, and Liv walked back in. It was so dark that I couldn't see her face; I could barely make out her shape moving toward me on the bed. I clicked off my phone, but she just crawled in and got under the covers, facing away from me.

I took a breath and tried to release it slowly. Then I got under the covers next to her. I wanted so badly to say something, anything: *I'm here. I love you. I won't let that happen again. I'll kill them.*

*No one else matters but us.*

*Let's run away.*

"Goodnight, Liv," I whispered to her back.

She didn't respond, and I closed my eyes.

But when I woke up in the morning, she was curled into me, sound asleep with her head tucked under my chin.

"Thank you so much, again," Eleanor says, pushing the plate of muffins toward me.

"Really," I say, trying to convince myself to take one. "It was nothing."

She blinks.

"I mean, it wasn't *nothing*." I look outside, at the sway of the leafless branches, instead of at her parents. "It's Liv's room. But . . . I just meant . . ."

"It's all right," Ramil says in his slow, easygoing voice. "We really appreciate your help."

I look back at them as Ramil places a hand on Eleanor's shoulder.

"We've just been having a . . . a really hard time," she says, taking his hand in both of hers.

I look again at the trees, but they're not exactly helping me, so I look back at Liv's parents. Liv's kitchen feels different, her whole house feels different, and it's not just because they're starting to pack up. There's no air in here. There's no light. There's only them, Liv's parents, screaming without being heard, and me, the intruder, concave with silence.

This is the house of a dead person.

"Me, too," I say, just because I need to say something.

"We know." Eleanor straightens her back and regains some composure, although I don't understand how. Ramil takes his hand off her shoulder and rubs his neck. "I can't even imagine what it's like for you," Eleanor continues. "Having been—you know—"

"Her best friend," Ramil says, and I see him very subtly look at Eleanor and shake his head. *Don't say, "in the car."*

*Don't say, "with her when she died."*

But we're all thinking it.

"Yes," Eleanor says. "Liv trusted you, Rory. More than anyone else. Are you sure you don't want a muffin?"

My stomach lurches. I want the plate far away from me, but instead, I take a muffin, because she has a dead child. I swallow it down, and my stomach screams.

"Anyway," I say. "I should . . ."

"Right," Eleanor says, placing her hands on the table and looking down. "You need to go. Your mom is probably wondering where you are."

"No," I say quickly. "She doesn't care. Really."

Eleanor looks up again, her eyebrows folding. She mouths the word, "Oh."

"I didn't mean . . ." I start weakly.

Eleanor shakes her head. "It's getting late. But Rory, we actually wanted to . . ." Her voice hitches higher, and tears finally slide down her cheeks. "I'm sorry," she says, as Ramil places his hands back on her shoulders. "I'm sorry."

"Don't apologize," I tell her, feeling like a robot.

"It's just—" She sniffs. "We've asked you for so much. And we need to ask for more."

Somehow, I tell her that it's fine.

Ramil looks at her, but she is giving off zero signal

that she can speak, so he starts talking instead. "As you know, Liv's birthday is coming up."

I do know. Liv was born on December 18th. Sun and moon in Sagittarius, Leo rising. *Triple fire signs, bitch*, Liv used to say, nudging me.

If the Worst Night hadn't happened, Liv would be turning nineteen in three weeks. But she's stuck at eighteen, always in the first year of adulthood. Always at the beginning.

"It took us a while to figure out what to do for Liv's birthday," Ramil is saying. "But we decided . . . well, as you remember, we had the . . . the small funeral in February, but—"

Eleanor buries her face in her hands.

"But—we didn't really have anything for the community," Ramil says, looking at the wall next to me, continuing to clear his throat. "It was so sudden and so horrible, and you were hurt, and we just . . . we couldn't."

Eleanor looks up, wiping her eyes.

"So we thought," Ramil continues. "We thought we might have a little . . . celebration of life."

The wind batters the trees outside, and inside, it's still.

Eleanor finds her voice again. "We didn't want to make it necessarily a . . . a *sad* thing. Well, it's sad, but . . . we want to . . . to celebrate her. You know, Rory?"

I'm really cold.

"Yeah," I say.

"So," Eleanor says, brushing the blond hair out of her face. "We've been in touch with Principal Vance from Telsey, and the school board, and we decided to have a celebration of Liv. There."

I swallow. "Where?"

"At Telsey."

At Telsey. At our high school.

"Oh," I say.

"And Mr. Wong, from choir—you know him—he said he could put something nice together. A musical tribute . . ."

I haven't thought about school, really, in months. Everything having to do with Telsey seems so far away from Liv, from *my* Liv. I barely remember sitting next to her in choir, beyond it being how we met. Did we even enjoy choir, really? Did Mr. Wong know Liv at all? What did he think of her? Did he have even the faintest inkling that she was special, that she was different?

I try to pull myself back to the present, sitting at the kitchen table with Liv's parents.

"—honoring Liv," Eleanor finishes.

"Right," I say.

"So . . . is that something you think you can do?" she asks me.

"What?" I say.

"Give a speech," Eleanor says. "For Liv."

Everything in the world stops. I try to blink away the cold that is threatening to take over. Try to will away the shivers.

"I . . ."

"Just a small one," Eleanor says, her words quickening. "About Liv, about all of the special things that made her *her*. You know . . . how great she was. Smart. Kind. Happy." She sighs. "Fearless."

I swallow it all down.

"And . . . I can give you a list of accomplishments," Eleanor says, quicker still, like she's trying to get all the words out before another flood of tears. "I have all her report cards, so you can mention how well she did in school, all the colleges that accepted her . . . the Telsey Honors Society . . . the National Writing Competition . . ."

She looks down, and then back up at me.

"All you need to do," Eleanor says, taking my hand, "is talk about Liv."

I hope that my hand isn't shaking, and then realize that it doesn't matter, because hers is.

"Just tell the truth," she says. "About how she was perfect."

I want so badly to pull away. The ice is swirling around in my chest, in my stomach. Ramil whispers something to Eleanor, and she lets go and leans back from me, wiping her eyes, apologizing over and over again.

"I know it's so much to ask," she says.

"It's not."

"Are you sure?"

"Yes."

"So . . . you can do it?"

*Snow, humming.*

"Uh-huh."

"Write a speech? For Liv's celebration?"

*White snow, bright lights.*

"Yes."

"Oh, Rory," Eleanor says, and she gets up, walks around the table, and pulls me into her arms.

I don't throw up until I'm a block away from their house, far enough so that they can't see.

*four months before*

We sat outside Panera, blinking in the early fall sunlight. I licked cream cheese off each finger and then stuffed the rest of my honey-whole-wheat-everything-with-sun-dried-tomato-cream-cheese   bagel into my mouth.

"I can't even watch you," Liv said, her forehead in her hand. "I don't understand how you're eating right now."

"I don't understand how you're *not*," I said thickly.

"Roo, we finished an entire jar of crunchy peanut butter last night. I don't think I'm ever going to be hungry again."

"We also drank an entire six-pack. You need the electrolytes," I reminded her, wiping my mouth as a mom with her bathing suit–clad kids sat down at the table next to us. It was that frustrating time at the very beginning of the school year where it still felt like summer. My hair was lighter, and the freckles on my nose and elbows popped out vibrantly, and Liv was a perfect shade of golden brown, hair bundled magnificently at the top of her head. I kept feeling like we were about to head to Grace's house to jump in the pool or go bum around outside the secondhand furniture store where Jem worked, instead of what we were actually about to do: go to the library and work on our college essays.

Maybe that was why Liv was nauseated.

"Remember when I taught you the word *electrolyte*?" Liv said, taking her head out of her hands, the beginning of a sneaky smile spreading across her face.

"No," I said adamantly. "I refuse to—"

"When you were having explosive diarrhea at Barnes & Noble last month, and I was standing outside the stall door trying to give you Gatorade—"

"Nope. I don't remember that," I said, although crumbs were falling out of my mouth because I was starting to choke with laughter.

Liv's voice rose as she imitated me. "'*It's burning, Liv!*'"

"Oh, fuck you," I said, and the mom with the little kids looked at us angrily. "Like you didn't have explosive diarrhea at my house like four times this summer."

Liv accidentally barked with laughter, which made both of us dissolve, pounding the table with our hands and the ground with our feet. The mom and her kids got up and moved away.

"Stop," Liv squeaked. "I'm gonna vom, I'm gonna vom—"

"That was a bark! You just sounded like a St. Bernard!"

"Hey, guys," someone said. Ignoring Liv wheezing across from me, I squinted up at Jem, whose head perfectly blocked the sun. He'd recently taken out his braids, and he looked like some type of angel from my viewpoint, his curly black hair crowned in a halo.

"Hey," I rasped, bagel crumbs and phlegm lining my throat. I swallowed, trying again. "Hey."

"What are y'all howling about? I could hear you from, like, three stores down."

"Nothing," Liv said, controlling herself finally, tugging the scrunchie out of her hair and bending over to redo her bun.

"Rory'll tell me if you won't," Jem said, nudging me playfully, and I laughed again. In the few months since we'd kissed in his room and I'd backed away, he'd been just as friendly and jovial as ever. At first, I froze up when he'd start a conversation, thinking he'd try to ask why I'd acted that way, but I quickly realized he wouldn't. He'd just banter with me about music on the long train rides to and from Dreamtown, acting like nothing had ever happened between us.

"He still likes you," Grace had drunkenly told me at a party the week before, raising her eyebrows and nodding at Jem, who had been bopping around to a Childish Gambino song. "I can just tell. I think everyone can."

"That doesn't mean Rory owes him anything," Liv had said coldly, and Grace had responded with "Of course!" and "No worries!" before going off to dance.

I squinted up at Jem now, with his hands stuffed into his pockets. "Liv was just being an icon of beauty and grace," I told him, nodding at Liv as she blew her nose and gave me the finger.

"Okay, whatever," Jem said, smiling and shaking his head. "Are you guys going tonight?"

"To what?"

"Okay, you guys need to pull through," Jem said. "The Garbage Girls are in town for a night, and Natsuki's cousin knows them. They're having a show at her house in the city."

"The *Garbage Girls*?" I said. I remembered Liv showing that band to me on her laptop months ago, the glow in her eyes when she said, "This shit is next level. Just wait." I turned back to Liv, who now looked calm and collected.

"Sounds cool," she said. "We'll have to check."

"Okay, well, it's kind of a big deal," Jem said.

"Cool. We'll let you know." Liv smiled casually.

"Okay . . . just text me later if you're coming. By, like, five. I have to get you on the list." He ruffled my hair and then walked into Panera.

As soon as Jem disappeared, Liv slammed her hands flat on the table. "*Oh-my-god-Rory-the-Garbage-Girls-we-have-to-see-them-oh-my-fucking-god—*"

"That was a literal one-eighty reaction from what you just gave Jem," I said, and she laughed, her face beet red with excitement.

"Come to my house at eight," she ordered. "I'll do your makeup. Just tell your mom you're sleeping over!"

"Okay, but what about *your* parents?"

She shrugged, taking a large handful of my chips. "They go to bed at, like, nine thirty. I just have to be relatively functioning so I can go to church tomorrow." She smiled, and I could feel the excitement radiating off her. "Roo, we're going."

"Garbage girls supporting the Garbage Girls," I said. "Feminism at its finest."

She snorted at me and tore into her bagel, all remnants of her hangover magically forgotten. "Do you ever think about how our generation has reclaimed the word *garbage* to, like, fit into an aesthetic?"

"I . . . no?"

Liv dissolved into a philosophical monologue about language use, and I started nodding along, but then someone over her shoulder caught my eye. Someone getting out of a Mercedes with his mom, heading into Panera, dressed head to toe in Ralph Lauren.

A strange feeling shot into my chest as Stoff and I made eye contact. Instinctually, I raised a hand and half smiled at him, because Stoff was my friend, and that's what friends did.

But his stare was ice. And then I remembered.

*shit kind of hit the fan with this guy i like.*

*can we hang soon and i can tell u about it?*

I never responded.

Stoff stood there for an instant after his mom disappeared through the doors, folding his arms. He raised one eyebrow, just the smallest amount, and cocked his head. Almost like he was waiting.

I thought about pausing Liv in the middle of her monologue, running up to Stoff, and apologizing. Asking about drama camp, about the guy. Telling him I was there and wanted to listen. But then I looked back at Liv, oblivious to Stoff behind her, animatedly gesturing with the warm and familiar glint in her eyes. And I remembered something else from that cursed night, the awful way Stoff had held back laughter as he asked her:

*Why do you hate everyone?*

I kept my eyes on Stoff but flattened my mouth. I didn't get up.

Something registered in his face: almost a grim type of resolution. And without another glance, he followed his mom into Panera, and the moment was gone.

"—and it's almost like Gen Z has a completely different dialect," Liv observed.

"I agree," I told Liv, turning back to her. "But what about all the white Telsey kids who say, 'It be like that sometimes'?"

"Don't even fucking get me started," she fumed, and I laughed.

* * *

"Are you sure you don't want a bite?" I asked hours later as Liv and I sat in the dark of her mom's car, stalled in front of Natsuki's cousin's house in Lincoln Park. I was working my way through a burrito. Even though it was Liv's idea to go to Chipotle, at the last minute she hadn't ordered anything.

"I don't want even a possibility of weird farts tonight," Liv said, which made me snort out a black bean. "I can't with you, Roo. Almost ready?"

"I'm good. Just don't be crying on my ass later about how you're ravenous."

"I never do that," Liv sang as we got out of the car, even though she always did.

As we walked into the house, I could feel rather than hear the air pulsating with music. Warm bodies slithered around, and the thick smell of weed filled my lungs. Liv took my hand and led me farther in, and under the warm lighting, I could see her properly for the first time since we'd gotten ready in the dark of her room. She was wearing a velvet burgundy dress with a perfect V-neck and her shiny black Docs, and waves of dark brown hair spilled around her shoulders, spiraling down her back. She turned to me and grinned with excitement, and the fireworks in her eyes danced, and my heart pounded in my throat.

"What?" she asked.

*You're perfect,* I told her silently.

"Nothing," I said, willing my cheeks to cool. "You look really—I mean, your dress. It's just . . . yeah." I cleared my throat. "Can I borrow that?"

"Obv," Liv said, giving me a half smile. "Oh, there's Milo!"

The bubble in my chest burst as she wove her way through the crowd, but I still followed her.

"Hi," she said, and kissed him lightly.

We had been pretending that the Fourth of July hadn't happened. Not Hot Seat, not Milo cutting his hand, and definitely not the conversation Liv and I had after. Three days after that stupid party, we were all back in Grace's basement—the school picture now in a different frame—and Liv and Milo were kissing.

And it was okay, because she was happy, and I wanted her to be.

Even when Milo made her laugh harder than I did.

He kissed her back now, harder. When he pried himself from her mouth, he looked over her shoulder and smiled, nodding to me. "Hey, Ror."

"Hey," I said. He hadn't cut his hair in a while, and he'd started tying it up in buns. He'd also been working on transforming his junior-year stubble into a senior-year beard, which made him look at least five years older than us. Liv crossed her arms and looked up at him, one corner of her mouth tugging slightly upward. I knew she didn't want him to see it—the giddy butterflies spreading through her—and I knew he couldn't. Liv's face, to everyone else, was opaque. But me, alone—I could see everything. To me, she was like glass.

"It's loud in here," Milo said.

"I know," I said.

"No, like, it's *loud*," he said.

"What?"

"Let's go upstairs." He took Liv's hand, and they started walking away. I started to follow, but then my brain kicked in, and I realized that they weren't just going upstairs. They were Going Upstairs. Probably to hook up.

So I stopped, turned around, and faced the others. People milled around me, spilling drinks, shouting with laughter, and I stood there in my tiny Forever 21 dress and sparkly socks and Converse, my eyes painted with wings.

And, like I had been doing for two months, I thought about what Stoff said on the way to the Fourth of July party: *This isn't you. This is you trying to be Liv.*

The thing is, he wasn't entirely right. At first, I thought I wanted to be her.

But now, I think I wanted . . .

*Shut up*, I told the voice in my head. *Think about this later.*

Suddenly, I really wanted to be drunk.

"Hey, Rory!" came a voice. Instead of being excited—because this had *never* happened to me before this year, people "Hey, Rory!"-ing me—I felt my heart palpitate. I turned around to see Grace and Devon, just good old Grace and Devon, both smiling at me.

"Hey," I said, suddenly wondering what I should do with my hands.

"How's it going?" Grace asked.

"Wonderfully," I chirped. "It's going absolutely *wonderfully*! How about yourself?"

I was not entirely sure Grace had ever, as in *ever*, seen me smile this big. I could see from the shock on her face that I was correct. I tried to deflate a bit, pushing my shoulders in front of me and hanging my head. "I like your, like, haircut," I said, hoping that sounded better, less flustered. Hoping I sounded like I had no idea what Liv and Milo were doing upstairs, and even if I did, I didn't care.

Grace smiled and shook her now chin-length shock of blond hair. She had pulled some of it into a tiny knot at the top of her head, mastering the half-up, half-down bun, and let the rest fan out around her. "Thanks, Rory. Just needed some changes for senior year, you know?"

"Totally," I said.

Devon nodded his head to the music, holding his red Solo cup. "You excited for the Garbage Girls, Rory?"

"Um, *yes*," I said, accidentally chirping again, so I cleared my throat. "Yeah, should be cool."

They nodded, and then it was quiet. I needed to fill the silence immediately.

"Mostly because I *am* a Garbage Girl," I said, then quickly corrected myself, just in case. "Not like . . . I'm in the band. Obviously, I'm not. Just because . . . I dress like garbage."

*Why am I acting so fucking weird?*

"You do not!" Grace said.

"No, like, it's a look," I babbled. "It's my aesthetic." While Grace laughed, I turned to Devon. "Hey, man, could you grab me a beer?"

"Where's Liv?" Grace asked, as Devon dipped into the kitchen. "I actually don't think I've ever seen you without her."

"Oh, she's . . ." I trailed off. *Upstairs, hooking up.*

I suddenly realized David Bowie was playing from someone's speakers.

"You two are the cutest," Grace said, tipping her

head back and dancing slowly, completely offbeat. I could smell the alcohol on her breath. "I wish I had a friend like that."

"Totally," I said, wishing they would turn down the music. For some reason, it was getting under my skin in a way I never thought Bowie could.

"It's like . . . more than friends with some people, you know?" she said dreamily. "Like . . . *soul mates.* Or something. I don't know."

"Mm-hmm." I played with my nail.

"One beer for Rory," Devon said, pushing a cold can into my hand. I didn't even look at the brand; I simply cracked it and started swigging.

"I was just talking about how Liv and Rory are, like, friendship goals," Grace said, looking up at Devon, making him dance with her. "Aren't they perfect, babe?"

"No, like actually," Devon said.

"A literal *iconic* duo," Grace said.

The beer wasn't helping my brain turn off.

"I'm just gonna go find—" I started, and they were dancing and not paying attention, and I walked away. Then a warm hand wrapped around my arm and pulled me in, and I was staring straight into Liv's flushed face.

"The band's almost here," she said excitedly, squeezing my arm. "Let's go to the basement!"

"Yeah," I said. "I'm just gonna pee. I'll meet you."

"Okay." Her breath was hot on my face. "Don't take too long, sis."

"I'll try not to."

"Also." She tightened her grasp, holding my whole forearm. Her voice lowered, and I tilted my head to hear her. Her hair brushed my cheek. "Do you mind dropping me off at Milo's tonight and picking me up in the morning?"

"Um," I said. "Well, I can't really . . . drive. I just had a beer."

Her face fell. "I just—shit. Milo has these edibles his brother brought home from Colorado. I just took one."

I blinked. "We could Uber . . . ?"

"We'll figure it out," she said.

"Okay."

"You don't mind, right?"

"What?"

"That I'm sleeping at Milo's?"

"Dude," I said. "Why would I mind? Do your thing."

"I love you," she replied. "Don't take too long in the shitter."

"You never know with me, right?" I turned to go. "Hashtag Barnes & Noble–gate. Never forget."

"I love you!" she called again, disappearing.

\* \* \*

When I went downstairs five minutes later, the Garbage Girls hadn't arrived yet, and the smell of sweat and alcohol permeated the air like an atomic bomb. I moved through it seemingly in slow motion, trying to make out people's faces in the smog and wondering how the fire alarm in Natsuki's cousin's house had not already gone off, whoever Natsuki's cousin actually was.

Then I heard my name slice through the hazy air. I turned and felt my stomach drop into my feet. Liv and Milo were sitting on the couch, all snuggled up. But it wasn't Liv.

Well, I mean, it *was* Liv.

Except for her eyes.

They were someone else's eyes; that had to be the

only answer. They stared straight ahead, but didn't really stare, just *looked.* They were dark, too dark. One of them was more closed than the other.

Liv's eyes were always fully open.

*Something is wrong*, my brain said.

"Rory!" someone said again.

It was Natsuki, sitting on the other side of Milo, waving me over. Milo's arm was hanging loosely around Liv's shoulders, but he was fully engaged in something else—Natsuki? Something over Natsuki's shoulder? And his mouth was a little open, like Liv's. But he was smiling.

Liv was not smiling.

There was one more thing I *didn't* need to see, which finally set my legs in motion: Milo's hand. Milo's hand, literally resting on Liv's boob.

I walked up to the couch, ignoring Natsuki, and crouched down directly in front of Liv.

"Hi," I said. "Liv?"

"She's fine," said Milo, lifting his arm from Liv (thank fucking god) and waving it at me, laughing. "It might take her a minute to respond."

"*Liv?*" My voice hitched.

"She's fine, really," Natsuki said, giggling, from Milo's other side. "We did this shit all the time last year . . ."

Her voice faded. Everyone's voices and faces faded, except Liv's.

"Rory," she said. Or someone said, from deep in her throat.

*We're leaving*, I thought.

"We're leaving," I said out loud.

"The Garbage Girls haven't started yet," said Milo,

the same expression on his face from the Fourth of July: *Really? Are you serious?*

*Killjoy.*

"I don't care," I said shortly. "Get out of my fucking way, Milo."

"What's the problem?" came a voice. I turned and saw someone I felt like dealing with even less than Milo: freaking Harrison.

*Fuck off, Liv.*

*Selfish fucking bitch.*

"Bro." Milo, reached his recently-nonconsensually-feeling-Liv-up arm across to pound Harrison's fist.

"Yo, look at her right now," said Harrison, and I could hear a snicker in his voice that made me want to punch him. "She is *faded.*"

"Dude, I know, it hit her hard," Milo said.

"Wonder how it feels to shut up for once?" Harrison muttered, laughing.

"It's not funny," I spat at him.

"Uh, yeah, it actually kind of is," Harrison said, not even fully looking at me. "Chill out, bitch."

"Ex*cuse* me?"

Milo put his hand on Harrison's chest. "Dude, stop." He turned to me. "Rory, chill."

I turned back to Liv, my heart pounding in my chest. The corners of her mouth had turned down. Her normally golden-brown skin was ashen.

*Act now*, said my brain, and that was the last thing it said for a while. I pulled her upward into a standing position and, with every ounce of my lackluster muscle strength, I half dragged her across the basement to the staircase.

"We're going upstairs," I told Liv, but when I looked

at her again, I realized it was too late. She lurched forward.

"Fuck," I whisper-screamed, as vomit splattered all over the floor.

Ignoring everything that wasn't Liv, I pretended not to hear the chorus of "*Oh my god*" and "*Ew*" that surrounded us. I pulled her around by the shoulders and looked into her eyes. Her dark, drugged, terrified eyes.

"It's okay," I said, as she bent over again. This time, all over my shoes.

"Let me help," came a voice, and suddenly Jem appeared between us. I had no time to tell him to fuck off, or maybe the words got stuck in my throat, or maybe I was too scared to handle this alone. I let him lift Liv from my arms and carry her up the stairs, and I ran up behind him, leaving other people to deal with the mess.

"It was Milo," I panted, slamming the bathroom door shut a minute later. "He gave her something."

"Are you sure? Do you know what it was?" Jem asked, as Liv slumped over the toilet.

"Yes. No. An edible. I don't know."

Jem ran his hands over his face. I wanted to thank him, should have thanked him, but did not. I ran across the bathroom and knelt beside Liv, pulling her hair out of her face.

"It's going to be okay," I whispered into her ear. "I promise. I *promise*."

"I know what it probably was," Jem said. "Milo's brother brings back these crazy brownies from Boulder. Like there *has* to be something other than weed in there. It fucks you up even more if you don't have any food in your stomach."

I felt Liv shaking next to me; I could literally hear

her teeth chattering. She had barely eaten all day.

"Same thing happened to Natsuki's friend last year," Jem said, leaning against the sink. "It just has to get out of her system, and she'll be fine."

"Thanks," I said, not looking at him.

"Hey," he said, and I looked up. "She's gonna be fine, Rory."

"I know," I said, although I didn't.

"You want me to get you an Uber?"

"Um . . ."

The thought of not being near a toilet stressed me out. But I could hear noises below us. People yelling, laughing. The floor underneath our feet pounded with bass.

"Rory," came Liv's small voice.

"Yeah?" I brought all my attention to her once again. "I'm right here, Liv."

"I want to leave," she said. "Now."

I turned to Jem.

"On it," he said, whipping out his phone. "Just hang tight."

\* \* \*

It wasn't difficult to guess the passcode for Liv's phone: her birthday, 1218. I went to her text strand with Eleanor and hastily typed in, *Hey Mom, I'm sleeping over at Rory's tonight. See you tomorrow!*

I hoisted Liv up the stairs of my house and into the dark bathroom, thanking all higher forces that Mom and my grandparents were asleep. Liv's phone buzzed in my hand.

Eleanor: *This isn't Rory, is it? Lol.*

My eyes almost clouded over with panic.

Me: *No*

I needed to sound more like her.

Me: *Wtf mom*

Eleanor: *K. Thanks for letting me know. See u tomorrow. Love u*

Me: *Love u 2*

Eleanor sent three red heart emojis. I had the sudden urge to scroll up, to see what their text interactions usually looked like. Liv distracted me by throwing up again, and I put her phone down, rushing over to gather her hair.

* * *

Some point after three, when exhaustion was crawling between my eyes and my brain, and the bathtub had formed a substantial bruise on my ass, my own phone lit up in the dark. I checked on Liv first: she was curled asleep on her side on the bathroom rug, with an old pillow tucked under her ear, various towels draped over her shoulders and legs like blankets. I silently picked up my phone and curled back into my makeshift bed in the tub.

I would not be sleeping tonight. I had made the plan hours ago. At six, I would move us back to my bedroom, clean up any signs of human activity, and start feeding Liv Gatorade and toast, so that hopefully by the time my family woke up and started bumping around the kitchen, yelling about food, Liv would be relatively functioning. I hadn't forgotten about Liv's car, still at Natsuki's cousin's house, or about the fact that Liv needed to be at church with her parents by ten. I had not yet made a plan for these things, but I kept telling myself it would be okay, because it was the only way I knew how to keep going.

When I finally got around to opening my texts, I saw they were from Milo.

*Hey is liv ok/?*

*Im so sorry about tonight I thoguht she could handleit. Ive nevr seen someone react like that before Can u call me?*

When I hadn't responded, he'd sent two more texts:

*Talked to my bro. Shell be fine. Just needs to get it out of her system*

*Id appreciate if u called me tho*

I thought of Harrison's face when he saw Liv. Milo's face. Laughing. White-hot, exhausted fury flooded through my brain.

Me: *She's not fine. Check your shit before you give it to other people.*

When he tried to call me, I ignored it. I ignored the next two times also.

Some amount of time later—my brain had long since sacrificed its ability of measuring minutes versus hours—Liv spoke for the first time since we'd gotten to my house. Her voice was still a bit muffled, but she sounded closer to the real Liv than she had all night.

"No," she said. "No. *No.*"

I sat up in my bathtub bed and climbed to the edge, where I could see her curled right below me.

"You're okay," I said.

"Oh my god."

"The edible hit you really hard, but you're safe now. It'll pass."

I lowered my hand onto her shoulder, but she recoiled, curling away from me. My arm flinched away again.

"Oh my god, oh my god," she kept whispering, burying her face in her hands, and she started to cry.

I said nothing and let a million years go by. Then slowly, as lightly as I could, I lowered my hand back onto her shoulder, and she didn't push it away. She pulled it closer and squeezed.

* * *

Five hours later, the most perfect fall morning began— the sun beat down on yellow-tinged leaves, the wind lightly nipped our cheeks, and the sounds of Willow's soccer practice traveled across Evergreen Pond and into our backyard. Kids screaming, whistles blowing.

Life continuing in a way that, at three in the morning, I'd worried that it would not.

I looked over at Liv as we made our way out to Mom's minivan. She had managed to swallow down a few bites of toast before we left the house, but it had taken major begging on my part—and by major, I mean I almost cried with anxiety and exhaustion before she gave in. Even after the toast, she still looked gray and disheveled.

"Are you sure you don't want to borrow one of my dresses?" I asked as she swung into the passenger seat of the van and I twisted the keys in the ignition.

Liv didn't answer for a few minutes, just cradled her forehead in her hand.

"You know I wouldn't fit," she said finally.

"Dude, I borrow your stuff all the time. We're the same size."

"We're *not* the same size, Rory. You think I'd fit into one of your little plaid jumpers?"

Instead of answering, I turned on the radio. Mom always had it switched to the oldies station, and as soon as Fleetwood Mac's "Dreams" came on, I started singing along. As much as Liv didn't like to admit it, she loved this one; we'd sung it all the time on our way to Grace's or the beach over the summer. I sang along dramatically, but then Liv switched it off.

I sighed. We stayed quiet for a few more moments as I drove toward Liv's house, but after a short time, the silence became unbearable.

"So . . . how are you feeling?" I asked.

"You know," she said in a clipped voice, "I'd rather not talk about it, Rory."

*Okay*, I thought, feeling the coldness again in my chest. *That tone was uncalled for.* Before I met Liv, I'd ignored miles of passive-aggressive attitude from people in my life: Mom, my sisters, my old friends. But Liv had changed a lot of things about me. One of those things: I no longer tolerated being snapped at.

"I was just asking," I said. "You don't have to flip a shit."

Her voice elevated. "I'm *not* flipping a shit. I'm asking you to leave me alone."

We sat in more silence. I could still hear the ghost of Stevie Nicks's voice, singing of lonely dreams.

"Why don't you call me after church?" I said finally. "I can tell you exactly what happened, if it makes you feel any better, just so you know—"

"I know what happened," she said, her voice like a punch. "Milo gave me something. I got fucked up, and I puked in front of everyone in the middle of someone's basement."

"No one really no—"

"*Don't* tell me they didn't notice," Liv said, and I felt the venom in her voice, felt it plunge into my chest, like

I'd swallowed a handful of ice. "It's probably on a dozen Snapchat stories by now."

I tried to take a different tack, although I really should've just shut up. "Why do you care?"

"*What?*"

I tried to make it less obvious that I was taking deep breaths, that my hands were tightening around the wheel. "You're always telling *me* not to care what people think. So, I'm asking you. Why do you care?"

For a moment, she was silent, but when she spoke, her voice shook with rage.

"Rory, I fucking *threw up* on the *floor* in front of *everyone I know*!"

"Okay, but—"

"That isn't the same as you being fucking *shy*!"

"I didn't say—"

"It's senior year, and I'm the girl who still can't fucking hold her shit," she said. "I'm the girl who overdid it."

"They'll forget about it, Liv," I said loudly. "No one cares as much as you do."

But she wasn't listening. She kept talking. "This doesn't happen to me. This *never* happens to me."

"Liv, no one's above this," I said. "Not even you." And although my eyes were on the road, I could feel her freeze next to me. "It doesn't matter how cool and poised and emotionless you are. Anyone can get drugged at a party."

"You don't know what you're talking about," she spat.

"Yeah, I kind of do." I pulled over, because even though we were a block away from her house, I was getting too pissed off to drive. "I know what it looks like when someone's too fucked up."

"Oh, you know what it looks like? Really, Rory?"

"If Jem and I hadn't been there—"

"Okay, yeah, thank *god* for you and Jem. I don't know what I would have done if you hadn't been there to save me. Probably embarrass you more, since I'm clearly the fuckup that you have to take care of—"

"Liv, you couldn't even talk," I spluttered. "You needed *help.*"

"I *don't* need help," she yelled, unclicking her seat belt. "I can take care of myself, Rory. You think that just because you're some inexperienced saint, that gives you the right to get into other people's lives and decide whether they need help? Really?"

Tears rushed to my eyes, and I hated myself for it. *Don't let it show. Don't let her see.*

"Quit judging other people's choices," she said. "You don't know *shit* about Milo, or Jem, or any of them. You don't know shit about *me.* Stop pretending that you do."

I sat there, letting it all flood through me, and she opened the car door.

"I'm walking home," she said.

I watched as she did.

I waited until she was in her house, until the door slammed shut.

I waited three more minutes after that, just to be sure.

And then I hit the steering wheel as hard as I could and cradled my hand, so I could cry about that instead.

"*I* heard you last night, Rory."

I looked sideways up at Mom, my head slumping in the palm of my good hand. I sat at the kitchen table, a full plate of food in front of me, but dinner had been over for an hour. Willow and my grandparents had already gone upstairs, Saige was at a late practice, and Mom was clearing away the plates. They still set one for me, every night, even though I couldn't bring myself to touch it.

"Heard me doing what?" I asked, my voice in monotone.

"Limping around at three in the morning."

"Oh," I said. "Yeah. I was looking for a book downstairs."

"Why?"

"Because I wanted to read it."

Mom joined me at the table and ran her hands through her messy dark hair. She hadn't gotten it cut in way too long, and her bangs were growing out over her eyes like mine. With her tattoos and my casts and scars, we looked like an alt girl band from the nineties.

"I meant, why were you walking around in the middle of the night?" she asked.

"I can't sleep."

We'd had this conversation many times in the past

eight weeks. I had to tell her repeatedly: can't eat, can't sleep. Not *won't*. *Can't*. For a while, in the hospital, I needed a feeding tube. Not because there was anything wrong with my stomach, but because everything I tried to put in my mouth suddenly turned to wet cardboard. The thought of *biting* and *chewing* and *swallowing* was enough to make me gag.

As for sleeping, it's not that I didn't *want* to—I did, so badly—but the most I could manage was an hour here and there, and usually in the middle of the day. I was so tired that everything was a nightmare: the snow falling outside under the dim porch lights, the shadows under Mom's eyes, my constantly buzzing phone. *Thinking of you. Thoughts and prayers.* None of it seemed real anymore. Colors blurred and sounds linked together and everything was made of sharp edges.

"Rory, you're going back to school tomorrow," Mom said. As if I needed reminding. I hadn't been back to Telsey since before winter break, before the Worst Night, but I'd finally gotten clearance from the doctor. *She'll be fine*, he'd said at my last appointment.

"I'll be fine," I said now, to Mom.

She looked at me hard. "I keep telling you, if you simply lie still and tense your muscles one at a time—"

"That hurts way too much," I told her.

"Well, count sheep, then."

"Mom," I said, in the same flat voice. "I can't."

"I'm telling you, your body will listen, if you just think peaceful thoughts and—"

Heat rushed to my chest. "I don't have peaceful thoughts. Every time I close my eyes, I think I'm going to see it."

"See what?"

"*It*, Mom. I might see it *happening*."

I couldn't bring myself to say "the accident." I couldn't bear to say her name. I hadn't said her name in weeks. I looked up and saw that Mom understood what I meant.

"I can't even turn off my light," I said, embarrassed at the pleading note my voice had taken. *Darkness means night. Night means the car. The car means—*

No. I couldn't.

Mom looked at me for a moment, then reached across the table and eased my good hand out from beneath my chin. She held it tightly, and I didn't have the strength to pull away.

"I want to help you," she said quietly.

"You can't."

Normally, I didn't like being touched. But because everything was a nightmare, and nothing made sense, right then I wanted my mom to hug me. I wanted to shove into her and bury my face in her bony shoulder like I used to when I was little, feeling her breathing evenly, and I wanted her to call me "Rory darling," even though it was so cheesy, and I wanted—I *needed* —for her to tell me everything was okay.

But that hadn't happened in so long. And so she stayed across the table, miles away, holding my hand.

"Rory, you need rest," she said. "Especially tonight."

I stayed silent, and she let go.

"Come with me," she said, and she started heading toward the stairs.

* * *

In her bathroom, I watched Mom open the top cabinet and pull down an orange pill bottle.

"Xanax," she said. "Been on it since Willow was born."

My mouth fell open. The fact that Mom had been on an anxiety med for eight years without telling a soul baffled me. Mom, of all people. The same woman who mostly refused to take Advil, urged *deep breaths* when Saige sprained her ankle in practice, and thought listening to an earsplitting album on the treadmill would solve any and all problems. My Tough-It-Up, You're-Fine, Cut-the-Attitude mom took *Xanax*.

She twisted the bottle open and tipped a white pill into her palm. Then she pulled open one of the drawers, removed what looked like a tiny guillotine, and sliced the pill in half.

She looked at me, the severed pill in her palm.

"This won't fuck you up," she said. "It's such a low dose, it might not do anything at all. But it's worth a try, yeah?"

She tipped it into my palm. I stared at it, then looked back up at her.

And then she pulled me into her arms, slowly, so it didn't hurt as much. The shock of being touched sent chills down my spine, and at first, I stiffened. But the longer we stood there, the more the smell of her shoulder made me want to collapse. It was a few minutes before she whispered, softly, into my hair: "If you tell your sisters or grandparents I'm on an anxiety med, I'll kill you in your sleep."

A sound between a giggle and a sob escaped me, and she kissed the top of my head and sent me to bed.

For the first time in weeks, I slept for eight hours. I didn't dream about the Worst Night. I didn't dream at all.

\* \* \*

"Get up," Mom said the next morning.

"I can't."

"Yes, you can."

"It hurts too badly," I tried.

"No, it doesn't."

"Let me keep sleeping."

"Rory, it's time. We agreed." She pulled the covers off me. I tried to curl into myself further to preserve the warmth, but my arm and leg stabbed with pain. The worst time for the pain was in the morning, when my limbs had been stiffened in sleep for hours.

"I'm not going to school," I told Mom.

She sighed and sat down on the bed, putting her hand on my shoulder, but I pushed it away.

"I know you don't want to," she said. "I know you're scared."

"I'm not *scared*."

"You don't know how the other kids will react when they see you. That's bloody scary, Ror," she said. "But you just have to rip off the Band-Aid! And before you know it, those kids will have moved on. No one will care as much as you do."

This was basically the eight hundredth well-meaning-but-very-cringey thing Mom had said to me since the Worst Night, so it barely fazed me.

"Get up," she said again, tapping my hip before standing and walking out the door of my room. "Get dressed. Eat. We're leaving in thirty."

I barely got dressed and I didn't eat, but it was still an accomplishment.

\* \* \*

Telsey was the exact same as it had been before the Worst Night. Kids in Lululemon and Adidas, pep-rally posters and chorus concert flyers, and people jogging through the halls laughing, pushing each other, shouting about the obsolete things they cared about. Everything in a rich, loud, energetic bubble. Clarksdale: cars and golf and church and prom and lawyers and nannies and money, so much money, and names like John and Emily and Grace and—

"Rory?"

Grace.

"Rory?" she said again, moving toward me, approximately fifteen seconds after I limped into the building.

"Oh my god, Rory," she said, and tears rushed down her cheeks, and she moved up to me too quickly and wrapped her arms around my neck. My ribs hurt and I gasped, and she pulled away with her hands on her mouth.

We stared at each other, her hands on her mouth and my hands on my ribs. Kids walked slowly around us, flicking their eyes in my direction, turning to their friends to whisper, pulling phones out of their pockets. I couldn't hear what they were saying, but it wasn't hard to imagine it.

*She's back*
*Rory Quinn-Morelli's back*
*Ms. Quinn's daughter?*
*Rory?*
*The girl from the accident*
*The one who was with Liv when she*
*Yeah*
*That's her*
*That's the girl*

Grace looked around at the people staring at us, letting go of her mouth.

"Come on," she said, taking my arm—the one not in a brace—and leading me down the hallway, away from the sea of faces and phones.

"I'm sorry I didn't visit you in the hospital," Grace said. "I tried to, but they said you didn't want any visitors . . . Things got really shitty over here. Like, Milo almost had to go to rehab, and Devon and I are on a break, and our whole friend group kind of . . . you know . . . disintegrated. But my mom's like, this is just what happens during a tragedy, everyone processes it differently, but I'm really glad you're back, Rory, 'cause this fucking blows, and I miss Liv so much. Like you have no idea, I've known her since first grade, and it's so unreal that she's like, I just like, I can't even say it, I can't even get through the day without crying—"

I didn't know where she was taking me. My mental map of Telsey had somewhat dissolved. All the lockers looked the same.

"—don't even know if I'm going to prom, I know that sounds stupid, but I can't imagine doing any of these things without her, and did you read the *Gazette* article when it happened? Natsuki and I got interviewed for it, I guess 'cause they saw our posts about Liv or something, and I told them to interview you but they couldn't reach you, and have you been in touch with Liv's parents? My mom was bringing them food, but I never went with her. I don't know what to say to them, like, this entire thing is just completely unreal, I keep thinking it's a nightmare, I keep thinking I'll just see her at school—"

I stared at the ground, at my uneven paces: right,

left, right, left. Sneaker, boot, sneaker, boot.

"—and I keep thinking about our friend group, and like, I wish we had hung out more this year before it happened, but it feels like she was kind of distant during the fall after that Garbage Girls party, you know? She seemed like she didn't want to hang out . . . She seemed different in the last few months, like more serious, I don't know why, I swear I was inviting her to everything still. You know?"

We'd stopped, and I realized Grace had taken me to my locker.

"Yeah," I said, not moving. I couldn't remember the code to my lock.

The bell rang.

"What do you have first period?" Grace asked, wiping her eyes. "I'll walk you."

"Uh," I said. "I have to go to my advisor."

"Oh, no worries, I can walk you there, too."

"No," I said.

Grace looked at me as people milled around, walking to first period, giving us some more prolonged stares.

I could tell what she was thinking: *But I want to be with you.*

*You're the only one who's feeling this worse than me.*

"I'll see you at lunch," I told her, trying very hard to smile.

She nodded shakily, turned on her heel, and joined the crowd.

The truth was that the entire friend group had all texted me, multiple times, after the Worst Night. And I *did* have my phone, and I *did* read them. But I didn't respond to anyone. I couldn't—first because my left hand was broken, and then just because my entire being was numb. I knew they'd stop eventually. And, after a few weeks, they did.

Jem was the only one who kept going.

He'd send me music recs and pictures of puppies from the internet, random thoughts and funny Tik-Toks. He never asked me to reply. He never said the generic, "Thinking of you. Hope you're okay." He just stayed there reliably in my phone, his name popping up at random hours, making sure I still existed. He never stopped.

\* \* \*

I went to my first four classes, which was miraculous in and of itself, although I didn't have anything with me. No pencils or paper, no books, and absolutely no inkling of what was going on. The teachers seemed not to know what to do, so they mostly ignored me. Mrs. Galvez in third-period psych pulled me over and gave me the Grief Lecture, handing me a list of possible counselors I could see, telling me there's a bereavement group that met on certain days in certain rooms. Warning me to say something to a trusted adult if I start feeling too hopeless.

I told her I would, and then she let me draw while the rest of the kids took a test.

Fifth period was when it happened.

I was chugging along on my route, not really thinking—my Telsey map had come back to me after all—until I realized where I was going: the music wing. To choir.

*It doesn't matter*, said my brain. *Don't make this a thing.*

*This whole* thing *is a thing,* I argued back.

*Well, don't make it MORE of a thing. Choir is just like any other class.*

I took a deep, rattling breath.

*You didn't even really like choir.*

*But . . .*

*You always sat in the back doing nothing anyway. How is this any different?*

I swallowed. *Liv won't be sitting there, doing nothing with me.*

I made it all the way to the door of the music room, my hand resting on the narrow glass window, fingers curling.

But then I gave up.

I gave up because, through the window, everything was the same: Mr. Wong was dramatically leading the choir into a warm-up, and Stoff was there, and everyone was there, holding their black folders. But there were two empty seats in the tenor section, right in the middle of the room.

So I turned around and started walking away without thinking. I walked down the hallways of Telsey, passing classrooms and the library and the writing center and everywhere else that didn't matter, and the world faded into black and white, and I kept walking.

I walked until I reached her locker.

This is where we sat in the mornings with our headphones on, where I met her after school to catch the bus.

This is where I found her, where I always found her.

But when I got there, it was no longer Liv's locker. It was no longer anything that I recognized. Because Liv's locker was now pink, and green, and purple-red-gold-silver and all these colors, all these flowers and Hallmark cards and candles and lots of different hand-writing. Ribbons. Paper stars. A teddy bear.

*You will never be forgotten, Liv*
*Fly high*
*Love you*
*Love you!*
*Luv u*
*ily ♡ iy*

When I got closer, I saw the pictures: pictures of Liv from before I'd met her, maybe freshman and sopho-more year, with various people I vaguely recognized. Liv, maybe fifteen, standing out in her vibrant clothes. The only one not making a duck face. There were a few of her from junior year, too, with Jem and Natsuki and the rest. One with me, one I'd never seen before, that must have been taken in Jem's basement. I wasn't looking at the camera; I was looking down at my hands. Liv was in the middle of a laugh, and that's why they chose it.

*Perfect-Happy-Sweet-Loving-Confident-Kind-Brave-Perfect-Perfect-Perfect.*

It seemed like only a minute that I stood there, but I guess it was thirty, because suddenly the bell rang and fifth period ended. People filed out of the classrooms around me, talking, laughing. Whispering.

*I should go to lunch*, I tried to tell myself.

I didn't go to lunch.

I spread my fingers at the top of Liv's locker, where the pictures and flowers and beads began, and I pulled down. I watched everything tear, heard the ripping, felt the softness of the flowers and the scratchiness of the fake flowers against my skin. I pulled it all down, tear-ing and scratching, and heat filled my fingers and my eyes. I started to kick, too, each *bang* punctuating the heavy air around me. I felt the bottom of her locker cave under my good foot. I picked up flowers and pictures from the ground, and I tore them apart, shredding them between my fingers. I scraped at everything I could, destroying it all. No sound escaped me except the heaviness of my breath, but on the inside, everything screamed.

When there was nothing left to do, I stared at the dented, destroyed locker. I felt the gazes of the crowd that had accumulated. The second bell had rung, but no one had moved. An odd silence fell in the hallway, but—yep, there it was: the whispering.

"Oh my god."

"Should I get Ms. Quinn?"

"Where's your phone?"

Then, another voice. A familiar one.

"Rory?"

My mind was so far away, my entire body was numb. But at the sound of my sister's voice, I still found myself automatically turning to face her. Saige stood just feet from me, arms crossed tightly, her brows folded up into a question. Everyone stood silently apart, giving us a wide berth, watching with unashamed open mouths, but Saige ignored them and stepped closer to me.

"Why . . ." she said, gazing at the mess I'd created. "Why would you . . ."

She bent down to pick up the picture of me and Liv, which I realized I'd torn straight down the middle. And she was only fifteen, but suddenly, my little sister's movements reminded me of Nonni's: frail, hunched over, aching. As she straightened up, I noticed the dark circles under Saige's eyes, and I thought of the way she couldn't look directly at me for weeks after the Worst Night. The way she took a break from lacrosse, and failed two classes, and curled up on the couch every day, biting her nails and obsessively scrolling her phone, but ignoring her friends.

I realized, *Other people are grieving, too.*

Saige gazed down at the picture for a moment, and then back up at me.

"Come on," she said, reaching for my arm. "Let's get Mom."

*Click.* The camera of someone's iPhone.

At the sound of it, Saige spun around to see what I was already well aware of: that not one, not two, but three separate people were filming us. She tensed, and I thought of all the times she obsessed over what other people thought. How much could I possibly embarrass her in the span of a single year?

But instead of running away, she snarled, "Mind your own *fucking* business."

Before she was even done speaking, a few people had already scattered. When she turned back to me, tears swam in her eyes. "Let's *go*," she said again, reaching for me.

I knew I should, but I couldn't face her. I turned away, pressing my back against Liv's locker. I pulled my headphones over my head, clamped them over my ears, and looked each of our spectators in the eye. The few kids who still stared, open-mouthed, at our scene, crowded around the locker of the dead girl, here for the drama.

No one met my eyes.

So I turned again and walked away, ignoring Saige,

ignoring them all. And then I started running, reveling in the pain pounding through my bad leg, my ribs, my arm, and then I was out the door.

It was the last time I stepped foot in Telsey.

"Rory and Saige are texting at dinner," Willow tattled, as she passed Nonno the salad bowl.

"Snitch." Saige pushed her phone back into the pocket of her sweatshirt.

"Saige," Mom said in a warning voice.

"Whatever." Saige caught my eye quickly and mouthed, *Okay, boomer.* I hid my smile, and so did she.

"Rory." Mom turned to me, bringing her wine glass to her lips. "Quit texting Liv and eat."

"I'm not texting Liv," I said, my smile flickering out. And it was true.

I hadn't texted Liv in two weeks.

I was flipping through Snapchat stories under the table, subconsciously looking for her, and ignoring all the stupid pictures Saige kept sending me to try and get me to crack. I found Grace and Natsuki at a pumpkin patch, Devon flipping Solo cups at some house party, Stoff skating with theater kids. Everyone at Grace's track meet, Devon's hockey game, Natsuki's art show.

No sign of Liv.

"Rory," Mom said, reaching across the table, palm up. "Phone."

I sighed and handed it over.

Before the Garbage Girls party, Liv and I had snickered behind our music in choir every day, doodling on each other's arms and chewing gum and whispering observations.

But since the party, Liv had been paying attention to Mr. Wong.

Before the party, we sat together in the hallway during lunch, listening to music.

Since the party, she'd been going to the library to do homework instead.

Before, we sent each other Snaps and memes throughout the school day. My phone would frequently buzz with Liv's words, or lack thereof: *Literally me. Omg I can't. I—*. Sometimes, I'd send her a meme and she'd just respond *SLDKFJSDLKFJSD*, and I'd know I got her good. Since last February—our very first show together—we had texted every waking hour of every single day.

But since the Garbage Girls party, my phone had been quiet.

"So," Mom said, as Nonni fussed with Nonno's napkin and my sisters started hitting each other. "What've you been thinking, Rory?"

I paused in the middle of chewing my bread. "About what?"

"You know." Mom gestured with her wine glass. "College."

The sounds around the dinner table mostly stopped.

"Well," I said.

"Because, you know, the first of November is approaching."

"Right," I said. "The Early Decision deadline."

About a month ago, Mom made me give her a list of my top schools. At the very top of my list was Ridgewood College, in upstate New York—probably the most expensive, far-from-home place I could have thought of. She asked me about eighty-five questions about why *there*, why not *here*, why New York instead of Illinois. She talked to me about in-state tuition and on-campus jobs and student debt. I told her I understood.

I still applied.

Mom's eyes glimmered across the dining room table. "Just making sure you're on top of it," she said, before taking another sip of wine.

Unsaid: *You'd better be getting those scholarship applications in. Keep your grades up. Do some social service. Do something, and write about it. Because we're not like the other families at Telsey. Because if you don't, we cannot afford this.*

"I'm on top of it," I said.

Mom looked at me for a moment and then nodded.

Saige gave me a look, like, *You're fucked.*

I narrowed my eyes back, like, *I know, but just fuck off.*

She shrugged. We moved on.

\* \* \*

The next day was the Friday before Indigenous Peoples' Day, and we had off from school. Mom, Nonni, and Nonno went to a distant cousin's wedding in New Jersey, and Saige and Willow went to sleepovers. If it had been three weeks earlier, I would have invited everyone over, but the Garbage Girls party was still fresh in my memory. I decided to parade around the house in my underwear instead, shout-singing the entire *Wicked* soundtrack, eating Willow's candy, screaming "*FIYEEEEROOO!*" at the top of my lungs over the banister, letting gummy worms fall out of my mouth. When, after hours of this, I tired myself out, I took a bath with the door wide open. I was blasting Stevie Nicks at full volume and thinking about making waffles when I heard a ding.

I climbed out of the tub, shivering, and walked naked up to my phone.

Liv: *can i come over*

I stared down at the text for a full minute. And then I brought my phone back to the tub, placed it at the very edge, and sank back into the boiling water. I scrunched my knees and lay all the way down, submerging my ears, staring at the cracked ceiling of the bathroom.

Another ding, but muffled. Then another.

Liv: *I don't have to stay, I know you're mad at me*
Liv: *I just wanna talk for a sec*

I sat with my chin resting on the edge of the tub, thinking about the last time I was in this bathtub, fully clothed, taking care of Liv. I'd slept here, sitting up, my head resting against the cold tile. I thought about her, looking at me in the dark of the bathroom. The look in her eyes: Confusion. Revulsion. Fear.

Me: *Sure. Come on over*
Liv: *Ok be there in 5*

* * *

I swung the door open to see Liv standing there without a bag, without anything at all. Her bike was on its side next to Nonni's garden. Her hands were in the pockets of a huge flannel—mine—and her hair hung loosely around her. No makeup. Worn-out sneakers.

She looked at me with her lips pressed together.

I looked back, my hand still on the doorknob.

She looked up, then to the side, then back at me.

"Remember after Grace's party on the Fourth of July?" she said finally.

I twitched.

"When you said something rude, and then told me you didn't mean it?" she continued. "That you just took out your anger on me because I was your best friend?"

I nodded.

"You did that because you felt safe with me," she said slowly. "Because you knew I'd love you no matter what."

I pressed my lips together tight.

"I'm not saying it's right," she said, "but that's what I've been doing to you."

I stayed silent. She sighed and looked all over the porch, the yard, the doorway. Anywhere but my eyes.

"Look," she finally said. "After that Garbage Girls party, I wasn't just embarrassed. I was scared. I've never felt that way before. That . . . out of it." She finally met my eyes. "Every time I drink or smoke, I'm *always* in control. And this time, I wasn't. And if I don't have complete control over something, my brain just . . . I freak out."

She pressed the heel of one hand against her eyes.

"I know," I said.

"Just, the thing with those guys at the pond and . . . and . . ."

"I know," I said again.

"Trust is really important to me," she said, bringing her hand down. "So, I broke up with Milo."

I sucked in my breath. "I'm sorry. I should have—"

"No," she said firmly. "No. You were there. *You* took

care of me."

"I know," I said. "But lately, I've been feeling like I just . . . I'm not really supposed to be there. At these parties, with these people." I took a breath. "I'm not chill, Liv. I don't handle things in a cool way. I don't know how to do that. I try to listen to this new music and smoke weed and wear bold makeup, and it . . . it feels . . ." I had no idea where I was going with this, but I couldn't stop talking. "It feels fake. I can't be like you guys. It's not me. I'm sorry, but none of this is me. When we go to shows and parties, sometimes I just want to stay in and watch, just, dumb-as-fuck movies. I don't want to get drunk or go to Dreamtown, I want to—I want to eat cereal and listen to old bands," I said, my voice starting to peter out. "And it's boring, and I'm sorry."

Liv stared at me, and for the first time, I couldn't read her expression. Then she took a step toward me.

"Don't apologize for who you are, Rory," she said, her eyes wide. "Don't ever."

I nodded, but a lump formed in my throat. "I just . . . I think I came in and messed everything up."

Liv closed her eyes and shook her head. "Don't. Don't think that."

I didn't say anything.

She heaved a big sigh. "I mishandled the situation," she said, her eyes still closed.

"You were upset," I managed.

"That doesn't justify it. What I said, about you thinking you were a saint and not knowing shit about me? That was *really* fucked up."

"I know you didn't mean it," I said, so quietly that I could barely hear myself. I cleared my throat. "No, actually, I thought you did mean it. That really hurt."

Liv looked physically pained. "You *do* know me," she said. "You know everything about me. Sometimes it scares me, how much you know."

*Stay chill*, I told myself.

"Everything I do," Liv said, now looking me straight in the eye, her voice slow again, "you're just . . . there. With me. For me." She paused. "No one—I mean, I . . . I've never . . ."

She cast around again, biting her lip, looking frustrated.

"I don't know what to do with that," she finally said.

"Well . . ." I said, trying to pretend that my heart wasn't sinking. "Do you want me to go away?"

Liv gripped the sides of her head, closing her eyes again. "*No.* No, I'm just saying . . . I lashed out at you and pushed you away because I . . . I knew you'd still be here, in your fucking David Bowie shirts and high-tops, just—waiting for me to get over my bullshit. I knew you'd be here anyway." She swallowed. "And that's unfair, and I'm sorry."

We stood there, blinking. Liv, my confident friend, standing in front of me like she would rather disappear than keep talking. I thought about the past two weeks. How miserable I was. How I'd missed her with every fiber of my being. How relieved I was to just see her standing in front of me.

"I forgive you," I said. "It sucked how you treated me. But . . . I forgive you. You're my—" I swallowed. I couldn't find the word for what she was, so I ended up saying, "You're my Liv."

She nodded, exhaling, and stared at her feet.

"So . . . can I, like . . . come in?" she said.

"I don't know," I said. "I might need some time."

She nodded again, very solemnly, and started turning toward her bike.

"Liv?" She turned back to me. We stared at each other for an eternity. I wanted it to last longer.

"I'm fucking kidding. Come in," I finally said, and I couldn't help it. I smiled.

Her eyebrows rose in surprise. And then she broke out into a smile, too, and that familiar laughter bubbled out of her.

"God, I hate you for that," she said, as we slammed the front door behind us and walked into the kitchen.

* * *

We sat at the counter, shouting over each other, trying to make up for lost time. We yelled about *Stranger Things* and how we would've written the latest season. We grumbled about the first month of senior year, how everyone seemed to have upgraded to the next level of bitch-ass over the summer. We stalked each other on social media, liking Instagram posts that were 107 weeks old. We ate peanut butter straight out of the jar, dipping in anything we could find—carrots, pear slices, pretzels—while fighting over who was better, Beyoncé or Solange.

"*LEMONADE*," I kept shouting.

"Yeah, but Solange doesn't give a fuck. She colors completely outside of the lines. And she calls out white people on their bullshit."

"But *LEMONADE*!"

We talked about eyebrows, planets, and American Girl Dolls ("Kit was where it was fucking *at*," I argued, but she insisted on Samantha). We talked about maxi dresses, maxi pads, llamas, the Common App, spandex, deodorant, Chipotle, the shapes of our butts, baby names, singing, and sharting. How we both failed our driving tests the first time but were too embarrassed to tell our friends. Her dad's unbelievable level of patience, even when she was being horrible, and how both our moms occasionally made us want to claw our eyes out. Our friend group, what we loved about them, and what we hated about them. How Devon was a fuckboy sometimes, and Jem was so sweet it hurt, and Natsuki and Grace were unfairly prettier than us.

"Okay, false," I said, when Liv expressed this last view.

"I wish I had Natsuki's cheekbones," Liv said, leaning on her elbow.

"Bitch, I want *your* cheekbones." I dipped my fifty-eighth pretzel into the peanut butter jar. "Every picture of you is perfect."

She sarcastically smiled and batted her wingless, scrubbed eyes. "I'm really into this shapeless flannel, greasy hair, no makeup look. I'm trying this new thing where I haven't plucked my mustache in four days?"

"It works on you," I said. "I'm going with the unintentionally-resembling-a-seventh-grade-boy-at-all-times look. You don't have to do anything, just don't grow boobs, and you're good to go."

"You have *breasts*!" Liv shouted. "And seriously, Roo, just say 'breast.' I'm so done with the word *boob*."

"That word is so . . . *clinical*, though," I said, earning myself an eye roll and a grumble about the patriarchy from Liv. "Okay, fine. I don't have *breasts*."

"They're there, Roo. You just have to believe."

"Whatever," I said. "I *wish* I looked like you."

"No, you don't."

"Yes, I do!" I said. "You're perfect."

Except that it got weirdly quiet when I said that. And something in her face shifted—hardened—and her eyes fell to the counter, to the remains of our peanut butter massacre, and then to her lap, and her mouth twisted into a frown.

*No, wait,* I thought blankly.

"You're like the Beyoncé of Clarksdale. No, the So-lange," I invented, searching chaotically for the right thing to say. "You and Grace and Natsuki should just join a club of pretty, perfect people."

She laughed again, her face melting back to normal, and I released the breath I didn't know I'd been holding. "Only if you're in it, too, queen," she said, and then her whole face brightened. "I almost forgot! I taught myself another song on the uke. Can I play it for you?"

A few minutes later, we climbed onto my bed, Liv clutching Mom's old, scratched ukulele.

"Okay, promise not to laugh," she said.

"I don't know if I can promise," I said. "How emo is it, one to ten?"

"It's, like, eleven."

"I'm so ready." I lay down on my side, propping up my head.

She started strumming, closed her eyes, and sang.

It was "A Case of You," the Joni Mitchell classic we'd listened to last year on long bus rides after school. But she made it different. It was something separate. *More.* It was like listening to the cello in a hot bath with lavender, like settling comfortably in a dark corner under neon lights, like coffee and rainy mornings and standing at the edge of water. The way it must be to see a sound and hear a feeling. She wove the still sadness of the song into a bold, sharp, breathing-and-beating cover, eyes closed, lips curved into a smile, the light pouring from her mouth and hands. It filled me to my brim.

She stopped playing suddenly.

"Are you *crying*?" she asked, putting down the uke.

"No," I said, my voice cracking.

She started laughing. It was not the low, controlled laugh that she had at parties, but the one she let loose when it was just us. It bubbled out of her, wave after wave, making me giggle, too. She dropped the ukulele and collapsed onto the pillow inches away from me, hiccupping and snorting, until we were both literally hollering, hitting the pillows.

"You're so *weird*," I said, wiping my eyes, when what I actually wanted to say was, *I'll never let you go again.*

"I can't believe you *cried*," she huffed, controlling herself.

"There was something in my eye."

She raised a finger between us and tapped my nose, and when I flinched, she gave me her twisty, cunning smile. But then a line appeared between her brows, and the corners of her mouth twitched.

I felt a tug of fear in my chest. "What's wrong?"

She closed her eyes, but she didn't turn away. "I'm just sorry," she whispered.

I didn't realize I'd reached for her hand until she squeezed my fingers back, hard. A tear slid down her cheek and onto the pillow between us. Without knowing what I was doing, without thinking about really anything at all, I reached up and brushed the next one away.

"It's okay now," I told her.

"Are you sure?" she asked, her voice small. She opened her eyes to meet mine. We were so close, I was seeing double: four shining brown eyes, four sparks of green.

"It's like you said. I'll be here in my high-tops," I whispered, tapping her nose back, and she smiled. "Always will."

She nodded and closed the space between us, wrapping her arms around my waist. I hugged her back tightly, scratching her back and wondering if she could feel how hard my heart was beating. I didn't know if I wanted her to.

"I'm gonna play another angsty song," she said eventually into my shoulder, her voice muffled but steadier.

"Okay," I whispered, her hair tickling my nose.

Neither of us let go.

*J*ust before Thanksgiving break, Mr. Wong read out a list of names from his iPad.

"If your name is called, please stay after class—I'll give you a pass for next period." He took a breath and started calling out a few people from each section, concluding with, "Liv Martinez! Rory Quinn-Morelli!"

We looked at each other. A thin-lipped smile appeared on Liv's face, and her eyes bulged out, and she looked at me as if to say, *If we're in trouble, I'm going to fucking murder someone.*

In the six weeks since we'd made up, Liv and I had been barreling through school with our heads down, ignoring everything and everyone except each other. We were doing our same old stuff from junior year—sitting by her locker listening to music, cracking each other up in the silent study room, chewing gum in choir—except, this time, it was just us. Our other friends seemed to be busy with college apps and sports games, and even when they weren't, we just . . . didn't see them much.

*It happened organically*, I would tell myself, as I scrolled through social media. Liv and I ditched homecoming, and Dreamtown started carding and had a bad fall lineup, and it was too cold to go out, and then suddenly, it was just us. Liv-and-Rory. Listening to music. Huddled together, watching movies. Helping Willow with her homework, helping Nonni make dinner. Helping Saige get ready for her first "real" party, covering for her as she snuck out, then driving to pick her up, tipsy and giddy, at one in the morning.

"I truly don't miss it," Liv sighed, taking on the air of a wise elder, as Saige stumbled through the back door. After making sure Saige brushed her teeth and drank some water, Liv and I tumbled into my bed, giggling. The heat didn't reach my room, so we snuggled together under the covers, cheek to cheek, and talked ourselves to sleep.

We hung out every day, and no one bothered us.

So we floated, together, in peace.

* * *

When the bell rang after choir and most people filed out of the room, looking at us curiously, Mr. Wong led us to the piano.

"Okay, folks, so we've got something really cool up our sleeves," he said. "Every year we have nursing homes and country clubs contacting Telsey, asking if we do any caroling."

Liv sucked in her breath next to me.

"So this year, I decided to get a group of seniors together to learn some holiday songs to perform around the community."

I stole a glance at Stoff a few feet away. The smile was frozen on his face, a sarcastic glint in his eye, and I wanted to laugh. I looked away quickly before he could see. We hadn't talked since the Fourth of July, and he'd been flat-out ignoring me since that moment outside Panera. Sometimes I really missed him, but I didn't know what to do about it. Or maybe I did, but it felt too scary.

*I'll fix things soon*, I thought, vaguely.

"You'll get two all-day field trips and ten points of extra credit for choir," Mr. Wong continued. "So if anyone needs a GPA-booster for those college apps . . . " He chuckled, shuffling his music, and then surveyed us all. "Just let me know by tomorrow morning if you're in or out. If you're in, I'll give you the music to learn over Thanksgiving. Cool?"

As he wrote us passes, Liv focused her entire repertoire of sassy eyes and venomous, having-absolutely-none-of-it expressions into one stare at me.

"*NO*," she said, as soon as we were out the door. "Kill me with a spoon."

"I'm confused about which part of spreading holiday cheer to old people makes you want to die," I said.

"Holiday cheer," Liv said, "and old people."

"Ooh, we love a Scrooge-y witch," I said, as we rounded the corner of the music building, and she snickered. "If you really don't want to do it, then just opt out."

"I can't," she said.

"Why?"

"The extra credit."

We arrived at the staircase. We both had lunch, but she was going to spend it in the library doing work.

"I need those ten extra points," Liv said.

"You're getting straight As," I replied. This was not an assumption. Last Sunday, while we worked on our safety school apps at a coffee shop (Liv making fun of me relentlessly for my gingerbread latte), she checked her grades online and showed me, her face glowing with pride.

"The average GPA at Blackwell is 3.98," Liv said,

starting to walk up the stairs.

"You've already applied," I reminded her.

"Colleges can revoke their decision if your grades slip, you know," she said over her shoulder. "Besides, I'm only at 3.95." She trilled, *"Not satisfactoryyyyyy!"*

I trilled back, *"Perfectioniiiiiiiiiiist!"*

A group of girls walked past us, all wearing matching Uggs, leggings, and large cashmere sweaters. One of them gave us a look that could have started World War Three.

Liv smiled pleasantly. "Why are we so fucking *popular*, Rory?" she said, before walking up the rest of the stairs to the library.

\* \* \*

The next three weeks sped by in a blur. Colleges promised to release their early admission decisions on December 15th. Liv and I had applied to our top schools eight weeks earlier—Blackwell for her and Ridgewood for me, a three-hour drive away from her—and we knew on that mid-December morning that we'd be drowning in either celebration or sorrow by nightfall.

December 15th was also the day of our first caroling gig at the Clarksdale Country Club. When we'd gotten our schedules the week before, Liv had groaned and said, not bothering to lower her voice, "This *truly* could not be scheduled on a worse day." Mr. Wong had pretended not to hear.

We started that anxiety-ridden day standing outside the school at seven thirty in the morning, in black suits and dresses, freezing, no one talking.

"The bus will be here any minute, you guys," Mr. Wong said cheerfully, although I couldn't fully hear him because of the wind. I stood there shivering in a black dress that Liv had lent me.

Liv scooted sideways so that she was standing directly next to me, shoulders bunched up to her ears, a painfully angry and bored expression on her face.

"Fuck this," she growled, by way of greeting.

"Ten extra-credit points," I replied, my teeth chattering.

"I thought we would at least sing for *needy populations*," Liv said. "Not rich, judgmental old people who eat caviar for breakfast."

A school bus swung around the corner, and everyone moaned in relief.

When we entered the club, a weird cluster of sleepy teens in funeral wear, I had to keep my jaw from dropping to the ground. Everything inside was wooden and polished, dozens of gigantic portraits of old white men hung plastered to the walls, and a real bear—as in an *actual taxidermied bear*—casually stood in the corner of the front room.

"Not the bear," Liv breathed in my ear.

"I think they want us in the dining hall," Mr. Wong whispered, bursting with excitement.

"The 'dining hall'?" Liv said. "I actually can't."

Stoff sidled up to the kids in front of us as we walked down the hallway, which featured more portraits of rich old men and some extravagant Christmas decorations.

"Quick pause," he said. "Can we talk about the literal bear in the foyer?"

Then Liv, Stoff, and Mr. Wong spoke at the same time.

Liv: "This is the epitome of old white privilege, and it disgusts me."

Stoff: "I'm pretty sure my grandpa, like, shot that bear."

Mr. Wong: "Okay, team, we're gonna go ahead and start with 'Carol of the Bells'—formation, please!"

\* \* \*

During our fifteen-minute break between sets, we were instructed to meander around the tables and socialize, an order that made me want to barf up the stale Cheerios I'd had for breakfast. Socializing was easy for most of the kids in our little caroling cluster: if their parents weren't there, then their uncles or neighbors or friends' parents were, because everyone in the Clarksdale hierarchy knew each other—everyone's dads golfed together, everyone knew that one business professor at Yale, everyone talked about prestigious colleges and frats and lacrosse teams. I had little to talk about with anyone, as I didn't play lacrosse or shop at Nordstrom or have any relatives who went to the Ivy Leagues, so I mostly wandered around humming our songs to myself, as if I missed our carols dearly. As if I couldn't get enough of that fucker Good King Wenceslas.

I passed Stoff, who currently held the attention of no less than eight club members and was talking joyously about college as if he hadn't angry-cried during choir two days ago about his ACT score.

"—Stanford's my top, obviously, but I'm also looking at a few eastern schools—Duke, Tufts, Dartmouth. I'm really looking forward to this next year. I think I'm definitely ready for the transition—"

I found Liv, who was being similarly interrogated by an elderly couple near the back.

"So, where did your parents go to law school?" asked

the surly man, who had a bit of caviar quivering on his chin.

"Loyola Chicago," Liv said. I noted her talking-to-old-people face: eyes slightly narrowed, lips curved upward at the ends, everything sculpted into a distantly pleasant expression that gave off a politer vibe of *Would you kindly fuck off?* than the one she wore at school.

"Oh, then I wouldn't know them," said the man. "Harvard man, myself." He seemed to pause for effect, which he disguised by cracking his neck. The piece of caviar fell off. "You're thinking of going into prelaw, then?"

"No," said Liv. Not *I'm undecided* or *You know, it's not really my thing.* A literal hard pass.

The couple blinked in tandem.

"Oh," said the woman.

Bing Crosby's voice sang dreamily from speakers somewhere above us.

Liv turned to me. "I need to go reapply my lipstick, Roo," she said, smiling, as the older couple started talking to each other again. "Wanna come?"

In the single bathroom, which was larger and fancier than basically my entire house, Liv rolled her eyes to the ceiling.

"This place is toxic," I said.

"Right? I'd almost rather be at school."

Liv leaned over the sink with the tube of lipstick in her right hand. The dim lights around the mirror framed her face, creating gold streaks in her hair. She puckered her newly wine-red lips at me, arching her eyebrows to look like she belonged in an old French painting, and then popped a piece of gum in her mouth.

"God, I don't want to go back," I said.

"We still have break time. Let's just post up here."

We sat down on the ground of the bathroom, which was probably cleaner than our entire high school. Liv sighed, straightening her back and tilting her chin upward.

And then she said, suddenly: "I didn't get in."

"What?"

"To Blackwell." She kept her eyes closed. "I checked my email on the way here."

I sat in genuine shock. Liv, with the perfect grades and the million hobbies, languages, and instruments. The fact that anyone would deny her anything baffled me. I thought back to the many weekend afternoons we'd spent in cafés, editing each other's college essays and stressing about scores and fantasizing about the trips we'd take to visit each other the next fall. She'd prowled through Blackwell's website every time, pointing out different things to me: This is the dorm she'd choose. That's what their dining hall looks like. This would be her major, with a minor in that.

I hadn't known about my chances with Ridgewood, but I'd known, without a doubt, that Liv would get into Blackwell.

And I'd known she wanted it more than I could want anything.

"Liv," I said, and that's all I could come up with.

"I shouldn't have even applied," she said. "It was out of my reach."

She started to take those long, shaky breaths, and I thought, *Not a panic attack. Please, not here.*

In spontaneous problem-solving mode, I began the most compliment-filled speech I'd ever said in my life. "Liv, you don't even, like, *know* how special you are.

Dude! You can play five instruments! You build lofts in your spare time! You've read *Anna Karenina* twice out of sheer enjoyment. You're getting straight As while doing all these things, *plus* teaching yourself Swedish *and* doing perfect makeup every day. I deadass don't even know how to put on lip gloss. You're like Beyoncé slash Eleven slash A.O.C. You're the smartest and funniest and coolest and wokest person in our entire school. So, like, what-the-fuck ever about a college of smartasses who probably were too busy riding their high horses to actually read your application. They're going to hate their lives in four years when you're literally the most famous person on earth and speaking at, like, Google headquarters and shit about women's rights, and they're still sitting in an admissions office scratching their pretentious, bleached assholes."

She gave the tiniest scoff, but it didn't reach her eyes.

"Fuck them," I said firmly, resisting the urge to grab her hand. "They don't deserve you."

Her shoulders were still rising and falling, but she wasn't pale and shaking like last time. She closed her eyes, took three breaths, and then opened them again and faced me. Her breathing slowed.

Then she broke into a tight smile and said, in a voice I didn't recognize—small, gentle—"Thanks, Roo."

We sat in silence for a bit. I felt my phone in my pocket, but I didn't take it out. Didn't open my email.

*Wait*, I told myself. *Just wait until you're alone.*

\* \* \*

After the break, we sang through a few encores of the club members' favorites: the jazzy version of "Sleigh

Ride," the eight-part harmony of "Hallelujah Chorus," and that super slow "Silent Night" that made everyone cry. On the bus ride home, Liv leaned against the window, and I faced forward, and we shared her ancient iPod. I let her pick the album, and Maggie Rogers serenaded us through the afternoon.

I tried to walk casually instead of sprint into my house when I got home. Tried to be patient when I was immediately bombarded by what seemed like every member of my family: Willow wanting me to take her to the *Nutcracker*, Nonni demanding to know what happened to the tiramisu, Saige needing help with her English paper. I walked past them, bounded up the stairs, and locked myself in my room. I didn't turn on the lights; I just collapsed on my bed with my phone.

Took a deep breath. Logged into my email.

*From:* Undergraduate Admissions, Ridgewood College
*Re:* Your Admissions Decision

I fumbled around, my hand shaking so hard I could barely open the email.

Dear Rory,

Congratulations! On behalf of Ridgewood College, we are delighted to announce your admission for next school year!

My heart flew into my mouth. I couldn't breathe.
*Okay, Rory*, I told myself repeatedly. *Okay. Keep reading. This doesn't mean anything until you keep reading. Don't get your hopes up yet.*
I flew down the email, reading until the end.

And there it was. Two sentences:

> Due to your prestigious academic records, we are pleased to award you the Presidential Merit Scholarship. As you may be aware, this scholarship accounts for the entirety of your tuition at the College.

I jumped out of my bed and ran out of my room. Ignoring Saige and Willow again, I flew into the family room where Mom was posted up, surrounded by piles of tests. She looked up at me, startled, as I flung myself onto the couch next to her.

"Jesus, Rory, you're messing with my—" She clutched at the tests until she saw the email I was thrusting in her face. She grabbed my hand to steady it, brought my phone up to her nose, and read. At the first line, she turned to me and planted a huge kiss on my forehead.

"Oh, my love. I'm so proud of you," she whispered into my hair. "But—"

"Keep reading," I said. I wished she weren't reading on my phone, so I could film her reaction when she read about the scholarship. Every muscle in my body tensed with anticipation as I watched her eyes speed down the lines.

Then, suddenly, she was off the couch and jumping up and down, screaming. And I was up there with her.

"The bloody *Presidential Merit Scholarship*!" she bellowed, hugging me tightly, as my heart exploded with joy. "Fuck! That's my girl! *Fuck!*"

My grandparents and sisters came into the family room, and soon we were all jumping around the Christmas tree like kangaroos and screaming, except for Nonno, who sat in his chair happily watching.

When Mom regained her breath after yelling herself hoarse, she turned to me, a glimmer in her eyes. "We should celebrate! Nonni and I will whip something up. Come on, invite Liv over!"

I felt the tiniest deflation in my stomach.

"I think she's . . . busy tonight," I said.

Mom shrugged and turned to Nonni, pulling her into the kitchen and happily shouting something about letting me try my "first sip of wine." I looked down at my phone again. Liv and I hadn't texted since we got off the bus.

I knew logically that I'd have to tell her soon that I got in. But tonight, just tonight, I wasn't going to worry about it.

I shut off my phone and picked up Willow, spinning her around until we both felt sick.

April has put up a tiny Christmas tree in her office. It makes me feel even more depressed, which is hard to do these days.

We've gone through our usual routine—check-ins, questions, mantra—and now we're silent. In the past month or so, we've continued to talk about Liv, but I've also started telling her about other things: Mom's intensity, Willow's clinginess, Nonno's silent worry. Saige's various micro-dramas about boys and grades and JV lacrosse. I still come to our appointments with protective walls built up around me, but she usually gets me talking within the first five minutes. In fact, she's pretty much the only person I talk to these days.

But today, I'm tapping my foot, waiting for time to move faster.

"That caroling gig sounds terrible," April says. "Was there really a taxidermized bear in the foyer?"

"Yeah. The Clarksdale Country Club was bougie as hell," I say, looking at the clock.

"Well, I'm glad not to be a member," April replies.

Then we sit in an uncomfortable silence again.

"Rory," April says.

"Yeah?"

"You're a little tense today."

I refrain from biting the insides of my cheeks.

"Really?"

"Really." She fixes me with a very intense stare. "Is there anything I should know about? Any . . . triggers? About the accident, or Liv?"

*I just have to write and then present a speech about my dead best friend at our old high school on her first-ever missed birthday in front a hundred people.*

"Not really," I say.

"The holidays can be hard, especially the first ones without her. And it sounds like you and Liv had a lot of fun last year."

I think of that Mariah Carey song about missing her boy toy at Christmas.

"It wasn't exactly fun," I tell her. "We had a million caroling gigs, and she was really put out about Blackwell. She got into a fight with her parents about it. They said they weren't mad that she didn't get in, but she thought they were. She slept at my house for, like, three days. Including her birthday." I swallow.

"Are you going to do anything on her birthday this year?" April says. "It's next week, isn't it?"

I clear my throat. "I'll probably, like . . . light a candle or something."

"Okay."

More silence.

"Rory," April says again, leaning forward and fixing me with an intense, no-nonsense stare. I hate it when she does that. "We've talked a lot about Liv, and I think that by revisiting these memories, you've made some great progress. But there's something else we haven't talked about, and I really think we need to."

"Is it my sexuality again?" I ask. "I told you, I'm

really not feeling anything—"

"No, not that," April says. "It's the pills. The Xanax you took back in August."

I stare at my hands.

"That's partly why we're here, after all," April continues. "Your mom signed you up for therapy right after your stay in the hospital."

I puff out my breath.

"How long had you been taking your mom's Xanax before then?"

The small bit of warmth and comfort I've started to feel around April has evaporated. It feels like our first appointment, when she drilled me.

"My mom gave me half of one before I went back to school last March," I say tonelessly. "I wasn't sleeping. Like, at all."

"And it helped you?"

"Yeah."

"So, how frequently did you take it after that?"

"I . . . well, the sleeping got better after a while, but whenever I had a rough night, she'd let me take half."

"Okay. Did you ever take a whole one?"

"Yeah," I say. "But she called her doctor to ask if I could first."

I'm perpetually annoyed with Mom, but I don't want to throw her under the bus. She did ask her doctor, and her doctor said yes. But he also recommended that I come in to get an evaluation, and I refused.

"So, if you'd been taking half a tablet, sometimes a whole . . ." April says, "why did you take three on that one day in August?"

"It . . . I . . ."

She stares at me. My throat closes.

A million years go by.

And to be honest, I'm so tired. It's December, and Liv's birthday is next week, and I've been trying to write this speech. Trying to keep getting out of bed in the mornings, trying to smile in front of Saige and Willow and my grandparents, trying to pretend that I'm not disappearing slowly, fading into nothing.

"I know you by now, Rory," April says softly, maternally, and it makes me freeze up harder. "I know this feels impossible. Let me see if I can help, okay?" She opens a drawer and pulls out two coloring books and a pack of markers. She slides one of the books over to me, then sits down cross-legged on the floor and opens her own book to an unfinished page. She looks back up at me.

And the colors and sounds around me have been fading for a long time now, and I'm too tired. So I give up and grab a marker.

"That day in the summer . . . Mom was driving me home from physical therapy," I say finally, the truth sliding off my tongue. "And while we were going down Evergreen Lane, someone texted her. Her phone went off. And . . . she checked it."

I shove the purple marker hard into the flower petals spread across my page.

"She checked her phone while driving?" April says.

I stay quiet.

"The person who hit you on the Worst Night was texting behind the wheel," she says.

I switch to green, to color in the leaves.

"What happened, Rory?" April asks.

I take a deep breath. "Mom started to veer left, and I couldn't control it. I felt this jolt in my chest and I freaked out, screaming at her. And it caused her to jerk the car back, hard. And I . . ." I swallow. "I went back."

"You remembered the Worst Night?"

"No," I say. "I was *in* the Worst Night."

We're quiet, quiet, quiet, and snow is swirling around my brain.

"Hon, can you tell me about the Worst Night?"

"No," I say.

She raises her eyebrows.

"It's not that I won't," I tell her. "I can't." I take another big breath, but it doesn't help. "After the pills, I kind of . . . forgot again."

I'm positive she's going to test me. She's going to tell me that I can't just *forget* what happened on the Worst Night. That brains don't work that way.

But she surprises me again: she keeps coloring and says, "Okay." And underneath the snow swirling around in my brain, I'm grateful for her. I wish I could give her more.

* * *

Back at home, I try to motivate myself to work on the speech for Liv. The list of accomplishments from Eleanor is still crumpled up in my jeans. Thinking I might as well blast some Bowie and get it done, I put on my headphones and go into Mom's room to use the laptop.

It takes some fishing around on Mom's overflowing desk to find her old MacBook. Bowie is screaming about rebels in my ears. I open the laptop and power it up, but because it's so old, it takes about a million years to reach the home screen. Tapping my feet, I flick my eyes around Mom's tornado of a room, from her pile of blankets on the bed to the stacks of old bio textbooks in the corner to the cracked drawer underneath the desk. Peeking out of the drawer is an envelope with a familiar picture in the corner: a yellow-and-black lion. It takes my brain a few moments until I realize why I recognize this: it's the Ridgewood College mascot.

I tug on the envelope, pulling it out until I see the front.

It's addressed to me.

Without a second thought, I tug it completely out of the cracked drawer, turn it around, and see it's already been opened. The letter is from last July. I take off my headphones to read.

Dear Rory,

My name is Aisha Smith, and I work in the Ridgewood College Admissions Office. We recently received your spring transcript from Telsey College Preparatory and were surprised to see a significant decline in your grades during the second semester of your senior year. As you may already be aware, like many other colleges and universities, we cannot allow the entrance of students who perform poorly in their last year of high school after receiving admission decisions.

However, we were subsequently informed by Telsey's counseling office that you were involved in a life-threatening car accident in January, causing you to miss several weeks of school to undergo medical treatment. I wanted to personally offer my deep sympathies for what must have been a difficult experience.

Because of the nature of your academic decline, we will not consider your spring-semester grades at Telsey as due cause for the withdrawal of your admission at

Ridgewood College, nor will your Presidential Merit Scholarship be rescinded, on the condition that you maintain a qualifying grade point average while at the College.

We look forward to seeing you on campus this autumn, and again, welcome to Ridgewood.

Regards,

Aisha M. Smith

I stare down at the letter. *It can't be real*, I think, repeatedly.

I hear a *ding* and look at the laptop screen, which has finally loaded. Heart pounding, I go to Gmail and log into Mom's account. My lips press together as I type in her password: *RorySaigeWillow<3*. I remember sitting with her as she set it up years ago, groaning about how she needed a capital letter *and* a lowercase letter *and* a number *and* a symbol. We laughed about it together.

In the search bar, I type Aisha's name, and a single email thread pops up. I click on the latest message, dated August 24th, almost four months ago.

*From:* aishasmith@rc.edu
*To:* eve.quinn@gmail.com
*Re:* my daughter rory

Hi, Ms. Quinn,

Thank you for filling us in about the state of Rory's well-being. We understand your concern, as well as Rory's, and at your request we will withdraw her from the College. Health takes priority over academics, and we are glad Rory decided to postpone the start of her college career to focus on wellness. Please inform her that she is welcome to reapply for next school year, and that I will personally review her application and place it under special consideration.

I wish the best for you and Rory during this difficult time.

Sincerely,
Aisha M. Smith

*No*, says my brain blankly.
Yes.
*She didn't.*
She did.

Four months ago, right after the Xanax Incident, Mom told me that she'd gotten an email from Ridgewood saying that my scholarship had been taken away and that I couldn't go. She said, *I'm sorry, Ror. I know you were so excited. I'm just as disappointed as you are.*

But it was all a lie. Ridgewood sent *me* a letter, saying that I *could* still go to the school. That my scholarship was safe. And it was Mom who hid it from me, Mom who emailed them and said that I'd decided not to go. That *I'd* decided to take a gap year and stay in this miserable town.

*I'm so stupid*, I think. *I should have asked to see that email.*

But who would need proof of that type of thing? Who would have any reason *not* to believe their own mother?

At that moment—at that *very* moment—the door slams shut downstairs, and I hear busy footsteps in the hall. My family's voices float into Mom's room, where the door is wide open. I hear Mom saying something to Willow as she climbs up the stairs. At the sound of her voice, my blood boils. I sit there, waiting.

She walks into her room and throws her briefcase on the bed before noticing me, then presses her hand to her heart.

"Jesus," she says. "You scared me to death."

I just stare at her.

"What are you doing?" she asks, unbuttoning her tattered green coat. "What's that you're holding?"

I stomp up to her and thrust the letter in her face. She looks at it for less than a second before her eyes dart over to the computer screen and she sees the open email. She looks back at me then, and I meet her eyes for the first time in months.

My voice comes out in a bleat. "How . . . how *could* you?"

She could sigh and apologize, and it wouldn't affect me. She could completely defend herself, and I wouldn't care. But what she does somehow makes me even angrier: she takes the letter, walks past me casually, puts it back in the cracked drawer, closes the computer, and then shrugs off her coat.

She *ignores* me.

"Really?" I shout, as she busies herself with unpacking her briefcase. She won't look at or acknowledge me, and my insides are shaking with rage.

I walk right up to her face and say, "I hate you."

She throws some papers down on her bed. "You can do that," she says. "You can hate me." She starts sorting her papers. I hate that I know exactly what she's doing: sorting quizzes and homework into class periods, and then into alphabetical order. And then she'll warm up a bagel downstairs and start at the top of the class list for first period, then go all the way down until she's at ninth.

I hate that she's doing this right now. I hate that she's not hurt by what I said.

"I could have *gone to college!*" I shout.

"You still can," she says, refusing to raise her voice. "Next year."

"That's not the point! You had *no* right to do this behind my back! They said I could still go, and without asking me, you emailed this Aisha person and told her to *withdraw* me?" I've never yelled this much in my life, and it takes me by surprise when my lungs run out of air. I take another deep breath before spilling out, "You straight up *lied* to them! You told them *I* wanted to withdraw, but you never even asked me! How could you do this to me?"

She throws her briefcase down to the floor, so hard that I flinch.

"How could *I* do this to *you?*" she says, jabbing a finger into her chest and then at me. She runs her hands through her hair. "How could you do this to *me*, Rory?"

"Do what?"

"Those *bloody* pills!" she shouts.

"I didn't mean for that to happen," I say, grinding my teeth harder. "I told you it was an *accident.*"

"Let me tell you about that accident, all right?" she says loudly, drowning out my voice. "I'm sitting in the family room, and Willow runs up to me, snot gushing down her face, so hysterical she can't talk, and pulls me up to your room, where you're—" She runs her hand through her hair again, closing her eyes. I think she's going to cry, but when she takes a deep breath, her voice is loud. "You're lying there in your own fucking *sick*!"

My brain feels like it's being pressed from all sides. Lying in my own vomit? It was only three pills. I thought I'd just gone into a deep sleep.

And . . . Willow?

*The clinginess*, I think, burning up with shame. *The way she follows me everywhere. The way she always tries to hold my hand. Like I'll disappear if she lets go.*

"You told me Saige found me," I say, my voice shaking.

"I BLOODY LIED, DIDN'T I?" Mom yells. "Rory, you don't understand what we're dealing with—"

"Oh right, all the shit I've dragged the family through this year?" I say, regaining strength, trying to file the Willow information far away in the corner of my brain. "My bad that you had to pay for all that physical therapy. My *fucking* bad that I was hit by someone who was *texting while driving*, just like *you* do!"

She covers her face with her hands. "It's a habit I've quit. I put my phone on airplane mode now—"

"I don't care," I say loudly. "You're avoiding the topic. You literally lied to a *college* to make me stay home. You never even wanted me to go in the first place. You thought Ridgewood was pretentious and I should just stay in the Midwest so you wouldn't have to pay so much, and—"

"Oh, cut the self-pitying, Rory, you know it wasn't that."

"Really? Because you never gave a shit about what I wanted until I started getting interested in Ridgewood. Until it seemed like I might actually *not* follow your footsteps and live a pathetic, miserable life, never trying to make it any better. You *never* wanted me to go to that school, and the accident was just an excuse for you to pull me out. Now you just want me to stay here and stew in the past like you do. And you want me to never move on, like you never moved on from Dad."

It's like I've slapped her. Mom blinks slowly, taking a step back, the color draining from her face. "Be quiet," she whispers.

"*NO*," I bellow. "I *hate* you. I hate the way I fucking idolized you for *years* and you never even smiled at me, you never asked shit about my life unless it had to do with money, school, or those old bands. Do you realize you haven't asked Saige, Willow, or me about anything else in years? Do you know how much I used to *crave* attention from you? How much Willow still does? I'm not one of your bumfuck hippie mates from your past life that was so much better when you had Dad instead of us."

Her mouth moves; she might have just said my name. But I'm still going, the words still spilling out of me like water from a busted fire hydrant, and it's like I've fully left my body, like I'm just listening to my own yelling. I can't stop.

"Dad's *dead*. He's been dead for fifteen years, Mom. Those times are over. You know who's been here for fifteen years? Us. Your fucking kids who fucking needed you. And still, you didn't give a shit about *my* life until I started wanting more. Until I wanted to leave your toxic nest."

Mom just stares at me with her mouth open, unable to speak. For the first time in my life, she's unable to come up with some sarcastic, witty remark. To brush it off with ease.

Unable to stand the silence, I keep going. "You know, Liv's mom was always obsessed with her hobbies and her interests and *her* life," I say, my volume finally lower. "And guess what? She knows more about me than you do. She *cares* about me more than you do."

Mom finally flinches, and her senses seem to come back to her. I know I've finally gone too far. She walks toward me and shoves her finger in my face. "*Enough*," she seethes through clenched teeth. "My turn."

"Get out of my—"

"*No*." She grabs my wrist, and it's not hard enough to hurt, but the shock of her grip makes me fall silent. "I listened to you. Now you'll listen to me."

She takes a breath. "I may not be the perfect mother," she says in a trembling voice. "I may have let you and the girls down. I may even have to go see a shrink about it, myself." And then she whispers, keeping her eyes on mine: "But *parents. Do not. Bury. Their children.*"

She lets go, and I fall back.

"The car accident and the pills. That's two times I almost had to bury you," Mom says, and her voice catches. "I've buried my parents, and I've buried my husband. But I will *not* bury you."

She looks down, and then at the wall, and then she turns around and lets out a hoarse sob as she sits down on the bed. Underneath the boiling anger in my chest, I feel a weird clench of panic: Seeing my mom cry has always made me feel sick. Moms aren't supposed to cry. Moms are supposed to listen to you holler at them, and they're supposed to holler back. They're not supposed to *cry*.

"D'you know that I sat there with her at the hospital?" she asks suddenly in a very broken voice. "Eleanor. The perfect mum."

Ice floods through my body.

"We didn't know, for the longest time. We'd just heard that you and Liv had been in a crash. Her husband was on a business trip, so it was just the two of us, sitting there for hours, waiting. We were in our pajamas. She had her big, fluffy robe on under her jacket. Her hair was standing on end. I remember it. We were holding hands. I can still *feel* her hand in mine." She swallows. "I can still hear the footsteps in that hallway. I can see the two nurses heading toward us. One for each of us. I don't even remember how I felt. I just remember *her* stiffening next to me, squeezing my arm."

My whole body is shaking. My knees are knocking together. I don't want her to keep going, she *can't* keep going, because otherwise, I'll go back again. And so will she. I try to communicate this with my eyes: *Stop. Please stop.*

"They started to take us into separate rooms, and that was when I knew. One of us was going to have to bury her child." She muffles another sob and says, "I just followed my nurse, praying to every god and saint above that it would be Eleanor, and not me."

Mom closes her eyes and clasps her hands under her nose, like she's praying right now, but I know she's not. She's trying to keep it together, and she can't.

"The thought that you might be gone," she says, and that's all she can manage.

I stand there for a long time, the voice in my brain urging me to *say something. Say, "I'm not gone. I'm right here." At least touch her arm.*

I know so distinctly that I should, but I physically can't. I can't touch her. I can't even look at her.

I run back to my room, aiming to cocoon myself under the covers. But at the last minute, I grab my keys and barrel out the door.

I need another mom.

*three weeks before*

*T*he day after I found out I got into Ridgewood, at precisely 11:11 p.m., I turned onto Liv's street in my family's minivan. Just like she'd instructed, I pulled in a few houses down and turned off the engine and the headlights.

*Here*, I texted.

Nothing.

*Still coming?*

Nothing. The car was getting steadily colder. I could see my breath.

*Did you fall asleep? Cause I'm freezing*

The three dots appeared, showing that Liv was typing.

*My mom caught me leaving*, she said.

I tensed. *Fuck*.

A few more minutes of nothing. I started blowing on my fingers, wishing I'd worn gloves. She'd texted me in the middle of the night asking me to come get her, so I'd simply thrown my winter coat over my pajamas and jumped in the car, thinking I'd be there and back before my extremities caught on that it was below freezing.

I finally texted, *Should I just go back home?*

When thirty more seconds passed without Liv's bubbles, I turned on the engine. It wasn't until I was clutching the gear shift, preparing to reverse, that I saw it: the rectangle of light from Liv's house, and her small silhouette against it. She shut the door and started walking toward me, hugging her huge burgundy coat to her sides. I turned off the engine again and, not really knowing what I was doing or why, got out of the car.

I stood there, rooted in the snow, and watched her tiny shape grow larger, until she was feet away. Her street, like all of Clarksdale, was quiet and dimly lit. I couldn't see her face, just her silhouette.

I said, "I'm sorry."

"Come on, Roo. Stop saying that."

I cleared my throat.

She took a step closer. "I'm really proud of you," she said. "You deserve this. Don't apologize for something you worked hard for."

"I'm not sorry I got the scholarship," I said. "I'm sorry that—"

"It's fine." She stomped her feet a little in the snow. "Shit's been tense between me and my parents forever. Not getting into Blackwell was just the tipping point."

"Did they try to stop you from leaving?" I asked.

Liv shrugged. "Not very hard."

I stepped closer and hugged her. She tensed, keeping her arms folded. But after a moment, she rested her chin on my shoulder.

"Come on," I said, resisting the urge to hold on forever, pulling her back toward the van. "I have warm spaghetti."

"God, Roo." She tugged on the passenger door. "Stop trying to turn me on."

\* \* \*

It wasn't until we were in my kitchen, jackets peeled

off to the floor, unceremoniously ravaging my cabinets, that I saw the change. I don't know how to describe it.

Liv was just . . . less.

She pulled out two plates, talking to me about something unimportant, and suddenly I saw the way the ceiling light cast shadows on her cheeks, how they seemed hollowed out. She sat at the counter, running a hand through her hair, and I looked at her eyes. Wingless and bare.

I'd seen her without makeup before, but it wasn't that. It was something inside.

"What?" she asked.

"Wh—huh?" I flipped my bangs out of my eyes and pulled open the fridge.

"You were just staring at me like I grew another head."

"My bad," I said. "Tired."

I spooned leftover spaghetti onto two plates and took them to the microwave.

"I get it," Liv said. "I'm not wearing makeup and I look like the cast of the *Walking Dead*. Move on."

I turned to defend myself, then I saw that she was smiling. It didn't reach her eyes, but it was something. Better than nothing.

"Hey, can we go Christmas shopping tomorrow?" I said, turning back to the microwave.

"My parents are probably gonna make me come home tomorrow morning," she said, yawning. "They're pretty sick of my drama."

"Well, good thing I'm not."

"I'm a lucky bitch, aren't I?" she said in a fake sweet voice.

\* \* \*

Twenty-four hours later, I was on her dark street again, and she was climbing back into the car.

"I'm fine, and I don't want to talk about it," she said briskly, buckling up.

"Okay," I said. "Are you sure?"

"Yes."

"Positive?"

"Yep."

"*Positive?*"

"I'm gonna kill you."

"Okay. Well, the good news is Nonni made fettuccini."

Liv sighed, leaning against the headrest. "Can we just drive for a bit?"

Without speaking, I handed her the aux cord and started up the engine.

"Can you do something really big for me that you're not going to like?" she asked.

"Of course," I said quietly. "Anything, dude. You know that."

"Can we just fucking blast heavy metal right now?"

I leaned my head on the wheel.

"I need this," she said.

"I know," I said, sitting up again. "Okay. Fifteen minutes of heavy metal."

"I love you, Roo," Liv said, cuffing my shoulder as an ungodly sound exploded through the speakers.

* * *

At 11:59 p.m., I pulled over and turned down the volume.

"You said fifteen minutes!" Liv protested.

I pointed to the clock.

"What?" she said, and I watched the wheels turn in her head. "Oh. Can we just not make this a thing, right now? Please?"

12:00.

"HAPPY BIRTHDAY!" I shouted, throwing my arms in the air.

"Jesus Christ," Liv muttered, pressing a hand to her ear.

"You're an adult, Liv!" I said, pounding the wheel. "You're eighteen! You're an actual, fucking adult!"

"I think you need to be sexually active to be a *fucking* adult, but okay."

"Don't downplay this," I said. "I'm ordering you to celebrate yourself. Come on, Liv." I reached into my coat.

"Oh god," she said. "Don't give me a present. Please. I didn't do shit for your birthday."

I brushed her off. "It was in January before we became friends. You can do something for the next one. It's in a few weeks."

"But—"

"Look, this is really small."

She looked at me helplessly until she saw how small it really was, and then she relaxed. It was a sticker saying *Fuck this!* ☺ in sparkly letters.

She burst out laughing.

"Tell me it's not perfect," I said.

She kept laughing, turning toward the window. Trying not to let me see her wipe her eyes.

I wanted to hug her forever.

Instead, I busied myself with the car, turning the heat higher and adjusting the mirrors.

"I know it doesn't need to be a big thing," Liv said

eventually. "But, just, like. I wish I wasn't fighting with my parents on my birthday."

Her voice cracked, and she leaned farther into the window.

"I know," I said. I put my hand on her elbow, holding my breath. She didn't pull away, but she didn't move toward me, either. I thought of the night we made up from our fight, when she played ukulele on my bed and we held each other, laughing and then crying and then laughing again. I longed for that. I longed to take her back to my house, bundle us both in blankets, and never leave again.

"It's fine," Liv said.

"It's okay if it's not fine."

"It is."

"Okay," I said. "But I know they'll call you. It'll get better."

She sat back up and rubbed her face. "Can we just keep driving?"

\* \* \*

We didn't talk for a while, until finally I convinced her to let me play the Christmas music station. Liv spiritedly hated on most of the songs, making fun of me for enjoying them, but we both sang along to every single one anyway.

"Wait—Philippa's about to come on!" I said.

"Whomst?" Liv said. "The *fuck*? Is named *Philippa*."

"The radio show host!" I said. "She takes people's calls during Christmastime and gives them a song—listen—"

"—and who may I ask is calling?" came the singsongy, sugary voice of Philippa.

"Hi, I'm Katie?" said a woman from the phone line. "And I'd just like to, like, give a shout-out to my boyfriend?"

"Rory, no," Liv said.

I shushed her.

"Young love," Philippa cooed on the radio. "And what a perfect time of the year to be with the ones you love! Bless you, Katie. Let me see . . . ah, I have the perfect song for you!"

"Like, thanks!"

"I've Got My Love to Keep Me Warm" came on.

"This fucking song," Liv said. "If we have to sing this in choir again, I'll—why are you pulling over?"

I shifted into park and then whipped out my phone, typed in a number, and put it on speaker.

"*What are you doing*," Liv said in a low voice.

"Hello?" said a man's voice from my phone.

"Hi," I said. "Is this the right number for Philippa?"

"Yes, this is the caller queue."

"How long do I have to wait to go on the air?" I asked, as Liv frantically shook her head at me. I gave her a thumbs-up and then blocked her attempt to swipe my phone.

"It's pretty late, so you're up next."

"Sick."

We sat there, and Liv put her face in her hands. "You fuck," she whispered, shaking her head. "I swear to God."

"You love me," I whispered back.

As soon as Katie's song ended, Philippa's voice spoke through my phone.

"Hello?" she asked. It echoed through the radio.

"Uh . . . hi," I said, and I heard the shaky, awkward

sliver of my voice blare out of the car speakers. Liv dissolved in silent laughter as she took out her phone to film me.

"Who am I speaking to on this lovely night?" Philippa said.

"Rory," I said.

"Well, good evening, Rory."

"Good evening. I—I just wanted to, well, it's . . ." I couldn't focus, hearing my voice echo through the radio. "It's my friend Liv's birthday."

"Wonderful! Happy birthday to your friend!"

"Thanks. She's a huge fan of you," I said, at which point Liv had to bury her face in her coat to stay quiet. "So I, like, um, just wanted to play . . . her favorite holiday song."

"Well, I would love to, Rory," Philippa said sweetly. "Friendship is so important, especially around the holidays. You girls are lucky to have each other."

"Um, yeah," I said.

"What's her favorite holiday song?"

I cleared my throat. "'Merry Christmas, Happy Holidays' by NSYNC."

Liv yelled into her coat.

"A family favorite!" Philippa said. "Well, I hope you and Liv have a wonderful holiday, and we're wishing Liv a very happy birthday and a successful, thriving year ahead."

"Thanks," I squeaked, and hung up.

The opening notes to NSYNC's holiday jam filled the car, and we keeled over, howling.

"Shut *uuuuuuuup*," Liv said, but I pretended not to hear her, roaring along with Justin Timberlake.

"You know this part, come on!"

"I hate you," she said, and then she shouted the rest of the lyrics with me. We threw ourselves around in our seats, clapping hysterically to the beat. When the song finished, we were both winded.

"Literally the best song of all time," I panted.

"Everything good happened before 2005," Liv said. "Like: me, you, this song."

"Tea," I said.

"*And that's the tea!*" Liv trilled.

I doubled over laughing. Suddenly, she leaned over and hugged me.

"I love that weird-as-fuck hyena laugh, Roo," she said into my coat.

My chest swelled, but before I could extract an arm out to hug her back, she let go.

"This is the worst, but can we go home?" she said. "I'm dead."

"Only if we get to listen to Philippa's station for the rest of the ride."

"I *hate* you."

We pulled back onto the road, Liv rebuckling her seat belt.

"I love your weird-as-fuck laugh, too," I said, as the Beach Boys' Christmas song hit the radio. "Only yours is more like an elephant's."

"*Thank* you," she simpered. "You're making me feel really attractive and datable tonight."

"Always my goal," I said, as we plowed down the road for one of the very last times.

*eleven months after*

*F*or some reason, I pick up fifty dollars' worth of groceries before I get to Eleanor and Ramil's house.

Standing on the front step, laden with bags of food that they don't need, I'm still breathing heavily from my fight with Mom. I can't stop thinking about what I said, how cruel it was. How her face paled and crumpled, how she looked like she was struggling to breathe. I've never seen her dissolve like that, and now I'm trying desperately to push it out of my mind. To help, I look around, remembering the first time I ever met Liv's parents.

For the first few months of our friendship, Liv had made sure we avoided Eleanor and Ramil. I'd been to her house secretly, late at night and early in the morning, while they slept soundly or made breakfast and listened to NPR. They sounded fine in those moments, when they were downstairs, unaware that Liv and I were silently laughing and simultaneously suffering through massive hangovers in her bedroom. While lying on the floor, willing my migraine to dissipate, I'd listen to Ramil's calm voice below the hum of the espresso machine, and Eleanor's cheerful responses. I'd catch snippets of their conversations: a coworker is having a baby next month; the Syrian Refugee Crisis; he would make chicken adobo tomorrow night. They talked about Liv—filling each other in about her classes, the next choir or cello concert, the foods she no longer liked.

I had pointed out to Liv that her parents sounded nice enough through the floorboards. She'd retorted, "They're obnoxious."

"Really?" I'd asked, doubtfully.

And she'd come up with a multitude of reasons: They were bougie. They stayed in their comfort zone. They listened to NPR and sighed about the news, but they didn't *do* anything about it, because they didn't have to. They knew Liv's every class, every grade. They wanted her to grow up "well-rounded," so they made her do cello and soccer and all these other activities.

"And the worst part," Liv had said, smoke spiraling from her mouth, "is that they just shamelessly assimilate to all the other Clarksdale parents. They actively *try* to be like everyone else."

So, that day when I waited with Liv on her doorstep (she'd forgotten her house key), I was extremely aware that I was about to meet the supposedly bougie, fake Eleanor and Ramil. And I was *anxious*. Liv stood next to me, impatient.

"Whatever they say," she whispered in my ear, "don't take it to heart."

*Shit*, I thought. *They must be really cold.*

The door swung open then, and there they were: Liv's parents, the very first time I saw them.

They were both small, like Liv. Liv's resemblance to Ramil struck me immediately, especially when he smiled, placing an arm around Eleanor's waist. He had Liv's bone structure, her dark eyes and brows, and her warm brown skin tones. Eleanor was everything Ramil was not: her hair, which fell just below her shoulders, was blond, her eyes were wide and green, and her smile was completely different from Liv's. But something in her—I couldn't put my finger on what—was exactly the same.

Before I could register their warm expressions, Liv spoke. "Sorry I forgot my keys," she said distantly, pulling me in behind her, trying to push past her parents.

"Wait," Eleanor said, and then she took my hand. "Rory! We've heard so many wonderful things about you. It's so good to finally meet you." She squeezed my hand before letting go. "I'm Eleanor."

"Nice to meet you," I said in a weird, breathy voice. Ramil swooped in to shake next, smiling.

"How was your day, honey?" Eleanor asked Liv as Liv kicked off her boots.

"It was eh," Liv responded.

"What's 'eh'? Bad?"

"No. I mean, just . . . eh."

"Was school okay?"

"*Mom.* Can we not, right now?"

"I'm just asking," Eleanor said with a hint of annoyance. "Do you ladies need anything before dinner?"

I followed Liv's example of removing my shoes and hanging my coat, which suddenly felt very grungy, on a hook near the door.

"Cheese and crackers?" Eleanor persisted. "Pop?"

"Mom, it's *soda*," Liv said. "We're fine. We're going upstairs."

"Tell us if you need anything," Ramil called after us.

Liv didn't answer. I looked behind my shoulder and smiled briefly, then followed Liv up.

\* \* \*

Now I'm standing on the front step again—but it's no longer *Liv's* front step, it's *their* front step. I've gotten used to coming to this house in the past few months to help clean up Liv's room, but this time feels worse, scarier. I still don't really know why I'm here.

Before I can think anything more of it, Eleanor swings the door open. She's wearing business clothes— probably working from home, like she often does now— and I see myself through her eyes: the messy best friend, the one who was spared. And fifty dollars' worth of unasked-for groceries, as if that could somehow make up for it.

"Rory!" she says in surprise.

"Sorry," I respond. *Damn it. Another dollar.*

She shakes her head and tries to smile. Eleanor didn't have room to shrink, but after the Worst Night, she did anyway. She's smaller and smaller every time I see her. Her blond hair hangs limply, her face pale as ever.

She steps back and helps me with my coat, not asking why I'm here. "Just me today," she says instead. "I only had one call. The firm's been going pretty easy on me." She helps me unravel my scarf. "Sorry the house is such a mess; we're closing in two weeks."

Together, we look around what used to be the front of Liv's house. The walls are bare and lined with boxes. Cleaning supplies are everywhere. But I notice they've left the dining room still intact, because the table and chairs are still—like they have been for eleven months— lined with condolence gifts. People must *still* be sending flowers, because the Martinezes have more than they have vases for. There are flowers stuck in random cups and bowls from the kitchen, more laid on plates and in newspapers; there's even a small bouquet of lilies stuffed into an old sippy cup, one with teeth marks at its edge. And the cards: boxes of cards. Rows of them, like I've stepped into the inner room of the post office. Trays upon trays, with odd labels sticking out. And pictures, pictures everywhere. Some of Liv. Some drawn by children. Some collages made by teenagers, who must not have known what to do with their hands. A poster from their church. A poster from Ramil's family in the Philippines. A banner from Telsey.

For a moment, I cannot interact or function. I just hang there, the life sucked out of me long ago, no feelings, no thoughts, nothing.

But across from me, I see that Eleanor has already taken that role: nothing. Nothing inside.

And so, before I know what's happening, my spine straightens.

"It's not a mess," I say, and my face cracks as it shifts position, as my cheeks and eyebrows lift for the first time in so long, and I take a step forward. "Do you want me to show you what I brought?"

Eleanor looks at me, her eyebrows slightly raised, her mouth turning upward: the faintest shadow of a smile.

"I mean, there are, like, six different types of pasta in here alone," I say, and she laughs a little, or at least makes a sound with her throat. "Let me bring it into the kitchen and you'll see. Do you have room in your fridge? If not, no worries, we can just eat it all right now."

I make Eleanor laugh ten times during the first hour, and every time I do, my chest turns over and expands, like it's been underwater and is coming up for air before another trip deep down. I tell her all the funny stories I had with Liv—cutting my bangs, racing to the train, tandem biking—and while I talk, I help her cook. We make enough pasta to feed a small country, bathing it in so much cheese that even Nonni would freak. With every minute we cook, every story I tell, she moves faster—or at least less in slow motion.

"Oh, that's awesome," she laughs, sprinkling salt into the boiling water, after I tell her about the time Liv forced me to watch three hours of *The Bachelorette* because it was her "guilty pleasure" and then yelled at the TV the entire time. Eleanor wipes her hands on the dish towel and wraps an arm around my shoulders, giving me a quick squeeze. "I don't know how you tolerated that. You're such a good friend."

She lets go just as easily and keeps cooking, but I'm stuck for a moment. I realize, with shock, that I haven't been *hugged* in so long. My skin feels cold where she let go, and I get the wild urge to ask her if she can put her arm around me again, if I can just rest my head on her shoulder for a bit.

*I want a mom hug*, I think, and my eyes prickle.

But then I shake it off. *This isn't about you.*

"And did I tell you that we called Philippa?" I say, swallowing, pretending nothing happened.

"What? Philippa from—"

"The Christmas radio," I tell her. "We called in. Or—well, I did."

Eleanor laughs again. "Oh god, don't tell me it was a prank call."

"No, it wasn't! It was Liv's birthday, and I was genuinely trying to make her feel better."

Immediately, *immediately*, I wish I could swallow

back those words.

The edges of Eleanor's mouth slide down and she starts to shrink more, losing color. She crosses her arms tightly around herself and looks away.

"I'm sorry," I say breathlessly. "I just meant . . . she wasn't . . ."

She shakes her head and mouths that it's okay. I want to disappear.

"That week," she whispers. "Her birthday. I—I . . ."

"Don't worry," I say meekly.

She kneels to the ground in the middle of the kitchen, breathing deeply.

*Help me*, I beg Liv. *Help me.*

I kneel next to her, but I don't know what to do next. I try to get her to stand up, but she won't. So I sit there, at a loss, with my hand on her shoulder.

"I'm sorry," she chokes.

"Don't apologize," I tell her.

"I just . . ." She crosses her hands over her chest. "Oh, god. I feel so horrible about how . . . how it was that week. With Liv. We fought so much, and it was so. *Fucking. Stupid.*"

The shock of Liv's mom saying "fuck" eclipses the shock of her collapsing in the middle of the kitchen. I nod and awkwardly rub her back.

"I never meant . . . I think Liv thought I . . . she thought Ramil and I needed her to be perfect. And . . . I know we were pretty intense. We signed her up for all this crap growing up, and we pushed her to take those APs and apply to those schools. But we did it because Liv was so . . . *much*. She was so bright and expressive and energetic, and so *smart*. I mean, it scared us how smart she was. She had to be busy, ever since she was a kid. Otherwise, she'd just . . . I don't know. She couldn't stand being bored."

She sniffs and wipes her nose on the sleeve of her blazer. I've always seen Liv's mom as the exact opposite of mine: Neat and clean. Calm and professional. Polite. Now she's sitting on the floor in her work clothes, make-up smeared.

*Parents should not have to bury their children.*

"In high school," Eleanor continues, "she . . . she just *changed.* So moody all the time, and she never communicated. She never wanted help with anything, she was so independent. I tried so hard to understand her, but she was stubborn. She wouldn't talk. And we stopped asking." She closes her eyes. "And when she didn't get into Blackwell, she was so angry, and she came in just . . . yelling. At us. For pushing her, for wanting her to be perfect. She said . . ." Eleanor shakes her head, squeezing her eyes shut. "It doesn't matter what was said. We were all angry, all three of us, and it had been building up for so long. We fought that whole weekend. Two nights in a row she stormed out, and she went to you. And it was only after she left that second night that I realized . . ." She folds in half, arms around her stomach. "I realized the next day was her birthday."

I can tell that she can't breathe.

I can tell that an avalanche is coming, and it's not mine.

"Try to take a deep breath," I say, as gently as I can.

I want to tell her that it's okay. That Liv was fine. That she was being dramatic that week, that it was nothing. But I remember Liv curled up against the window, trying to hide her emotions from me, trying to be strong. I remember her voice—tiny—when I was used to it filling the space around me: *I wish I wasn't fight-ing with my parents on my birthday.* I remember how small she looked in the dark, and how angry I'd felt *for* her.

I don't want to lie. But Liv's mom is crying, gasping for air.

"I . . ." I say. "She . . ."

She squeezes my hand so tight that it hurts.

"She was okay," I tell her. "Liv. She was fine. We just . . . we kept losing track of time. Because we were celebrating her birthday."

Eleanor breathes a little easier, still in the fetal po-sition.

"We had a lot of fun," I tell her, continuing to rub her back. "We danced to stupid bands. Like NSYNC."

She chokes. The good old cry-laugh. "NSYNC? That was *my* favorite band. Like, in the nineties."

I nod eagerly, although this is news to me. "She knew all the words to the song."

Eleanor clasps her hands under her chin, closing her eyes and giving the smallest smile.

"I'm sorry we didn't call you," I tell her.

"It doesn't matter," she says. "Just . . . was she okay? Not just that night, but . . . all the time she spent with you. Toward the end." She lifts her head again and looks at me with Liv's face. It's the shape of her eyes, I realize. That's what they share.

"Was my baby okay?" Eleanor whispers.

Liv's eyes, with their fireworks of green.

It's too much.

I just nod.

*liv's celebration of life*
*eleven-and-a-half months after*

*H*ow does it feel to walk into Telsey for the first time since I ruined Liv's locker?

How does it feel to walk through the halls, a year after she last stepped foot in them?

How does it feel to step into the atrium and see a two-foot portrait of her—her senior yearbook photo, the one that she never saw, because it didn't even get developed until After? To look at her too-big brown eyes with their sparkles of green, and her twisted, close-lipped smile, the smile that says, *I am thinking so many intriguing thoughts right now, and I simply can't be bothered to tell you any of them*—to look at her, and squeeze the paper in my pocket, knowing what I'm about to do?

I can't say how any of it feels. I can't feel anything. Not today.

\* \* \*

It's snowing outside, and our town is in full Christmas mode again. Inside the Telsey atrium, there are eight small trees, glimmering with Clarksdale-themed ornaments, each one topped with an angel. I remember switching classes with Liv this time last year, her begrudging comments about how *Not everyone here is Christian* and *This is so fucking WASPy* and *All these angels are white.*

Each tree is centered on a table. Last year, those tables were full of flyers for sports teams and bake sales and tutors. But tonight, the flyers are gone. Instead, there are pictures of Liv, two on each side of each tree, all encased in the same golden frames.

For some reason, the uniformity of it, the organization, is what gives me tremors deep in my stomach.

People are everywhere, moving around in fuzzy blobs, and I haven't really noticed their faces yet, but with a sudden rush, I see so many of them: Mr. Wong, Liv's English teacher, her elderly neighbors. Jem's parents. The school librarians.

And kids. Kids from Telsey. Kids from our *group.* I see them all at once: GraceDevonJemNatsuki Stoff. *Milo.*

They're all crowded around one table, looking at the pictures. Devon's arm is around Grace's waist, and she's giggling but also wiping her eyes, while Jem points at a gold-framed photo and talks. Natsuki's standing with Stoff and Karim, who I met on Black Friday; their fingers are interlaced. And Milo is there, a little behind the group, hands in his pockets.

His eyes swivel to mine, and I feel knives in my chest. I haven't seen him since before the Worst Night.

For a moment, everything freezes, and I just hear my heart beating. My eyes are open, but I don't see Milo. I see Liv, curled up on the bathroom floor so many months ago. I hear Milo's voice, lined with confidence and laughter: *Dude, I know, it hit her hard.* I feel Liv's shoulders rise and fall under my hand; I see her face crumple with embarrassment and fear.

I shake my head at Milo now, ever so slightly.

He opens his mouth, and I shake my head harder.

But then Natsuki notices me, and she strides toward me, and Devon, Jem, and Grace follow, and Stoff and Karim are behind them. I'm engulfed in arms.

"I'm so glad you're here, Ror," Natsuki says in my ear.

"How're you doing?" asks Devon. "Holding up okay?"

"Ugh, Rory," Grace says, leaning her head on my shoulder. "Just you *being* here is bringing me comfort."

They let go but still encircle me. I don't know why this is the first time I notice, but every one of them is taller than me. My hands are cold.

"This is weird," Grace says, her eyebrows knitting together.

"Yeah," Jem agrees. "This whole week I've been looking forward to it, 'cause it's Liv's celebration, and, like . . ."

"Yeah, like it felt like we would . . . *see* her," Natsuki says. "I know that sounds stupid."

"You miss her," Karim says. "It's not stupid. It's—"

Stoff squeezes his hand and looks at him, and Karim nods slightly and stops talking.

They're all looking at me expectantly, so I clear my throat. With every ounce of strength I have, I produce words. The words are both audible and English, and I mentally send a little prayer of gratitude for that, because it's more than what I feel capable of right now.

"Hey, yeah," I say awkwardly. "What are you guys up to?"

"Oh," Natsuki says. "The usual. Winter break."

"Yeah, break."

"Just flew in this morning."

"Right," I say, holding my arms tightly around my stomach. "How's . . . how's school?"

They don't know who I'm talking to, and neither do I, and there's a little confused laugh when they all start talking at once. And then, for the next few minutes, I hear about everything: the best bars in Ann Arbor (Natsuki) and whatever "Fighting Illini" means (Grace) and weird roommates (Jem) and hockey (Devon) and another praise of econ (Stoff). They all talk fast and with very few words, as though the less time they take up, the less obvious it'll be that they know I'm *not* in college. That I *haven't* moved on.

That I haven't moved, at all.

"So, yeah," someone finally says, and then we're quiet again.

The current Telsey carolers—kids from the year below us, who are now seniors—are singing mellow songs in the corner. They're dressed in pristine black suits and dresses, swaying their heads, raising their eyebrows. I wonder which ones just got into their top schools, and which ones didn't. I wonder which ones, if any, think of Liv as more than "the girl who died."

"So, how've you been?" Natsuki asks, bringing me back. They all look at me hopefully. And our friends—they look, like, *so* good. Why haven't I noticed until now how beautiful everyone is? Grace with her long eyelashes and wavy blond bob, and Jem with his smooth dark skin and light brown eyes. I look at the choir again and realize that they are all beautiful, too. Clear skin stretching into grins, white teeth flashing, delicate hands folded behind their music.

Telsey is full of symmetry. Full of perfection.

Full of straight lines and tight spaces.

Everything Liv was not.

Before I can answer Natsuki with some bullshit that's flowing numbly through my mind—*Oh, you know, I'm doing all right, getting a lot of support*—I feel a warm hand on my elbow. I turn around to see Eleanor.

"Rory," she whispers. "Thank you *so* much. Is your mom here?"

"Oh, uh, she's at a conference. But she sends her love," I mumble. I hadn't wanted to tell Mom about this event, but Eleanor had asked me to invite her, so I awkwardly did—without mentioning the speech, of course—the day after our huge blowout. I'd already known she had the conference, so I'd known she wouldn't be here, but as she furrowed her brow in confusion ("Why didn't you tell me about this before?"), I was filled with fear. I didn't know if I was afraid that she'd cancel the conference to come, or if I was afraid that she *wouldn't*.

She didn't.

A crease appears between Eleanor's brows, and she wraps her arms around me. I can barely talk because she's hugging me too tight. I feel her breath constrict, and I know she's trying not to cry, so I attempt to hug her back. Over Eleanor's shoulder, I can see the rest of their faces: Jem and Devon are looking down respectfully, and Natsuki's eyes have filled with tears. When Eleanor lets me go, it seems like the whole circle of people holds their breath at once.

"Do you know what Rory's doing for us?" Eleanor says in a shaky voice, turning to them. Ramil comes up in his dark suit and places a hand on her shoulder.

"Mrs. Martinez?" Natsuki squeaks.

"Oh, call me Eleanor," she says. She tightens her

arm around my shoulders, and the tremors spread from my stomach all the way down to my ankles. "Rory's giving a speech. A birthday speech, for Liv."

Their faces freeze and then, one by one, break into smiles.

"That's so sweet, Rory," Natsuki says.

"She would," Devon says, nodding.

"Yeah," Jem says, and he looks directly at me. "Heart of gold."

Eleanor simpers and hugs each of them, thanking them for coming, and I feel myself backing away. I bump into someone, but I don't know if I have the strength to turn and apologize.

The person takes my shoulder gently and mutters an apology, and I turn. It's Milo.

And I need to disappear but can't.

"Rory," he says.

"I—"

"Look, Rory, I'm really sorry about what happened last fall," he says quickly. He's cut his bun off and shaved his scruff. He's wearing a suit. (*Why are they all wearing suits? This is a celebration. Not a funeral.*) Milo takes a breath and keeps going. "I just—I literally think about it every day. I'll never forgive myself for— for betraying her trust. It was a fucking shitty, asinine thing for me to do, and I'm not expecting you to forgive me. I just—wanted to tell you that I'm sorry."

He presses his hands against his eyes.

I feel my mouth and hands twitching, but I don't know what they want to do. Hug him? Strangle him?

I don't know. My mind is blank.

"She loved you, dude," Milo says to me, from behind the palms of his hands. "She did."

I know he wants me to say, *She loved you, too.*

I don't say it, and somehow, Stoff and Karim appear beside me. Stoff doesn't know about Milo and the edibles, unless he does, because he knows everything. I don't know. I don't care. He takes my arm and leads me away.

We stand in a corner, and Stoff doesn't ask me how I'm doing.

He asks, "What can I do for you? Just, right now?"

I look at my feet.

Stoff's questions end in periods: "Do you need to sit down. Have you eaten. Are you hydrated."

I say, "Water would be good."

He looks at Karim and says, "Water." Karim nods and walks away. Stoff and I don't talk while he's gone, and I focus on a tiny crack in the wall.

It's the best thing anyone has done for me all night.

* * *

The moment comes quickly, which doesn't surprise me, because as far as I know, time has stopped functioning. There are no more clocks. One minute, everyone's hugging, talking about Liv, and eating on plastic plates, which Liv would hate because they're bad for the environment. Then Eleanor is at the microphone, welcoming us to Liv's nineteenth birthday celebration. Crying. Telling a story. Laughing.

The choir sings. A cellist plays. Then Eleanor's at the mic again.

And, suddenly, so am I.

"As many of you know," Eleanor says, holding my elbow lightly, "Rory Quinn-Morelli was Liv's best friend. She was . . . well, she was like family to our girl.

Like a sister." She looks down, and then looks at me. She smiles, and I can see through it to the twisted pain in her chest, a cataclysm. I think about Mom, the other day, speaking to me through her fingers: *We were both in our pajamas. She had her big, fluffy robe on under her jacket.*

I squeeze Eleanor's hand below the podium, and she squeezes it back.

Her eyes say, *I love you.*

*I love you, even though if this had to happen, I'd rather it have been you.*

I nod, taking out the crumpled paper from my pocket. Liv's mom hands me the mic and steps away.

I just stand there and look at everyone else looking at me.

"Um," I say, and my voice reverberates through the mic. "Hi."

A few of them chuckle and say, *Hi.*

"I'm Rory," I say. "Um, well, you already know that."

More polite laughs.

I make eye contact with people: Eleanor and Ramil. Jem. Stoff. Mr. Wong.

Liv, smiling crookedly at me from her senior portrait, larger than life.

I take a deep breath.

"Eleanor very kindly asked me to write a speech about Liv for her nineteenth birthday. And first of all, I want to echo her and say thanks, everyone, for coming. Liv would be happy to know she's being celebrated. I mean, she loved a party. I can feel her squeezing my arm and whispering, like, '*Look* at this shit, Roo.' I mean—" The mic squeaks out some feedback as I catch the disapproving frown of Principal Vance and a few other teachers. "My bad. I wasn't supposed to swear. Um . . . okay. Well, anyway. She would be happy to see you all here.

"Anyway, Liv was a lot of things. Right? I mean, she had so little time on earth. But somehow, she was everything. All at once. All the time." I'm improvising here, before I dive in.

I look into her eyes again. Big, brown, with fireworks of green.

I say, without moving my mouth or making a sound: *I'm sorry.*

I take a breath, my stomach plummeting to the ground, and look down at what I've typed out. *This is for your parents*, I tell her. *Not you.*

"From fifth grade onward, Liv got straight As in every class. In sixth grade, she was the only one in her class to get one hundred percent on her research magazine, which she wrote on the topic of women in World War Two. That same year, she played the title role in Clarksdale Junior High's production of *Annie* and started volunteering at a soup kitchen with her church on Saturdays. In seventh and eighth grade, she continued her years-long hobbies of playing the cello and piano, as well as taking up guitar and ukulele, and joining the school's JV soccer program. By age twelve, she was taking high school–level math, and by the end of eighth grade, she'd won six cello competitions, a service award at church, and the Clarksdale Youth Leadership Award for being captain of the soccer team.

"During her first year at Telsey College Prep, Liv was one of only four freshmen to maintain a 4.0 GPA for all four quarters. She balanced honors classes with playing in the symphonic orchestra, volunteering, and singing in the Telsey Choir. During her sophomore year, Liv traveled to New Orleans with her church to help rebuild a house damaged by a hurricane, an experience that she then wrote about for her sophomore portfolio, which got submitted by her teacher to the National High School Writing Competition and subsequently won second place in the country. During junior year, Liv committed tireless hours to her five AP-level classes, competed in two more cello competitions, and was soon hearing from colleges across the country, practically begging her to apply. At the end of her junior year, Liv was recognized by the dean of student affairs at Telsey for her impressive academic achievement. By the middle of senior year, Liv had been accepted into Carleton, Swarthmore, Wellesley, and Vassar, but, in a humble move, she decided to keep these college acceptances to herself." I take a deep breath, daring myself not to look up. "In fact, I didn't know any of this until Eleanor told me last month. Liv was posthumously accepted to five more schools that she applied to, including Amherst, Macalester, and Smith.

"But even more important than Liv's measurable achievements was her shining joy."

Another deep breath. *Don't look at her eyes.*

"Liv exploded with happiness and a zest for life that went unparalleled among her peers. She had the ability to turn anything into a positive situation. She seemed to possess endless joy and patience, never once losing her temper or letting the pressures of school and life get to her. She took everything by force, head-on, and never doubted herself."

My stomach is twisting so hard. I catch Eleanor out of the corner of my eye, nodding quietly, and I genuinely hope she feels some relief. I hope she thinks that this is true, instead of just partly true. Because Liv *did* explode with joy and zest, sometimes. She *was* confident, sometimes. But we're ignoring an entire part of her.

"Liv loved so much," I continue, willing my voice not to shake. "She loved her friends. She wanted to be with as many people as possible, all the time—she never got tired or frustrated. She was always the life of the party. She loved our school. This place, where we're standing."

*Lol*, I think humorlessly.

"She loved our town."

*Lol again.*

"And she loved her parents, who she trusted and respected." This one, at least, I know is true. Because as many times as Liv fought with Eleanor, as many times as she tried to pull away, I know what it's like to be an eighteen-year-old girl with a mom. And I know that, just as much as I'd cease to *exist* without Mom . . . Liv would be nowhere, completely lost, without Eleanor.

I will the tiny lump in my throat to go down. *Don't think about Mom.*

I hear Eleanor choke back a sob, and although I know I shouldn't, I finally look up. I gaze into the sea of faces, most of them beautiful but crumpled, and let my heart pound louder in my ears. Looking at them, it almost feels okay that we're ignoring this huge part of Liv: the part that obsessed over grades and couldn't turn off her thoughts and tried, so very hard, to not show that she was scared. Tried to be fierce, cold, powerful, when sometimes all she felt was the opposite, and all she wanted was to curl up and have her back scratched.

Yes, it almost feels okay to ignore this part of her. She would understand.

But I really shouldn't say what I have written next.

"She . . . Liv . . ."

*Don't. Don't say it.*

"Liv didn't have to try."

Pounding heart, shivers down my spine.

I swallow. "She was just . . . perfect. Liv was perfect."

Except that the core beauty of Liv, the part that makes me miss her with every fiber of my being, is that she *wasn't* perfect. And all I want to do, really, is show the world that instead. I want to tell her, *It's okay that you aren't perfect.*

*I love you because you aren't perfect.*

*I'm sorry,* I tell her instead. *I'm sorry. I'm sorry. I'm sorry.*

*I*t was weird, showing up at Natsuki's house alone. Not carpooling with Liv for the first time. She'd texted me that she was getting dinner with her mom, who'd drop her off after. I'd said okay and begged Mom to let me take the van anyway, which, after some grumbling, she did.

"Be back by midnight," she'd said as I opened the door, but she and I both knew that she didn't mean it. It was almost the second semester of senior year. She fixed me with a pointed look that said, *Do whatever you want. Just don't be a complete dumbass.*

I grinned and buckled in.

When I got to the party, Natsuki swung open the door and hugged me. "I *missed* you!"

"It's been four days," I said, laughing, as I threw off my coat.

"Yeah, did I see you on New Year's?" Natsuki said, linking her arm in mine and leading me downstairs.

"I held your hair, remember?"

She laughed. "I'm kidding, I know you were there. But I completely blacked out."

"Same," I lied. Liv and I had taken a shot each and were the only ones without our heads in the garbage by the end of the night.

"Fuck New Year's," she'd muttered to me, pulling me

upstairs to listen to music.

Tonight, everyone was in Natsuki's basement, passing drinks around, laughing, nodding their heads to the music. I felt my usual wave of social anxiety—even now, after a year of knowing all these people, my stomach still shrank into a tiny knot at parties—and Grace made her way over and squeezed my hand briefly.

"Your soul mate's over there, FYI," she said, pointing to the couch before leaving to get a drink.

Liv was sitting, hugging her knees, talking to Jem. I walked up to them, feeling the fist in my stomach relax slightly. Her eyes flicked to me, and she reached her arm out and squeezed my hand before turning back to Jem to keep talking. I took her hand and then fell on top of her, just to be annoying.

"But yeah," Liv grunted to Jem, nudging me away. "The album can't come out soon enough. I need those tunes, like, *now*."

"Whomst are we talking about?" I asked, settling in beside her.

"Maggie Rogers," Jem said.

"*Oh* yeah," I said. "Maggie's our queen."

"I can tell," Jem said, cracking a smile. "Beer, Rory?"

"Can I just do a ginger ale?"

"For sure," Jem said, scooting off the couch.

Liv turned to me, and I saw the change again. Her cheeks were even hollower, and although she'd painted her wings of eyeliner, even those looked thin and deflated.

"How was your day?" I asked.

She shrugged and looked away.

"Liv?"

"It was fine."

Jem sat back down with a beer for himself and a ginger ale for me, and started talking about another album.

The interaction was nothing, meaningless.

But the whole time, her shoulders were falling and rising, higher and higher.

*liv's celebration of life*
*eleven-and-a-half months after*

When my speech is over, the applause sounds muffled. Someone walks me down from the podium. The noises around me blend together, but I think there's music, dim chatter, and sniffles.

I look at Liv's portrait again, not really knowing what I'm searching for. Some sort of comfort. Something to laugh about, only with her. But when I meet her eyes, mine blur. I feel a swirl of warmth between my ears and a frog in my throat.

*No*, I think blindly. *Not here. Not now.*
*Stay cold.*

I look around for the exit, but without warning, I'm suddenly buried in Eleanor's arms again. Ramil wraps his arms around both of us, and I stay, locked in their embrace. They tell me it was perfect. They say, *Thank you*. They say, *I love you*. They wrap me up in warmth and black fabric, and everything is even more muffled. I breathe in the scent of Eleanor's shoulder. Perfume and tears. I breathe in, and out, in and out. *I should cry, too*, I think. *I should just cry. It's okay to cry.* Eleanor rubs my back, and my throat is about to burst, but I close my eyes tight and swallow it down.

Liv's parents are crying, so I can't. I don't know why. They loosen their grip on me, and Eleanor holds me at arm's length. I try to smile.

"Are you okay, honey?" she says.

"Yes," I answer, my voice coming out high and weirdly enthusiastic.

Someone else takes Eleanor's arm gently to give her a hug, and I try to inch away.

"Are you sure you're okay?" Ramil asks me, eyebrows folding in concern. He looks exactly like Liv. I imagine her looking at me the same way, all the times I said nothing, and she still read me like a book.

"Yeah," I gulp. "Just need some air."

I walk to a clearing near one of the tiny Christmas trees and try to gather my breath. When I look down at the pictures, I see us in Grace's pool. Us at Dreamtown. Liv and me, somewhere, just the two of us. A frozen Snapchat that someone stole.

Heat continues to flood through me. I swallow again, so many times.

People are coming up and congratulating me on the speech. Praising me for my courage. Telling me they would never be strong enough to do what I did. Somehow, I respond. When they tell me I must have been a great friend, I thank them and say that Liv was, too. When they ask me how I'm coping, I respond that I'm doing what Liv would want me to, and trying to enjoy every second. The whole time, my voice is climbing higher, but no one seems to notice.

Then I step backward onto someone's foot and almost fall, and they catch me. The someone is Jem. He is the only one who doesn't talk or smile.

He holds my elbow and looks down at me with those light brown eyes. His eyebrows are raised.

Because he heard the speech, and he knows every

single word of it was fake. He knows that she did those things, maybe all of them—but that none of it matters. None of it was *Liv*.

I look up at Jem, and our entire friendship passes across my eyes like a newsreel: the bands we bonded over on the Metra, the way his lips tasted salty on mine. The way, as soon as I said no, he never tried again, never acted weird or embarrassed or hurt. I think of Jem against Milo: the way Milo looked at Liv like she was something he wanted to consume, the territorial way he'd always have a hand on her shoulder or pull her onto his lap. The way Milo didn't listen, after all, and he didn't know her.

But Jem knows me. Jem never stopped sending me silly notes and pictures after the Worst Night. Never too much, just enough to make sure I knew that he was here. That he'd be here, no matter what.

And seeing his face now, something happens to me: I start to white out. It's strange, because my body is still working fine; it's not like I'm about to faint and need to sit down. But everything around me is white, except Jem.

And then I'm back in Natsuki's basement, Six Hours Before.

Jem asks me, *What's wrong with Liv?*

I respond, *What do you mean?*

And he says, *She was talking to me on the couch, and then she just . . . ran upstairs.*

The choir starts again, so loud, and the lights are so bright.

I take Jem's hand and pull him, quietly, to the door.

"Rory," he says, as I tug him through, and the sounds disappear behind us.

I don't answer; I just lead him to the nearest exit.

"Rory," he says again. "Why are you doing this?"

*Why are you doing this? Why did you fake it instead of shoving your middle fingers in the air like she would? Why did you survive in the first place, if you were just going to live a fake, bullshit life like everyone else?*

We're outside, and it's snowing hard.

"Where's your car?" I ask him.

"Um, I'm just down the road." He points. I follow his finger to the black Volvo that he shares with his mom, and I pull him toward it.

Me, Six Hours Before: *What do you mean, she ran upstairs?*

Jem: *I mean, she was in the middle of a sentence, and she kept fumbling over her words, kind of breathing heavily. And then, without a warning, she just got up and ran. Rory, I swear I didn't do anything. We were just talking about music. I don't know what happened.*

We sit in the car, and Jem turns on the engine and blasts the heat. He grabs a snow brush and starts to open his door again, but I pull it closed.

"I need to be able to see, Ror. We're buried," he says quietly.

"I want to be buried," I whisper back.

He pauses, then takes his hand away from the door. We sit.

And then he hands me the aux cord, asking silently

what I want.

"Anything," I say.

"Anything?" he responds. "I mean, there's so much new shit. Are you in the mood for, like . . . Mitski? Phoebe? Maggie?" He's babbling. "Give me a hint."

"Surprise me," I say.

Jem scrolls through his phone. "Here. I know you like this one."

Before I can stop him, I feel the quiet words engulf me:

It's Joni Mitchell. "A Case of You."

Next to me, Jem blows on his hands and leans back, getting comfortable.

I want to say something kind, at least thank him. But it doesn't come out. Instead, I blurt, "Can we kiss again?"

He blinks at me, shocked. "Do you . . . I mean, do you *want* to?"

I imagine standing on my knees, pulling his face toward me, and pressing my lips to his. I imagine him surprised at first, but he quickly relaxes, snaking his hands around my waist and pulling me closer. Feeling his tongue pushing against my teeth. I imagine feeling what I need, what I've needed all night:

Numbness.

Spreading down my legs and arms, a large dose of nothing, like novocaine, or anesthesia, or whatever they use to make the pain go away.

I want to feel numb. But do I want to *kiss* him?

Did Liv want to kiss any of those boys before Milo?

And what does *Jem* want? This human next to me, who also has feelings? Who also has a heart pounding underneath his winter coat?

"I don't know what I want." The words don't feel like they came from me.

Jem nods, putting his hand on my arm. "Maybe we could just hug?"

I should answer, but I can't speak anymore, so I just give a paltry nod. He wraps me into a bear hug, and Joni Mitchell sings to us, and the notes fill my chest.

*So bitter.*

I think of the last time I heard this song, the way Liv smiled, eyes closed, as she strummed her ukulele.

*So sweet.*

And then, with absolutely no warning, I feel at the very core of my numb body the beginnings of an avalanche.

*Stop*, I want to say. *I can't breathe.* But it's not that he's hugging me too tight, because he isn't.

Something is different about this avalanche: softer, limper, like it's at half-capacity. It's growing and falling, but not in my stomach, or in my chest. It's in my throat. Behind my eyes. Stuck, physically, inside my head.

My hands are on his chest now, pushing away. I try to say something.

"You good?" he says.

"Please," I gasp.

"Please what?"

I mumble, "Please stop."

He immediately lets go.

"I can't breathe," I say, pushing into the back of my seat. "I—can't—I can't—"

"Hey, you're okay," Jem says.

Foreign sounds are tumbling out of my mouth now: coughs and gasps and strangled moans, like someone is holding my neck with one hand and pulling at my larynx with the other, and everything blurs, and I feel a rush of heat on my cheeks.

"I need to get out," I somehow tell Jem.

"I'll drive you home."

*No*, I say without sound, as he pulls on his jacket and turns on the ignition. *No. You misunderstood.*

I need to get *out*.

\* \* \*

Ten minutes later, I wait at my front door until Jem's taillights have disappeared around the corner. Then I step back into the snow. I start walking away from my house.

In the woods near Evergreen Lane, where they don't plow, the snow reaches my ankles. It soaks through my shoes and socks, and it drips down a crease in my jacket, causing my shoulders to shiver violently. I move through darkness, my face stiffening with cold. With leftover tears. With all the feeling that I can't hold down for much longer.

I don't stop walking until I reach the bank of Evergreen Pond, frozen over. There are no stars. Everything is black. So I take a deep breath and—

I am up, and I am up, and I am away.

*five hours before*

*L*iv is sitting on her knees, alone, in the middle of Natsuki's bedroom floor. She's clutching at her neck, telling me she can't breathe. I am sitting on my knees facing her.

*What happened?* I ask. *Did Jem say something to trigger you?*

She shakes her head.

*Who did what?* I press. *Tell me, Liv.*

I pry her fingers away and hold both of her frozen hands in mine, pressing them tightly.

*Nothing happened,* she says. *I just—can't—*

She closes her eyes, and pain is written all over her face.

*Breathe,* I whisper. *Breathe.*

Her shoulders rise sharply, fall, rise again.

*I-can't-get-out-of-my-head,* she says, the words tumbling out in one breath.

I nod, squeezing her hands.

*Rory,* she says. *I don't . . . I don't want to go to college yet.*

I stare at her blankly.

*But . . . you'll get to leave,* I finally say.

*I know.* She looks at me, eyes shining. *But I'm . . . it's like I'm frozen. It's so hard sometimes.* Her big, shaky breath.

*Liv, you just have to get out of here, and it'll get better.*

*I'm scared of going*, she says, not listening to me. *I want to, but I'm scared, Roo. Sometimes I think about the boys at the pond, and Milo, and the drugs, and I can't even move. What if it happens again? What if it happens, and you're not there?*

Our friends pulse and dance one floor below us, and Liv squeezes her eyes shut, her hands tense in mine, and keeps talking: *I try to control everything, but I can't, and that terrifies me.*

*It's okay*, I say.

*No. It's not*, she says.

*Okay, it's not*, I say.

Liv holds her breath.

I tell her, *Just be here with me.*

Her face pinches, her eyes shut tight. Her hands in mine are shaking, hard. I want to do something, but I don't know what she needs, and I'm scared.

*Can I hug you?* I ask finally, and she nods.

So I pull her into my arms, and I hold her against my chest.

When I was little, I dropped Nonni's favorite vase, and it didn't shatter: it broke, neatly, into six or seven pieces. I ran with them to the basement, digging until I found Mom's hot glue gun. I glued the pieces together and then held them, waiting for them to dry. They shook with my hands. I was afraid to let go, so I stayed, my hands holding the broken pieces in place.

We're leaning against Natsuki's bed now, and Liv's panic attack is easing, but it still feels like she's broken into pieces.

I hold and wait, hold and wait.

Her breathing starts to slow again as I rub her back, her body curled into mine. Her face against my neck. We breathe together; we don't talk. When she lifts her head, her makeup is smeared, and her eyes are tired. My chest feels tender.

*I'll be okay,* she says, managing a tiny smile. *I just . . . I don't want to go to college without you.* Her voice is small.

I want to say one thousand things in return, but I stay quiet. I take her hand in mine and bring it up between us, squeezing her fingers.

She looks at me for a long time, and says nothing, but I hear everything.

So, finally, finally, I put a hand on her cheek. She closes her eyes. She's calm now, breathing deep, but her heart is pounding.

And I know this, I *know* her heart is pounding, because she takes my hand and slides it down to her neck.

My mind races.

*Does she know?*

She takes a deep breath, and she presses her own hand against my heart. And when she feels it pounding, her mouth twists into the tiniest smile.

*She knows.*

She exhales quietly, slowly, and leans her forehead against mine. Her neck is so warm under my palm. I close my eyes, because electricity is humming under my skin, a flash of lightning that I've been pushing down for far too long, and maybe I shouldn't be, maybe I should just let it happen. Her heart is thumping, and so is mine, and maybe I should just go, follow the electricity, because—

But I think about her stories. The boys at the pond.

Harrison. Milo. Everyone who hurt her. Everyone who betrayed her. Who wasn't who she thought they were.

I *won't* be one of them.

So when she moves forward, just the tiniest amount, her breath tickling my nose, I don't lean into her. I don't take a breath and leap forward into what I've been craving for so long, even though every part of me wants to.

I take her hand away from my chest, squeeze it, and pull away.

And instead, I say, *Let's go dancing.*

She opens her eyes and surveys me. Golden brown and green, shining. A look I've never seen before . . . a question. Almost like she's surprised. She bites her lip, and I think she's going to cry, but then she starts to laugh.

I laugh, too, and she says, *We're hot messes.* I say, *You're my hot mess*, and she says, *Don't leave me.*

I tell her I won't.

We stand up and get our things. Then I drive us to Liv's, and we sneak up the stairs to her room.

*I fucking love this skirt*, she says, twirling around, and we're in the sixties, not some cold night in the present, and I watch as the light catches the sparkle in her eyes. *It's like a cave. I don't have to bring an actual bag, I can just keep all my shit in here.*

I watch as she fixes her makeup in the mirror one more time. Erasing the smudges. Erasing the last hour, or maybe the last week, or maybe the last four months.

She takes a tube of lipstick—wine red, her favorite—and stuffs it into another pocket. She grabs her gum and her coin purse. Then she looks up at me and grabs my arms, spinning me around, her eyes bright.

And it's as if the vase never broke at all.

\* \* \*

During her last hours on earth, Liv and I dance under blue lights at Dreamtown. We hold each other to Stevie Wonder and the Ponderosa Twins. I twirl her. She twirls me. Stars line the ceiling, and lights come and go, and she circles her arms around my waist, pulling me tight, and I press my cheek against hers.

I don't know if it's real: that I'm *this* in love with her. That she pressed her hand against my heart, felt it beating for her, and smiled.

It is real.

Maybe it isn't.

Maybe it doesn't matter.

\* \* \*

*You tired?* Liv asks, after we have danced and swayed and twirled and jumped for hours. She's sober still—we both are—but her cheeks are flushed, her face relaxed, eyes gleaming under the glow of Dreamtown.

*Yeah*, I say. *Yeah, I'm tired.*

She takes my arm the way she always does and leads me toward the door.

She says, *I'll drive.*

And I say, *Are you sure?*

And she says, *Yeah.*

*eleven-and-a-half months after*

*F*reezing wind scratches at my face. It was always colder by the pond.

I walk, and walk, and walk. The icy air fills my body from the bottom up, and I take off my coat. Snow is falling heavily now, and it bites at my neck. I am at the very edge of the pond.

But I'm still remembering.

I'm remembering so much.

I need to get colder.

So I close my eyes, and I step out onto the ice.

Almost immediately, a spiderweb of cracks fans around my boots in every direction. I shouldn't have worn my heavy boots, or maybe I should have, because if I hadn't pulled away from Liv that night, if I had just kissed her, instead of panicking and saying we should go dance, then maybe this wouldn't have happened. And if *I* hadn't let her drive after, if *she'd* been in the passenger seat instead of me, then *I* would've gotten hit harder, then *I* would've died, then this would've been *my* Celebration of Life and she would've been making a stupid, pointless speech for *my* mom.

I look up into the inky black sky instead of down at the jagged ice, and then I close my eyes. I imagine myself falling through into the freezing water, the way my boots would pull me to the bottom so easily. I imagine each of my muscles seizing, not standing a chance, and I imagine my entire body filling with ice. And she is at the other side, leaning toward me, a question on her face, and this time I'm *not* pulling away, and she's taking me by the waist, and we're rising up as my body falls. We're finally, fully entwined, and I'm finally pressing my lips against hers, and she's running her fingers through my hair and kissing me back the way she would have that night, because we're the only ones who matter, and they can't touch us, and they can't find us, and all that matters is us. Together.

I imagine these things so hard as my body shakes and the ice cracks further. I try, try, try to push reality away. But I'm remembering.

I'm remembering.

I remember

I remember


i don't remember *it happening* but i remember right before—

i remember the rumble of the engine and the heat blasting in my face and the snow like white flowers against the window and the feeling in my chest and the flash of her white teeth as she stared at the road ahead and laughed at whatever it was we laughed at—

lipstick like wine

hair piled up

six piercings in right ear

tattoos

brown eyes with green

big laugh

laugh made of bubbles, of velvet, of too much held in and not enough let go, of winter and summer and

all the in-betweens, of hiding, of lying, of singing, of
dancing, of screaming
    laugh
    *your hair is coming out roo*
    *it's fine*
    *i want food*
    *did you see*
    *i can't believe*
    *when we get home*
    *we should*
    *do you want*
    *okay we'll*
    laugh
    laugh
    laugh

and then, everything is just black.

My eyes are closed, and the ice is broken, and—
*liv, wait, i think i'm coming, too*
*i don't want to be here without you*
*there's no color*
*there's no sound*
*i'm sorry this happened*
*i'm sorry i never told you*
*i'm sorry i pulled away*
*sorry*
*sorry*
*sorry*

chapter thirty

Sorry?

A hand pressed against my heart.
   don't apologize for who you are, rory.
   don't ever. ever. ever.

## chapter thirty-two

*I* open my eyes to darkness.

My breath comes in loud, rattling heaves, and I feel my heart pounding against my throat. *Beat-beat-beat-beat. Beat. Beat. Beat.*

I'm too cold. I'm too cold, and my muscles are screaming.

*Beat. Beat. Beat.*

I turn around and throw myself back onto the bank, just as the ice breaks. My feet fall into the water, soaked, colder than they've ever been, but I'm army-crawling forward, and then I collapse back onto solid ground. I heave shattering breaths, covering my face and breathing into my palms. I try to blow on my fingers, but there's not enough breath.

I don't know if I can get up.

But I try, and I can.

I move to the edge of the woods, back to Evergreen Lane, shaking from head to toe. *Forty-nine fifty fifty-one fifty-two.* I'm counting my steps because that is the only way I can focus on my task: Go home. Go to warmth.

*Fifty-five fifty-six fifty-seven.*

Then there are headlights, and my frozen knees try to buckle but they can't, and light is everywhere, and tires screech just a few yards ahead of me, and snow flies in my face, and a scream sticks in my throat. Then, no longer stuck: flying away. I am screaming loud and long, everything inside my body unraveling, my lungs full of endless breath, breath that almost left me for good, three times, three whole times. Accident-Pills-Ice.

I'm screaming, screaming, screaming, as a smaller dark shape gets out of the bigger dark shape, and I realize it is a human coming out of a car, running toward me, and white is gathering at the edges of my eyes. My legs are crumbling. I am falling endlessly, but I don't hit the ground. In the end, I chose not to die, I *did*, but it's too late: I am dead.

But I am not dead.

I'm in Stoff's arms, and he's dragging me toward the car.

"I'm not okay," I keep saying, as he and Karim buckle me into the back seat. "I'm not okay. I'm not okay."

"Oh, queen, we know," Stoff says.

Somehow, he removes my wet sweater and boots and buries me in a blanket. Karim blows on his hands, mumbles, "Sorry if this is weird," and rubs them over my feet. Then he gets into the front seat.

"Get on the highway," Stoff says.

"I want to go home," I tell him, but my vision is white again.

"Hurry," Stoff tells Karim, and then it's quiet.

I come back for a bit. Stoff is massaging my feet now.

"Germs," I mumble.

"Bitch, you think I'm worried about germs right now?" he replies, his voice too high.

I close my eyes. "How did you find me?" I whisper.

"How did you—the pond—"

"We followed Jem's car," Stoff says. "I totally trust that boy, but you were acting *so* wack after that speech, and I just wanted to make sure you were okay—"

White again. So much white.

"Stoff," I whisper, later still.

"What?"

"Tell my mom."

"I did, she's coming back from her conference—we're almost at the ER—"

"No," I say. "Tell her she won't have to."

"Won't have to what?"

"Parents do not bury their children," I say. "Tell her that."

"Karim," he says. "*Faster.*"

I was born on January 8th, in the middle of a snowstorm. I have lived for six thousand, nine hundred and nineteen days. I've taken almost 150 million breaths. And my heart has beat almost 700 million times.

My heart almost stopped for the first time just after midnight on January 5th, three days before my eighteenth birthday. I was riding along in the passenger seat with my best friend, watching snow fly past the windows, listening to the perfect song, and a reckless driver sped through a red light and hit us.

My heart almost stopped for the second time on

August 16th, seven months later. My mom checked her phone while driving, and I remembered the Worst Night, and I learned that I had to face my pain. It was the middle of the day, but I wanted to sleep anyway, so I took three Xanax instead of one and fell onto my bedroom floor, where my eight-year-old sister found me.

My heart almost stopped for the third time on December 18th. Liv's first birthday After. I tried so hard, for so long, to run away from the Worst Night. But in the end, it caught up with me, and once the memories started coming, I couldn't make them stop. I thought of Liv, pushing her terror away with coldness, and I stepped out onto the ice of the frozen pond. I would say that I started to freeze, standing there on the spiderweb of white cracks, but I think I actually started a long time ago. The ice just kept doing its job.

I am eighteen years old, and already, three separate times, my heart has almost stopped.

And then pulled itself out of the thick, quiet darkness, for whatever reason, and kept on beating.

*T*he nurse calls Mom with one of the hospital phones, because mine died. When they pass it to me, my entire body tenses.

"Mommy?"

She exhales deeply. "Oh, Rory."

"I didn't . . ." I start, then swallow thickly. For the first time in years, I experience clearly that simple but petrifying fear of childhood: I Want My Mom, And She's Not Here. I try to bite down the frog in my throat, because there are doctors in this room, and I'm almost nineteen, and it would be stupid if I cried.

"I didn't want to *die*. I just . . ." And then I start to bawl.

"Rory, darling," Mom says, her voice crystal clear in my ear. The nurse moves around with her chart as though nothing at all is happening, as though globs of snot aren't sliding down my face and onto my hospital gown. "I know. I know."

"I w-want you to c-come home," I sob, my chest heaving underneath the scratchy heated blankets.

"I'm thirty minutes away. I'll be there before you know it."

"Okay."

"Okay. Shall I try to make you laugh now?"

"W-what?"

"I said, shall I try to make you laugh?"

I look down at the IV protruding from my wrist, the weighted blanket on my feet.

"It's not funny," I say through the mucus lining my throat.

"I know," she answers. "But this is what I can do *right* now, while I'm still pulled over to talk to you."

"Okay."

"Well, your dear old mum wore those Docs you've been stealing from me, thinking I'd be making a cool fashion statement, not knowing you'd worn a hole through the toe. Right as I was passing a bunch of administrators, I tripped and—"

"Mom," I say, through my blocked-up nose. "Mom, I love you."

I try to ignore the sound of her breath catching in her throat. "I love you, too, my sweet Rory."

We sit in silence for a few moments.

Then she says, "So anyway. I'm crashing to the ground . . ." And soon, I'm laughing, and a nurse finally can't stand it anymore and brings me an entire tissue box.

* * *

When I get released the next day, Mom drives me to April's office. We don't really talk much. When she puts the car in park, she kisses me on the forehead and brushes my hair out of my face, and I get out.

"I almost died again two nights ago," I tell April as she swings the door to her office open. I rush in, unraveling my scarf.

"H-hello," April manages, following me. "Rory. Wow. Okay. I wish you'd called. I have an appointment in—"

Concern folds into her face as she processes what I've said. "You what?"

Keeping my eyes on a Zen-ish painting above her head, I tell April everything in about thirty-five seconds: Liv's Celebration of Life, my speech, her parents, Jem, Stoff, the ice.

"I'm ready to talk about it now," I say. "I'm ready to talk about everything."

"Oh god," April says. "Rory, I—"

"I know you have another appointment, but I just wanted to tell you," I say robotically. "I didn't want to die, but I had to block it from coming back. So, yes, I took a self-injurious action by stepping out onto the ice."

"Okay," April says. "You know what? Sit down. This is an emergency. My next appointment is not. Let me just call . . ."

I rummage through my backpack like a squirrel while she's on the phone apologizing to her client. I need a fidget so badly, but I have none. My heart is racing in my throat. I have to tell her now, or else I will not tell her, and it'll slide down my throat again and settle into my stomach.

So, while April is still on the phone, I say, "Liv was my person."

April's eyebrows rise, and she nods. She brings up a finger as if to say "One moment" to me, and then changes it into a more supportive gesture that she invents midair, a kind of *Princess Diaries*-esque beckon.

I say, "I loved her."

"Yes," April says into the phone. "Wednesday. That's right."

I say, "I don't know what that means."

"Okay, thank you. Yes. Merry Christmas."

April hangs up as I start pulling a thread out of my sweater, watching it bunch around my elbow. She just looks at me for a moment, and then opens a drawer on her desk, drops a very squishy ball into my lap, and resumes her seat in front of me.

I sit down on the floor, leaning my chin on the coffee table between us.

She sits down on the floor, too, across from me.

"Rory," she says in her maternal, no-nonsense way. "I'm here."

"I know." I squeeze the stress ball and take a breath. "It was more than losing a friend."

She nods.

"I lost my person." I swallow. "I lost my reason for getting up in the morning."

She nods, slower.

"I can't deal with this by myself." For some reason, I'm nodding, too. I feel a tear trickling down, and I don't try to brush it away. "I need help. I'm so, *so* not okay."

She reaches across the table and lightly touches my arm. "Okay," she says. "Do you really, truly want to work on this?"

I nod harder, squeezing the stress ball.

April dips her chin. "Good. We're going to help you heal."

"We?"

She smiles and pats my hand. "Me and you, hon. You need both of us on your side to get through it."

* * *

Back at home, Saige and my grandparents skate around

me delicately while Mom takes charge of everything me-related, just like they did after the Worst Night and the Xanax Incident. Willow is the only one who acts normal, because we've decided not to tell her about the ice. I hate it, but Saige shuts me down immediately as we wash vegetables for Nonni in the kitchen.

"You're not telling her. Besides, she has her whatever thing tonight. Her choir show."

"Her what?"

"Her little holiday choir concert." She rolls her eyes at me. "The thing she's been talking about for two months?"

"Okay, well, I've been a bit busy," I reply, with a healthy amount of sisterly snark.

"Whatever," Saige says. "Just . . . please go to this concert, and leave those giant headphones at home and . . ." She gestures at me, my mismatched clothes and uneven bangs, seemingly lost for words for a moment. "Can you at least *try* to act normal?"

I feel guilt and anger rising in my chest, plus hunger, plus a weird urge to laugh, because I realize that I love Saige. It's confusing, having sisters.

"Being normal is overrated," I tell her, shrugging.

"Whatever," she says, going back to the zucchinis. "Willow's excited to sing tonight. And Mom and Nonni can't go, and I have practice, so you're going with Nonno."

"Wait, but—"

"You guys are leaving at five. Have fun!"

\* \* \*

It's snowing again, but it's not as cold as it was on Liv's birthday. Willow, Nonno, and I arrive early at the church where Willow's choir is supposed to meet. We sit at a small table among cheerful, chattering parents. A woman I vaguely recognize takes Nonno's arm and starts a conversation with him, and Willow immediately pulls out a book.

"You're not dressed very warmly," she says, her eyes skimming the page.

"Well, it's warm in here."

"We're singing outside, you know."

"What? *Why?*"

"It's the tree-lighting ceremony. *Duh.*"

I want to say, "Excuse me. Cut the attitude." Instead, I swallow three times and take a good look at my third-grade sister, with her big ears and old soul.

"Willow," I say, and she looks up from her book. It's suddenly very hard for me to speak. "Listen. I know I've been . . . bad, lately."

"Not just lately," she says.

"I know. It's not fair. You shouldn't have to be worried about me."

"I'm not," she says, but she's trying not to cry.

I drag my chair next to hers and pull her into a hug. She's stiff at first but then relaxes under my chin, squeezing a fistful of my sweater in her tiny hand.

"None of that is gonna happen again," I say into her hair. "I'm going to get better."

"How do you know?"

"Because I want to."

She pulls away. "You didn't want to get better before?"

I rub my nose. "I . . . I thought I wanted to. It's complicated."

Willow gives me a hard stare that, just for a moment, reminds me of Liv. The stare says, *Don't beat around the bush. I can handle it.*

But Willow is eight. And she's already had to handle so much.

I smile, reaching out my hand, and she looks down at it cynically. "This year, I'm gonna work really hard on feeling better," I tell her softly. "And I'm not going anywhere. Okay? I promise."

Willow looks up at me with her big eyes, and finally, she places her warm little hand in mine. Something passes between us, something very small, and she nods. When I let go and open my arms, she takes her book and plops onto my lap, continuing to read.

I tighten my arms around her and pretend to read over her shoulder, but the words of her chapter book are blurry. So instead, I close my eyes, and I think about my session with April yesterday. The mountain I seemingly climbed, cold and almost dizzy with pain, in that single fifty-minute session.

"Post-traumatic stress disorder," April said, calmly. "PTSD."

In many, many ways, I knew it already. The flashbacks, the avalanches, the sleepless nights; the way my stomach and chest seem to hollow out and cave in at the slightest trigger: the jerk of a car, yes, but also the specific, cunning look in Liv's eyes that I still see flashes of in Eleanor; a few single notes of Joni Mitchell or Maggie Rogers; the feel of a warm body pressed against mine. It all brings me back.

It brings me back, not just to the Worst Night, but to *her.*

And sometimes, I want it to.

I sobbed and wailed and resisted, yesterday, curled

up in a ball on the couch in April's office as she gently patted my back, but when I cried myself out—finally, *finally*, after almost a year—I lay there, exhausted, and started to understand: I have to start being *here*. I can't float through each day chasing the in-between space where I imagine her sitting, waiting for me. I can't refuse to see colors and hear sounds for the rest of my life because I'd rather tuck myself and Liv into a blanket of snow, just so I could see her firework eyes and hear her symphony laugh forever.

I can't refuse to live because she died.

When Liv was still here, we ran away from the hard things because we thought we had to. We put on a face. We said, *Don't fuck with us.*

But it's not sustainable, being that cold.

We could have learned that lesson together: That you have to feel things, sometimes. You have to struggle and cry and confront the bullshit in order to push through it. But now, I need to learn that lesson on my own.

"You *really* aren't going anywhere?" Willow asks suddenly, bringing me back.

I shake myself.

Being *here* starts now.

"I mean, eventually I'll go to college," I tell her, resting my chin on her shoulder. "But I have a lot of work to do before then. I won't leave until we're both ready."

She hesitates. "Do you promise?"

I nod and kiss her head. "Cross my heart. What are you reading?"

* * *

I navigate to the back of the crowd with my arm linked

through Nonno's. We climb the first few steps up to the church and then turn around to face the square. As we pass a few grandmothers Nonno vaguely knows, and they pull him over to talk, I'm surprised to see a familiar face.

"Stoff?"

He turns to me, the bored expression on his face shifting to a smile. "Um, hell*o?*"

"What are you doing here?"

He rolls his eyes. "My little cousin Margaret's in the children's choir." He's standing a few feet away from a group of grandparents, aunts, and uncles who share various things with him: his curved nose, his shock of dark hair.

"Same with Willow," I respond, checking on Nonno, who's now being fawned over by the grandmas.

"So . . . how're you feeling?" Stoff says. I hear a note of mild stress in his voice, and when I turn back to him, when I see the care in his eyes, it all comes to me at once: The way he found me, freezing. The way he massaged my feet on the way to the hospital.

I barrel into him, hugging him tightly around the waist.

"Thank you," I tell him, my voice muffled in his fashionable wool coat. There's so much more I want to say. *You saved my life. Not just at the pond, but all those months before, my very first week at Telsey. When I was completely lost, you saved me. You're beautiful. You deserve to be happy. I'm so glad you finally are.*

But as he tightens his arms around my shoulders, my throat glues together, and I'm too tired to even cry. I promise myself, and I silently promise him, that I'll tell him later. Maybe I'll even write it to him, so he'll never forget.

We have time, me and Stoff. We have time.

* * *

Standing there in the cold with Nonno and Stoff, I see everything: The swarming Clarksdale residents in their down coats and fleece hats. The children's choir making their way up to risers in front of the huge evergreen, their cheeks pink from the wind, frozen into excited, toothy smiles. Willow is in the second row, her ears poking out from underneath her hat. I point her out to Nonno.

"Big girl," he says proudly, squeezing my hand.

"Are you warm enough?" I ask. "*Sei caldo?*"

He shakes his head but smiles. "Rory," he says. "No more worry."

When the kids are finally in their riser spots, a round of applause starts at the beginning of the crowd and travels to the very back, where Nonno, Stoff, and I are standing. I didn't think to wonder who directed Willow's choir, but when Mr. Wong walks across the risers beaming, his cheeks flushed, I can't help but smile, too. He *would.*

My old choir teacher nods once to the crowd, turns sharply, and raises his arms to the kids. Their chests heave in a unison breath, and they start with a shaky "Angels We Have Heard on High."

It's really freaking cute. They sail into some less complicated renditions of the songs we sang last year in choir, and I clap with everyone and try to ignore my rumbling stomach and numb feet. When they finish "Sleigh Ride" and the evergreen behind them lights up, sending the audience into convulsions of applause, I let go of Nonno's arm and get my bag together. Mr. Wong turns around.

"Thank you, everyone!" he says. "We have just one more for you! It's been a tough year for some of us in the Clarksdale community, myself included, and we wanted to send you away with peace in your hearts."

*Jesus*, I can't help but think. I catch Stoff's eye and we share a mild eye roll. A moment of just, *Do we really have to?*

Mr. Wong turns around, raises his arms again. They sing "Silent Night."

While I stand in the snow at the back of the crowd, some parents wipe their eyes, and others turn around to face me. I close my own eyes against the bright lights of the tree and concentrate on finding Willow's voice out of the dozens. The song is beautiful, and it's for Liv, but it doesn't need to break me down. I'm just here with my sister, hearing her sing, and that's enough.

I hear a small gasp next to me and open my eyes. Nonno is standing a few feet away, both hands on his heart.

Everything inside me freezes, and I stumble toward him.

"Nonno," I say. "Can you hear me? Are you okay?"

He nods, his head wobbling up and down. Up close, I can see his face. My grandfather, crying.

"My Rory," he says, as I take his arm. "I am so proud. So proud."

We stand together, not speaking, as the kids' voices fill the space around us.

*my nineteenth birthday*
*one year and three days after*

*I*t hurts less than I think it will.

I keep up an endless stream of conversation for the entire session, which the artist probably hates, but it's how I get through it. I give them my opinions on various TikTokers, *Queer Eye*, and all of David Bowie's albums from the seventies. I share with them the food that I ate this morning and what Nonni got Mom for Christmas. I tell them the names of every family member, plus both cats. And I don't apologize.

When it's over, I look at Saige for the first time since lying down. The blood has drained from her face, but she's still holding my hand.

"How does it look?" I ask, before I look at my forearm to see for myself.

"Nonni's going to kill you," she responds, massaging her fingers. But she also smiles. "It's pretty badass."

As Saige drives us home, I check my phone and see that she sent me a silly selfie while it was happening, straight up the nose, even as I squeezed the feeling out of her hand.

* * *

Nonni is oddly cool about it. She only cries for two-ish minutes, and then she nods over and over again, more to herself than to me. She says, "You are my Rory. Okay. You are my Rory." Then she kisses me on the forehead and forces me to eat.

I'm waiting, though, for Mom to come home. It seems to take her forever: she and Willow are getting groceries and going to the dentist and doing seemingly every single boring thing you can think of. While I'm waiting, I send a picture to Jem.

He responds immediately: *Sick!!!!!*

When the door finally opens downstairs, I have to restrain myself from running down to greet Mom. Instead, I wait until she finishes talking to everyone and climbs the stairs up to my room, and then I turn off my Maggie Rogers album and face her. She leans against the doorframe, hands shoved into the pockets of her patterned pants, looking careless and cool. I love my mom.

"Let's see it, then," she says, her mouth twisting.

I pull up my sleeve, and she walks over to meet me on the bed. My new tattoo is covered in clear Saran wrap and red around the edges, but every time I see it, I feel a rush of joy in my chest. It's a pair of giant, chunky headphones, a lilac flower between them.

Mom stares at it for a long time, and then gently kisses my wrist, right above where the Saran wrap starts.

"Welcome to the club," she says, shaking out her sleeves so I can see hints of her tattoos.

"Well, I'm not going to look like *you*," I say.

"I should bloody well hope not." She smiles, and I think the conversation is over. But she comes to sit on my bed.

"Rory, I . . ." She stops, suddenly transfixed by her

hands. Her thumb pushes across the faded cursive writing on the inside of her wrist: *Rory. Saige.* And, the ink a bit fresher, *Willow.*

"I'm so sorry," she whispers, finally looking back at me.

I feel tears prick my eyes. "Mom, it's—"

"No." She puts a hand on mine. "No excuses." We sit in silence then because there's nothing else to really do. The past is over. She can't make up for what she did, and I can't make up for what I said.

"I'll—I'll be better," she says, finally, wiping her eyes. "For Willow. For all of us."

I nod.

She stands up, but I stop her.

"I—" The words suddenly get caught in my throat. Mom looks down at me, confused.

I stand up, walk toward my dresser, and turn around.

"I need to tell you something," I say. "Something . . . not so good."

She faces me squarely and crosses her arms. It's amazing how strict my mom can look with a simple change of body language. I take a deep breath, turn back around, and start rummaging through my sock drawer until my hands wrap around the little black book. I cross the room slowly, holding it against my chest.

"This is Liv's diary," I tell her.

I watch Mom's face as she realizes what I've done. She doesn't look angry. Her eyebrows rise, and she drops her arms to her sides again.

"Rory . . ." she whispers.

"I didn't read it," I say. "I don't want to. But . . . I can't give it back."

Mom closes her eyes for a few moments and then opens them again. "That doesn't belong to you," she says.

I hug it tighter to my chest. "You don't understand. Liv loved her parents, but she just wasn't as close with them as I am with you. There are things about her that they never knew. I'm sure she would've told them at some point, but she wasn't ready, and then . . ." I swallow. "There are things that would . . . it would kill them, Mom. She wouldn't want them to find out like this."

Mom sucks in her cheeks. She seems to take forever to respond, and when she does, I brace myself.

"Why are you telling me this?" she asks.

"Because I need you to keep it hidden."

Mom blinks.

"I don't want to read it, and I don't want *them* to read it. I need to know that it's safe in this house. But I can't know where."

Mom stares for a bit longer and then reaches her hands out. I drop the black diary into them and watch as her thumb grazes the sticker on the cover: *Fuck this!* ☺

Her lips curve up into a smile.

"Okay, my lovely one," she says, and she starts to turn around again.

"Mom?"

"Yes?"

I scratch my ankle with my foot.

"I loved her," I say.

She nods. "I know."

"It was more than just . . . well, we didn't . . . but . . ."

"No buts," she says. She tucks Liv's diary under her arm and walks up to me, placing her hands on my cheeks like she used to do when I was little.

"But I don't know what . . . what it means about *us*. About our friendship," I say. "I mean, *I'm* queer."

"Oh, my love, do I know."

I swallow. "But I don't know if . . . if *she* . . ."

"Here's what it means," she says softly. "It means Liv was loved by Rory Quinn-Morelli. It means she was the luckiest girl in the world."

epilogue

*I*t's stupidly beautiful at Ridgewood. I mean, it physically hurts my chest sometimes.

The buildings are old and Gothic; the library is so
cavernous yet cozy that it actually makes me want to
study. The leaves are already turning orange, way earlier than they did at home, and there's just the tiniest
sliver of crispness in the air. Like it's *almost* time for
sweaters and warm coffee, but not quite. We're still in
between.

My classes are hard. Some are in lecture halls, but
others are in small classrooms, and we sit in a circle
and talk about things that I never knew that I didn't
know. I've read three books so far, and I've already
gone to every single one of my professors' office hours.
They smile when they see me. They close their books
and say, "Come in, Rory. What can I help you with
today?"

It's Saturday morning, and I'm supposed to meet up
with Lou, Eliana, Katie, and Anna at our usual table
at PJ's before my Queer Alliance meeting, but I text
them that I'm having a late start. April says it'll take
more time before my medication actually kicks in, but
honestly, since starting it, I've been sleeping like a rock.
Most nights, for ten hours straight.

I don't hate it.

As I leave the dining hall alone, after shoving a few bagels into my bag for later, I stop by the mailroom for no other reason except that it's on the way out. Inside my mailbox is a huge, crushed manila envelope from home: my very first mail at Ridgewood. After grabbing it, I push back through the doors, and a pleasantly cool burst of air greets me. My phone buzzes with a text.

Nora (anthro 101): *yessss i love that album too!! okay also are you coming to lit mag tomorrow?! i'd really love to see you!*

I slide my phone back into my pocket, thinking I'll respond later.

Trying to ignore the smallest, slightest flutter of wings in my chest.

\* \* \*

It's chillier outside than I thought, so I stop back at my room to grab a flannel. While I'm there, I take my scissors, slice through the chunky envelope, and catch a faint whiff of tomatoes.

A note falls out:

Look, darling, I'm sorry, but I read some of it. The diary. Don't hate me. I promise I'll never tell a soul. Plus I'll take you for a bagel date when you come home, just the two of us.

It's just—well, Eleanor and Ramil came back to town for a visit and stopped by for coffee. Nonni obviously made them stay until they'd finished six helpings of food and I thought Eleanor was going to be sick, but they were very friendly regardless. The whole time they were there, I was thinking of you and Liv. The way you'd cackle behind your closed door, and I'd always feel ridiculous for wanting to know what was so bloody funny.

I know you are probably angry with me for reading it, but I'm sending this anyway. Hope your days are bright. Love you.

xx Mum

There are several sheets of paper attached to the note, smaller sheets with thinner lines. Clearly ripped out of the diary. I recognize Liv's scrawl immediately, and before I know what I'm doing, I'm closing my eyes and dragging my nail softly across the letters, hunting for the ridges where her pen hit the page: signs of life. I feel self-conscious, thinking of eight months ago when Eleanor and Ramil gave me that extra wool sweater of hers and I spent thirty minutes carefully picking out the few dark brown hairs that still clung to it, preserving them in a mason jar in my closet. *This is creepy*, the voice in my head said, but I overrode it: *I miss her. Very, very much.*

I take a breath and hold off from reading what Liv wrote, continuing with Mom's note instead.

PS: Right before they left, Eleanor pulled these out and gave them to me. She said she'd found them as she was cleaning out the last bits of Liv's room before the move. She'd kept them at first, but she said she realized that they're yours now.

Check the playlists, love.

I reach into the sliced envelope and pull out Liv's iPod and headphones.

I take another breath, but I can't stop shaking. I want to put off reading the pages from Liv's diary because if I don't read them, there will always be something left.

But then I'm reading them. I'm so hungry.

Jan. 2

Dear Rory,
Happy 18th

Dearest Roo,
Happy 18th birthday, queen girl!!! you fill my heart with joy and I'm so th

Dearest Roo,
I hope that the next year for you is filled with good tunes, happy times (#graduation, GOODBYE HIGH SCHOOL), and lots of me (which I know it will be).

omg

~~Dearest Rory~~

Dear Rory,
Remember when we were on the roof of Grace's house, and I was acting all cool? And I jumped into the pool? Dude, that was so fucking stupid.

Dear Rory,
Remember when we were at Grace's house, on the roof? Remember caroling at that club? Driving with the windows open in the snow? Lying on the floor, listening to Bon Iver, talking about life? you don't know what you've done for me. I mean, I'm

*overwhelmed writing this birthday note, because there are no words for*

~~To the queen of my heart~~

~~Roo,~~

~~I don't know yet but I think that maybe~~

*To my sweet Roo:*
~~you deserve~~
*I'd give you the sky, but that wouldn't be enough.*

I read them over and over again. For hours, maybe years, sitting at my desk. Her words, for me. When my eyes hurt, when my brain hurts, I take the iPod with shaking hands and pull her headphones over my ears.

I flip the on switch and watch as the screen lights up, remembering her voice in my head: *I've had this silver brick for years, but it works like a fucking charm.*

I go to *Music*, then *Playlists*. I scroll down, reading their alphabetized names, until I see it:

*Rory.*

I lie down on the floor, on my back.

Press *play*.

It's everything we've ever loved, all of our songs, all the heroes we scribbled down in the margins of our sheet music in choir. It starts with Bowie and Joni Mitchell, the very first songs I told her to listen to. She travels to Bon Iver, Sufjan Stevens, Mitski, Frank Ocean. Solange, Lucy Dacus, Phoebe Bridgers. Stevie Nicks, Billie Holiday, Billie Eilish. Florence + The Machine. Maggie Rogers.

While I listen, under my closed eyelids, I see everything: the bright oranges and yellows of fall, infinite snowy hills and trees, the way the grass looked so green when everything finally melted, the purple tinge of a summer sky at night—and her, laughing through it all. I see the wings flutter around her eyes, the way her head fell back into a smile, the times she forgot to cover her mouth or lower her voice. The way she sounded, laughing. The way it felt, lying next to her on the floor, sitting next to her in the car, feeling the warmth of her next to me.

And through a kaleidoscope of colors, all the shapes and sounds, I see the words:

*My sweet Roo.*

*I'd give you the sky.*

Music plays a huge role in Rory and Liv's year together, as well as Rory's time grieving and healing After. In addition to "Music We Listened to on the Train" (see Chapter Seven), here are some of the songs that meant the most to them, and to me while writing *Cold Girls*.

Hauntingly, this is the list *after* I heavily narrowed it down.

**THE VIBES, GENERALLY:**
The Aces / "Girls Make Me Wanna Die"
Angel Olsen / "Spring"
The Beths / "Little Death"
Brittany Howard / "Georgia"
The Cranberries / "Dreams"
David Bowie / "Rebel Rebel"
Florence + The Machine / "Free"
Florence + The Machine / "Sky Full Of Song"
HAIM / "Now I'm In It"
Lorde / "The Louvre"
Lucy Dacus / "Kissing Lessons"
Maggie Rogers / "Be Cool"
Maggie Rogers / "I've Got a Friend"
Maggie Rogers / "Symphony"

Mitski / "Geyser"

Mitski / "The Only Heartbreaker"

Nico Segal / "Wanna Be Cool"

The Ponderosa Twins Plus One / "Bound"

Sharon Van Etten / "Seventeen"

Soccer Mommy / "With U"

Solange / "Some Things Never Seem to Fucking Work"

Susanne Sundfør / "Fade Away"

**DANCING AT DREAMTOWN:**

Fleetwood Mac / "Dreams"

Florence + The Machine / "My Love"

Japanese Breakfast / "Be Sweet"

Jessie Ware / "Save a Kiss"

Kate Bush / "Running Up That Hill (A Deal With God)"

Kelsey Lu / "I'm Not in Love" (Cover)

Madonna / "Like a Virgin"

Madonna / "Lucky Star"

Mitski / "Love Me More"

MUNA / "I Know a Place"

Prince / "I Would Die 4 U"

Robyn / "Dancing on My Own"

**PARTIES, ETC.:**

ABRA / "VEGAS"

Billie Eilish / "when the party's over"

Chance the Rapper / "Smoke Break (feat. Future)"

Childish Gambino / "Redbone"

Kinneret / "No Wind Resistance!"

Labrinth / "Mount Everest"

MØ / "Pilgrim"
Rihanna / "Higher"

**RORY & MOM:**
Blur / "Coffee & TV"
Guns N' Roses / "Sweet Child o' Mine"
Joni Mitchell / "Both Sides Now"
Sonic Youth / "Teen Age Riot"
Wilco / "Heavy Metal Drummer"

**THE LAST DANCE:**
Barbara Lewis / "Hello Stranger"
Stevie Wonder / "Lois"
The Ponderosa Twins Plus One / "You Send Me"

**RORY'S QUEER AWAKENING:**
Ella Fitzgerald / "Happy Talk"
Florence + The Machine / "Between Two Lungs"
Florence + The Machine / "Girls Against God"
HAIM / "Hallelujah"
Lizzy McAlpine / "all my ghosts"
Lucy Dacus / "Christine"
Maggie Rogers / "Anywhere with You"
Maggie Rogers / "Fallingwater"
Maggie Rogers / "Say It"
The Mamas & The Papas / "Dedicated To The
    One I Love"
Nina Simone / "Why Keep On Breaking My
    Heart"
Sam Cooke / "Teenage Sonata"
Stevie Wonder / "Magic"

**AFTER:**
Andrew Bird / "Ethio Invention no. 1"
Bon Iver / "Woods"
Daughter / "Youth"
James Vincent McMorrow / "Red Dust"
Joni Mitchell / "A Case of You"
Jónsi / "Tornado"
Lucy Dacus / "Dream State . . ."
Nat King Cole / "It Happens to Be Me"
Phoebe Bridgers / "Smoke Signals"
Sampha / "Timmy's Prayer"
Sufjan Stevens / "Death with Dignity"

**FINDING PEACE:**
James Vincent McMorrow / "Post Tropical"
Jónsi / "Around Us"
Ólafur Arnalds / "Doria—Island Songs VII"

## acknowledgments

I've lately been thinking of myself as a well-cared-for plant that has been watered by so many incredible people through the years. If I'm thanking the people who influenced my writing career in chronological order, I first want to start with my grandparents, Dr. Donald Eugene Saunders Jr. (Umpapa)—the author of Liv's favorite *Christmas Thoughts about Love*—and Carol Cook Saunders. You knew I was a writer in fifth grade. Thanks for believing in me. Umpapa, I wish you were here to see this one. Carol, I'm so glad you are!

Snapping forward to the present, because this is important: Thank you so much to my supportive, enthusiastic editor, Ashtyn Stann. Thank you for cheering me on, for providing so much helpful feedback, and for sobbing over this book. Thank you to Meg Gaertner, for your endless help and wisdom, and for your uncanny attention to detail. (When I daydreamed about communicating with my future editors, I envisioned sending the most professional, grammatically correct emails. Cut to me sending you an email at 2:00 a.m. that is simply a picture of SpongeBob with a revised manuscript attached. Thanks for tolerating that.) Thank you to Heather McDonough, Taylor Kohn, and everyone at North Star Editions and Flux & Jolly Fish Press for taking on this book and treating it with the care of a newborn baby, because it is! Thank you so much to the incredibly talented Alisha Monnin for this gorgeous cover. You captured Rory and Liv perfectly.

Endless and eternal thanks to my agent, Maria Bell. When you took a chance on me and this book, my life changed for the better. Thank you for never giving up, even when I almost wanted to. Thank you for the tremendous amount of work you have done to get this book into the world. Thanks also to Elizabeth Bewley, Doug Stewart, and the rest of the team at Sterling Lord Literistic! My team, Maria, Ashtyn, and Meg: thanks for believing in me, and for tenderly loving Rory and Liv as much as these goofy and complicated teenage girls need to be tenderly loved.

Thank you to my writing teachers so far, in chronological order: Adrian Van Young, Jesmyn Ward, Charles Baxter, Abby Geni, Zoe Zolbrod, James Klise, and Rattawut Lapcharoensap. I wouldn't be here, writing this, without their valuable lessons and their belief in me. Jim, "thank you" can never be enough: for fielding my alarming amount of semiliterate texts and emails long after you stopped being my official teacher. For endless, valuable advice. For being the first person I called when *anything* happened. For the enthusiastic celebrations. For coming to the pride party at my parents' house in the suburbs, even though it took a huge chunk out of your day and you didn't know anyone. You are my writing champion.

Thank you to my StoryStudio Chicago family, the group of talented writers that I got to learn with and from: Klariza Alvaran, Candice Cusic, Dan Finnen, Jana Fredericks, Jane Hertenstein, Holly Jones, Ann Kaminski, Sonya Kenkare, Kristy Kennedy, Lauren

Mallik, Ansley Schrimpf-Haman, Chrissy Stephens, Ana Vargas, Teagan Walsh-Davis, Debbie Walters, and more. Look out for some pretty badass books coming from these badass humans.

Ansley, thank you for your very Ansley-esque response to my dream becoming a reality: congratulations, legal advice, and an extremely organized and COVID-safe gathering. (She's a powerhouse!) Klariza, thank you for helping me make sure my portrayal of Liv as a Filipinx American teenager—and her father, Ramil—was accurate. I also want to give a shout-out to Amelia Brunskill and Kimberly Gabriel, both Chicago YA authors who've given me wonderful advice.

To my full and partial readers, Sally French, Emily Goltser, Tessa O'Connell, Chrissy Stephens, Teagan Walsh-Davis—thank you for your kind words and constructive feedback! (Chrissy texted me eighty-five times in a row, everyone.) Thank you, Olivija Stephens and Jolie Armstrong, for filling me in on Gen Z slang, and for not laughing when I got it so wrong. Thank you, Paul Strabbing, for coming in clutch with that last-minute headshot—and for accepting smoked salmon as compensation instead of American dollars.

In my personal, nonwriting life: Thank you to my best friends on planet Earth and beyond, the truest of true gal pals, Glenna Siegel, Madelyn Miller, and Annie Carroll. You continuously help me to be a better person *and* make me laugh till I sob, which rocks. Sarah, for fundamentally changing me and for sitting with me in quiet moments, no words are ever enough. Ég elska þig. Tori, my gorl, and your parents, too: I love you; you know this. She lives on in every single laugh.

Other pals, near and far, who believed in me wholeheartedly and cheered the loudest, THANK YOU: Emma, Laura, Lauren, and Rachel, my college babes; Meredith, Ally, and Jen, my grad school coven who kept my goose self afloat; and my Chicago Ballet Arts family. My aunts, uncles, and cousins—both by blood and by choice—cheers! (Intense eye contact.) My kids (okay, so they're "not mine" if you want to get grammatical about it): Jacob, Kodi, and Ivy, I love you. And to their real parents, thank you—you cheered this one on for years. Thanks to Jane, my sixth-grade teacher who understood me so well, and her daughter Julia, too. Thank you to everyone on my chaotic-as-heck email list—friends and family, some of whom I haven't spoken to in years, who are now committedly in the front row, cheering me on. How lucky am I? And finally, to my amazing, iconic, talented, and hot friends and queer community in Chicago: dancing and laughing with you into the wee hours of the morning is the life I've always dreamed of.

A whole separate paragraph for my therapist: Queen, you have gotten me through. Thanks for understanding my brain, believing in my strength, and laughing at my jokes even when they're not funny (but I think the majority are? Let's bookmark this). Mental health care is so vastly important, and I hope we can keep reducing the stigma against it. Therapy rocks.

And lastly, most importantly, saying "thank you" could never adequately express my gratitude for my family, Mom, Dad, and Arden. Mom and Dad: Thank you for accepting your silly, moody, occasionally cringey oldest child and believing in me without fail, encouraging my love of books and writing, and helping me in every possible way you can. Thank you for never getting tired of this, for emailing everyone you know, and for telling the world how proud you are of your gay artist kids. Ardi: You are the funniest person I know on planet Ee-arth, and I wouldn't éxïst without you. Like, Yahtzee!

# about the author

Maxine Rae has studied writing at Tulane University, Sarah Lawrence College, and StoryStudio Chicago, where she trained under established authors such as two-time National Book Award–winner Jesmyn Ward. *Cold Girls* is her first novel. When not writing or working, she enjoys being a gay icon with her sister, dancing around to alternating ballet and disco music in her apartment, and snuggling with her two cats. You can find her on Instagram at @maxinerae_author.